FLASHBACK

OUT OF THE BOX
Book 23

Robert J. Crane

FLASHBACK
Out of the Box, Book 23

Robert J. Crane
Copyright © 2018 Ostiagard Press
All Rights Reserved.

1st Edition

1

Four damned walls.

That was what surrounded me as I sat, waiting, for something to happen.

Grey concrete walls, ten feet high, a ceiling of old, stained tile. Floor of concrete, dark as ground-out cigarette ends. The room smelled like it predated smoking bans, so maybe it came by that color honestly.

A table. Scarred white surface, a thousand wear lines and scratches suggesting long use. One chair opposite mine, the wooden back visible and reminding me of the kind I'd seen in a school the time I'd done a "Scared Straight" talk to kids in an outstate Minnesota school.

The wall across from me was mirrored, the entire length of it, a long strip of reflection that started waist-high and went to the ceiling, reflecting back everything in my half of the room.

And then there was me. Dark hair, pale skin, blue eyes, pissed off, impatient, staring at myself but really staring at the one-way mirror and the jackasses who were surely hiding behind it, wishing they would get. The. Hell. On with it.

How long had I been here? It was hard to say. It felt like months since the big, steel door had closed me in, since the stern government agent in the black suit with the ponytail had told me, "Just wait here for a minute," and disappeared.

How long had it really been?

Hell if I knew.

I'd gotten off a plane just before being brought here. A C-

1

130 Hercules had delivered me to Washington DC on the president's orders. The soldiers who'd escorted me home signed some paperwork when we'd arrived at Joint Base Andrews, we'd said our farewells, and I'd gotten into a black government SUV with black-suited government agents that had brought me...

Here. A shitty old government building on the outskirts of DC, where I now stared at myself in a one-way mirror wishing I had eyebeam lasers so I could blast through the assholes behind it. If only they'd get their damned thumbs out and move on with...

...whatever the hell this was.

Part of me wanted to stand up, raise my foot, and swing it back to kick my own ass. I'd bought into it when SecDef Bruno Passerini, the man they called "Hammer," had told me the president was ordering me home for...I dunno. Pardon. Absolution. Whatever the cross between forgiving me of my sins and dismissing the charges was.

Instead, I was locked in a cell, staring at myself.

Had Passerini betrayed me?

I kinda doubted it. He didn't need to, though. That was the problem with serving an immense Leviathan of a government. He'd just followed orders to deliver me to the next link in the bureaucratic chain; what happened after receipt of package wasn't his fault.

And I had been delivered to the shittiest place in the entire United States, the malarial swamp known as Washington DC. It didn't take much imagination to think I might just disappear into said swamp, especially given that less than a week ago the US government had tried to make me disappear in a prison for metahumans.

Was that really less than a week ago? Wow. I'd really been through the ringer since then. Prison break. War with my great-grandfather and his little country. Nuclear missile launches. Saving the freaking world. Again.

Hook. Line. Sinker. That was how my dumb ass had bought it, almost crying in front of Warren Quincy – the Terminator – and a bunch of Navy SEALs when Passerini had told me I was coming home a hero.

I said none of this aloud now. Showed no reaction but to glare at the glass.

Hell if I'd give these bastards the satisfaction of seeing my brain spin on a perpetual loop.

I gave good glare, though. If they were back there, I knew they had to be feeling the heat. After all, I'd recently massacred an entire metahuman Russian mercenary division. Only an idiot would be sitting behind that glass calmly knowing I was awake, irritable, and glaring at them through the glass. Like staring at the bobcat through the plastic divider at the Minnesota zoo. That animal was always pacing, looking at the people. If you didn't have faith in the guard between you, it'd be pretty damned unnerving.

Especially knowing the bobcat could probably bust out and rip you to pieces at any time.

And I was thinking about it. I'd have been a fool not to. If I got so much as a hint of gas pushing out of one of the vents, boom, I'd go through that mirror and then through someone's face, decisions to not run be damned.

I sat there a while longer.

How long?

Hell if I knew. I didn't have a cell phone or a watch. Felt like hours. Could have been minutes.

Glared.

Oh, how I glared.

There was no sound. Not even a chatter or a whisper from behind the mirrored glass. I knew they were there, but it must have been incredibly insulated for me not to hear them with my metahuman senses. Nothing but the hum of the overhead fluorescents kept me company.

There was a subtle distortion effect in the mirror. Probably a manufacturing thing, or something that happened during installation, a slight bending of the reflection at the level of my face. It was marginal but made one of my cheeks stick out farther to the right, the other to push in, and my nose to look a few degrees off axis. Without trying to be too obvious about it, I reached up and checked just to be sure I hadn't gotten my face mashed in my recent fighting. It felt fine, so I maintained my glare and tried to ignore the slightly funhouse-mirror quality of my own reflection.

Also, I kinda looked like hell. And would it have killed them to offer me something to eat? My stomach rumbled like slow thunder, and for a second I thought maybe I was hearing a storm in the distance. Then the vibrato shook the inside of my rib cage, and I realized I couldn't remember when I'd last had a meal.

Still, I stared. Never looked away. The key to maintaining your badass, fearless image was really just unrelenting discipline. If I could have cemented my eyes open, I would have, that's how committed I was to making these government types stew in wonder of what I'd do if they made a move against me. Would they make it out alive before they could put me down like a rabid dog? They'd have to put a big fat wager on the line to find out – their very lives.

It was funny how the prospect of being caged changed my attitude so quickly. Hours earlier, over Europe, I'd been ready to surrender to my fate and the possibility of prison again. But now, in the hours since I'd been told, "Nah, kid, you're going to be free!" my brain had quickly adjusted to the idea of what I could do now that my run was over. I'd spent the whole flight thinking about what would come next, of finding Harry, of reuniting with my friends. I'd started making plans. Now...

I looked at the four walls. The aged ceiling, scratched-up furniture, stained floor. Two chairs, table, mirror, me.

Freedom my ass.

I blinked. I had to, my eyes were burning. But when I opened my eyes again, after that millisecond of non-contact with the world visually...

Something had changed.

Something...swam across the table in front of me like a larger-scale version of the mirror distortion. It wasn't slow, it wasn't subtle, and if I'd been a slightly more excitable person I would have overturned my chair trying to get the hell away from...whatever it was.

But I was tired, and I was cranky, and hell if I was going to show whoever was behind the mirror that they were successfully getting to me with this...trick of light or whatever. I adjusted my gaze down, watching the table twist and shift colors-

And then...

I was suddenly not in the room anymore.

There were not four walls around me.

There was no ceiling. Grass as green as any I'd ever seen replaced the floor.

The table was gone, so was the chair across from me, and I was sitting on...

A bench. White concrete supports anchored either side, red wooden beams ran crosswise for me to sit on and lean back against. A mini billboard on the seat proclaiming the name of some realtor greeted me along with his cheesy smile. His phone number was right there, prefaced by a 515 area code.

I blinked, looking around.

The sky was blue, the dull cream ceiling replaced by bright cerulean, occasional puffy cloud catching albedo from the sun. Tree tops stirred with a sudden breeze that awakened the faint hairs on my forearms, sending goosebumps across my scalp.

"What...the hell?" I asked, looking around.

Someone shouted in the distance. A jogger went past less than ten feet away, shoes pounding against the concrete path that wended by me.

I sat.

Stared.

Waited.

To see if the mirror came back. If the room came back.

To see if anyone was watching me.

I don't know how long I sat there. Maybe an hour, maybe a few minutes.

People played. Jogged. A kid flew a kite across the meadow in the distance, dad chasing after him.

The gloomy DC office building was *gone*.

I was in a park, not a government cage.

I was...free?

"Huh," I said, looking around. "That...is a hell of a thing."

2.

Eventually I stood up, and eventually I moved around, and when I did, I found...

I was definitely not in DC anymore. And while that might have been cause for some celebration, under normal circumstances – being freed as I was from what was rapidly looking like a return to prison – disappearing from one, office-building place and appearing in another, park place? Of the non-Monopoly variety?

That was not normal, not even for weirdo metahuman me.

A mystery. Yay. Usually I got a little bit of a break between my various cases, but life sure was conspiring to keep me busy lately, throwing cartel metas at me followed by prison riots then a whole war and now...

Well, I didn't know what this was. A disappearing office building? A magically appearing park?

"Occam's razor," I muttered under my breath, pacing away from the bench as I looked around, trying to get the lay of the land. If I had indeed been pulled out of the government building, in my experience it would not be followed by a long rest on a beach with fruity drinks. Oh, no, any gift horse was immediately followed by a giant horse bite, laden with lots of infectious diseases. Or something like them, since I didn't really get sick. What was the metahuman equivalent of an infectious disease? Taylor Swift singing, maybe?

What was the simplest explanation for how I was suddenly in a city park, somewhere in America? Because this was plainly

America. I knew it for a fact as I walked the concrete path, leaving the bench behind, as I dipped under the shade of the trees straddling the trail. The real estate agent's telephone number was definitely American. Up ahead I could see shops, all the signs in plain American English. One of them was a diner, another was a laundromat. Taller buildings lurked beyond the edges of the park, though the trees did a pretty good job of obscuring them.

Some reasonably tall ones peeked out of the branches here and there. Which ruled out Washington, DC, where there were almost no buildings taller than about fifteen stories. There was a sizable downtown lurking in the distance, and I could catch glimpses of it here and there beyond the trees.

"Two possibilities," I muttered, as another jogger passed me, giving me a glance, then a double-take that confirmed that I was in fact here, that they did hear me, and that I might look slightly like a crazy person in my war-torn clothing. Shouldn't have passed on Warren Quincy's offer of a military flight jumpsuit that was twelve sizes too big for me. I would have looked slightly less crazy shuffling around in a city park, talking to myself, wearing that than the shredded garb I'd worn through the Revelen war.

"Possibility one...I just got teleported to...wherever this is," I said, picking up my pace so as to head toward the downtown skyline. If I saw it, there was a strong likelihood I could identify it. I'd been to a lot of cities in America and could identify quite a few of them on sight. "Possibility two...this is all in someone's head, maybe mine."

I liked that idea less. Because being delusional didn't sound like fun, unless you considered it in comparison to sitting in a government interrogation room, glaring at the one-way mirror. Being mindjacked might just be more enjoyable than that, at least in the short-term.

A car rolled by on a street ahead, just past the end of the heavy trees, and I stared. It was an old-model minivan, except it looked pretty new. Past it was a gas station at the corner of two streets, and a convenience store waited just beyond the pumps.

Hmm. Maybe that was a place to get some answers to basic

questions like, "Where am I?" I'd need to be careful about it, though, in order to avoid sounding insane.

The double doors clacked slightly on their tracks as they swept open in front of me. The sign above the door read "Mom and Pop's," in old-timey lettering. It was set up as a typical convenience store, coolers ringing the walls, shelves filled with junk food and other staples in the center, a nice coffee machine and soda fountain straight ahead. To my left was the counter, complete with a bored store clerk staring dully at me. Her name tag read 'Jane'.

Jane twisted her face into a smile, though it looked like it took some effort. "Welcome to Mom and Pop's. What can I do ya for?"

I frowned. I know that's a pretty common line among old oddballs but hearing someone ask what they could 'do me for' made me think – just for an uncomfortable second – she was propositioning me. "Hi. I was wondering..." Pause. Note to self: Try to sound sane. Force a light smile that probably looks terrifying. "...Where am I?"

She stared back blankly. "You're in Mom and Pop's."

"Yes, I know I'm in the store 'Mom and Pop's," I said. "More broadly, though...where am I?"

She stared back at me, eyes narrowing as she studied me with a little intensity. "Oh, I see. Philosophically. I understand. I did a couple years at the University of Chicago and those are just the sort of deeper questions we liked to contemplate-"

"No," I said. "I meant literally-"

"Hey, are you all right?" Jane asked, with a broad midwestern accent, scanning me up and down. "You look like you've been through it."

"I've been through it, all right," I said, and a thought occurred. "Do you...not know who I am?"

She looked kind of frozen, deer in the headlights. "Uhm...should I know? Are you on one of those new sitcoms? Because they've always got me working nights lately and my VCR is terrible-"

"VCR?" I blinked. "Who uses a – never mind." I shook my head. "No, I'm wondering, in the very literal, geographical sense – where am I?"

"Mom and Pop's," she said again, looking at me with the first, vague hint that I might be crazy. It was in the slight disengagement of her body as she took a half step back.

I sighed and slumped. "Third base."

"No, 'I don't know who' is on third," she said. "There is no 'where' in that skit."

"Well, at least you know your comedy," I said, and looked down past the counter. There was a stack of newspapers sitting there, with 'The Des Moines Register' blared across the top of the page. "Ah ha!" I said, then my shoulders slumped. "What the hell? I'm in Iowa?"

"Wait, you really didn't know where you were?" Jane had her elbows back on the counter. I guess I'd gone from dangerously crazy to unassuming kook with that admission.

"Do you think I would have been asking if I'd known?" I bent down to look at the newspaper headline, sure it'd have been something to do with the Revelen situation. I'd been on a plane and in that room for the better part of a day, plenty of time for the newspapers to bleat about nuclear war at the top of their lungs and get a new edition out. Instead, the front-page headline read, "State to study cities' impact on water." That was it. A secondary headline in the right-hand column read, "Killer quake rocks Taiwan."

I picked up the paper and stared. "That's...really weird." I looked up at her. "Nothing about the war, nothing about the nuclear missiles launching?"

She cocked a single, slightly frizzy eyebrow at me. "What are you talking about? The Cold War is over, lady. We won."

I stared at her, she stared at me, and once again, I felt like we'd had a clear miss in our attempted meeting of the minds. I glanced back down at the newspaper, another idle thought occurring as I looked to the top, left-hand side of the page.

Cold chills.

Yep.

It read, "Tuesday, September 21, 1999."

1999.

"What...the hell...?" I asked.

Jane leaned over the counter. "What now?"

"Nothing," I said, folding the paper and lifting it up so she

9

could see the left-hand column. It read, "Quality of genetic testing is under fire." "You know, I just get so...fired up about...genetic testing...quality." I knew it sounded lame, and I didn't care. I tossed the newspaper back on the stand and started backing away. "Well, Jane...you've been a huge help. Now that I know where I am, I'm going to go..." I kinda hit a wall there, because hell if I knew what I was going to do now.

In Des Moines, Iowa.

In 1999.

"Well, I'm going to go do something, for sure," I said, and snapped my finger her at her real quick, making a fake gun. "It's been real. Later."

She looked at me like I was out of my damned mind. Which, maybe I was, because people did not just randomly find themselves in Des Moines in the late 90's in a sane world. "Uh...good luck, then, I guess...?"

"Thanks," I said, turning around and walking out the door. "I'll probably need that." It whooshed shut behind me, leaving me in the parking lot just outside the convenience store. An old model pickup truck from the seventies rolled by, and it looked at least fifteen years newer than it should have if I'd been in the modern day. "Dammit," I muttered under my breath. "Options."

Mind jacking by a telepath to take me into a fantasy world of 1999 Iowa?

I'd been gassed to death and was now in Hell, which was, as I'd long suspected, Iowa?

Or...

I was actually in 1999, actually in Des Moines, in which case there was only one logical conclusion as to how I'd gotten here...

I looked left.

I looked right.

Up, down, and finally, straight ahead into the green, rolling grass of the park. With a tentative whisper, I called out, then again, louder.

"...Akiyama?"

3.

I didn't want to stand around in the parking lot of the convenience store, talking to the sky in hopes that a Japanese man would come popping out, so I cast a quick look over my shoulder at Jane, visible in the window, looking out at me, and waved, then quickly walked across the Des Moines street.

"Akiyama?" I called again, hustling to avoid getting run over by an 80's model pickup truck. "Come on, Akiyama. Either this is you or I'm crazy, dead, or a telepath is messing with me. Please let it be you."

I stopped on the sidewalk before the park, looking around. The trees swayed in a light, warm, summer breeze. In the distance I could hear children playing.

"Oh, come on!" I said under my breath. My brow furrowed deeply as I looked past the boughs hanging above me into the blue sky, as though he'd come dropping out of it any second if I just stared hard enough. "You can't just leave me here like this, without a word of explanation. That's not right, man. This is Iowa, okay? You don't drop people in Iowa without explanation, nineties or not. We have a constitution in this country, and there's one passage that specifically enumerates that cruel and unusual punishment is not acceptable, and I'm pretty sure Iowa qualifies in that regard."

I waited. The trees swayed again. A lone leaf came tumbling down in a slow twist, the smell of fresh air offset by a rumbling beater that went by behind me, spewing a black cloud in its wake that gagged my metahuman sense of smell. "Ugh.

Emissions standards must have been lower back here. Come on, Akiyama. You can't just leave me in Iowa, that's cold. That's beyond cold. That's Erich-Winter-in-Minneapolis-in-January-during-the most-brutal-day-of-the-season cold."

I looked around. Listened. The odd car in the distance was all I heard, save for those kids playing. There must have been a playground deeper in the park, though I couldn't see it from where I was standing on the sidewalk. The rumble of a train came from somewhere far, far off, miles away, carried in the morning calm. Or was it afternoon? It was surprisingly quiet, either way. This had to be a first-ring suburb of Des Moines, or damned near to the city limits, given how far I was from downtown.

"Fine," I said, looking at the sidewalk, at a couple spots where old gum had been driven into it over the years, black with age and being stepped on a billion times. "This is fine. In the same way that the dog in the internet comic in the fire is fine, Des Moines is fine. Better than a government cell, I guess. Even if I don't have the first freaking clue about why I'm h-"

A scream in the distance shattered the peaceful afternoon like a bottle breaking before a bar fight. It was loud and long and terrifying, not the laughter of a child or a shout of glee, but one of fear and horror and absolute, stark terror.

I snapped my head around, the direction clear. It was about forty-five degrees to my left, through the park.

Was this why I was here?

"No one ever brings me anywhere nice and peaceful," I muttered as I broke into a sprint, grass blurring beneath my feet and tree trunks whizzing by as I hit top meta speed, charging ahead to find out – hopefully – why I had been brought here.

4.

It didn't take more than a few hundred yards of sprinting before the playground came into sight. It was hidden behind a row of fat evergreens that didn't have much ground clearance at their bottoms. They were Christmas-y trees that weren't quite actual Christmas trees, being a little rounder than the kind that showed in our living rooms in December. They formed a kind of natural cordon around the playground, and the screaming was still in full force when I got there, shoving my way through tightly packed boughs, branches pecking at my exposed arms, finding the shredded gaps in my shirt and giving my skin a good brushing as I ripped through, uncaring.

I had saving to do. To hell with my arm skin. It'd grow back anyway.

One of the branches whipped me in the forehead, another damned near got my eyes, stinging my right eyelid and making me clench it closed. Bright sunlight shone through from the other side of the trees, and I muscled through, trying not to announce myself by screaming curse words at the top of my lungs at the indignities of being assailed by evergreens.

Also, at the top of my lungs near a playground would probably be bad, even given the circumstances.

About halfway through the thicket, I ran into a chain-link fence. "Oh, come on," I said under my breath. It was getting to be a common lament today. Not wanting to waste any more time, I closed my eyes, ducked my chin down to my collarbone, and leapt.

I burst out of the trees and came down on the other side of the thicket in a roll, landing on a patch of grass just before the playground. The merry-go-round was still spinning, kids were running in all directions, parents scooping them up and doing a little sprinting of their own as they bolted away.

It didn't take more than a second for me to find the cause of the disturbance. It was, of course, trouble of the Sienna variety.

Two guys with pistols out, trying to keep a mom at bay while they made to snatch a kid.

"You assholes," I said, and didn't waste a second charging in. They'd shot the mom a couple times; I could see the blood staining her blue blouse; a black spot on her jeans at the thigh. Her chest was still heaving up and down, her dark hair a stark contrast to the white sand that filled the playground area as it spilled across the miniature dunes.

One of the thugs whirled on me, the little girl's arm clenched in one hand, his pistol in the other. I was all over him like anorexia on a Paris catwalk during fashion week. He tried to bring the pistol around and I slapped it out of his hand, slamming the edge of my hand into his wrist and knocking it loose, then bringing my elbow up in a quick snap that cracked his mouth shut. He let out a sharp cry, and a little piece of his tongue came shooting out where I'd made him bite it off with my blow.

The little girl screamed as he tugged at her wrist, and I reacted by instinct, twisting to re-chamber my elbow and ramming it into his nose. That done, I snapped my hand down onto his and heard the mighty crack of his wrist as I convinced him to let the girl go. She toppled over, and I drilled a kick into his midsection, sending him flying into the solid metal piping of the jungle gym. The snap of bones as he hit was quite satisfying.

At least until the gunshot.

I'd kicked the thug out of our little struggle, giving his partner a clear shot at me. Which he'd taken, the bullet drilling me in the right shoulder. It felt like an angry stab, sharp and terrifying, the sound worse at first, the pain following and taking the prize for "Worst Part of This," a second later. I'd been shot before, and I knew it was going to be bad, but I didn't have time to stand still unless I wanted to get good and dead.

I hurled myself forward, years of training making me dive left, forcing the gunman to readjust his aim. The pain was going to be overwhelming soon, and if he'd hit an artery I was going to black out within thirty seconds. I was already oozing blood down the front of my shirt.

If I didn't want to die...I had to take him out before I passed out, leaving myself at his mercy.

I rolled and came up as he tried to track me with his human reflexes. He was pretty good, bringing the weapon down to line up with my head as I bounced back to my feet-

And caught his hands, driving them over our heads with my superior strength. I spun him into a pirouette, forcing him to go in the direction I pulled him. Once his elbows had reached maximum extension over his head, I brought a knee up into the base of his spine and savored the crack as I broke his back. He let go of the gun and tumbled to his face, and for good measure I drove the tip of my shoe into the bone behind his ear. It gave, and he went out, at least, died at worst, and I didn't care which.

"Shit," I said, clutching his pistol in one hand, covering him with it, and then putting a hand on my shoulder where I'd just been shot. I flicked my gaze between the two men and my hand, which came away from the wound seriously bloody. A little squirt of red came out of my shoulder with each heartbeat. "Dammit." He'd gotten an artery.

"Mommy mommy mommy-" the little girl said as she plowed into my leg, wrapping her arms around my waist, hugging me tight.

"I'm not your-" I started to say...

...And then I looked down at her.

Her eyes were bright and blue, with little flecks of green in them. She was fair-skinned and dark haired, and she was holding me tight as she looked up.

She stared at me and I stared at her, and it took her a moment for her brain to sort out the little things she was seeing-

15

And just like that, she detached from my leg, looking around.

"Mommy!" she shouted, bolting past me to the woman who'd been shot, the woman who was now rising to her feet, still bleeding out of her stomach and her thigh, whose dark hair and fair skin matched her daughter, whose blue eyes were also flecked with green like…

Like…

Like her daughter's.

Like mine.

Exactly…like mine.

I stared into the face of Sierra Nealon, some years younger than when I'd last seen her, as her daughter – only five years old – ran into her bloody arms. I stared as she scooped the little girl up, watching me all the while, tracking the threat–

Like I do–

-as she plotted her next course of action-

-The way she always taught me to-

-and I stared at her, stared, my gun still pointed away, my mouth hanging open, one word leaping out:

"Mom?"

She didn't answer. Didn't even seem to register my question.

What she did was clutch the little girl in her arms-

My God…that's me…

I'm so…tiny…

-and she turned, breaking into a run, as I pitched over, falling to the ground-

I stared into the sky as I passed out, wondering if I'd reached the end of the weirdest damned dream I'd ever had.

5.

"Sienna...*okiro*."

I awoke to someone slapping my face. A less pleasant way to wake up I could scarcely imagine, save for maybe a punch.

"Sienna."

Another slap. Pain in my shoulder like fire, like someone had driven a hot poker into it and was giving it a good twist for fun.

"We must depart this area immediately."

I caught the next slap because I'd gotten conscious enough to know it was coming, grabbing the wrist of my slapper before he could bring it to my cheek. The slaps weren't particularly hard, but they were especially annoying.

"Okay, I'm awake," I said, forcing my eyes open against the violently blue and sunny sky overhead. A shadowed face and bald head greeted me as I nearly pried them open, taking in the lines of a familiar face. "Akiyama."

"Sienna," he said, his thin mustache like a shadow on his upper lip. "I apologize for not greeting you earlier. It is taking nearly all my strength to maintain this..." He waved a hand around. "This."

"You brought me back to 1999," I said, clutching my arm. "To Iowa. And... I got shot."

"Yes," he said.

I looked up at him. "Well?"

His eyes were pools of shadow thanks to the sun behind him. "Well...what?"

"I hope you've got a damned good explanation for why I'm in Iowa," I said, trying to muscle myself into a sitting position and failing. He was of no help, so I rolled to my belly and just cringed at the pain. "Also...how?"

"How...what?"

"How am I in Iowa?" I asked, cringing. Sirens in the distance were the most familiar refrain of the soundtrack of my life, and of course they were getting closer. "You're a time...guy. Not a teleporting one."

"It has been some time since last I saw you," he said, putting a hand on my uninjured shoulder and helping me to my knees. "I have discovered a method of matching the time travel destination to the proper rotational position of the earth within-"

"Never mind," I said. "I hurt way too much for you to explain this to me right now."

"Perhaps I will try again when you are recovered."

"Then I won't care," I said, shaking my head. "So you can teleport now. Nifty."

"Not exactly," he said. "But...I can get you close, when coupled with an appropriate distance of time traveled."

"So you're in the DeLorean, *Back to the Future* business now?" I asked. Man, the shoulder. I felt like I was going to tip over any time. "Bringing me back to meet my mom?" I gestured vaguely in the direction I figured she'd run, then tossed a look over my shoulder at the two guys who'd tried to abduct...well, me. Little me.

Holy shit. That was a hell of a trip.

"There is a reason, of course," Akiyama said, slipping an arm under my uninjured one and dragging me to my feet. "I will explain-"

"Gah, I hope this doesn't set a precedent for this little tale, me getting shot this early in the game. Because I don't know if you know this, but I kinda just came out of a war and it was not easy, let me tell you-"

"I was watching," Akiyama said, taking up a little more of my weight and starting me forward in a run.

"And you didn't even offer a helping hand?"

He didn't shrug exactly, but he offered the ghost of one.

"You had it under control."

"You cannot possibly think there wasn't a second or two in there where I couldn't have used a time freeze? Maybe a breather to take a little break? You know, you show up with some orange slices, let me recover my stamina for a tick before throwing myself into a battle with a tank or one of the other hundred batshit crazy things that happened there?"

"Your worldly matters are your own," Akiyama said, dragging me into the cover of the trees as the sirens stopped a few hundred yards away at the road that ringed the park. "This, however...is a matter that I could not simply let pass."

"Lemme guess...it's a matter of time," I said, cringing. "And one that directly involves me, which is why you dragged my ass...to me."

"Correct," Akiyama said. "How did you guess?"

"Because I just met myself as a child and my mother was shot, and I don't remember any of this," I said, still stinging like crazy. The blood was not wildly pumping out of my shoulder now, though I doubted it was because it had completely clotted. More likely the angle Akiyama was holding me at was pinching the wound together. "Also, you're giving me some very legitimate reasons to hate Iowa this trip beyond just my natural Minnesotan disdain for our southern neighbor."

"I know nothing of what you are talking about," Akiyama said, "but the problem I have brought you here to deal with requires someone whose head is not fully pre-occupied in keeping time from crashing forward." He didn't even bother to cast me an accusing look. "Our acquaintance being somewhat...closer than my association with...anyone else, I assumed you would want to be involved in this. Especially considering it turns heavily upon your previous involvement."

"My head aches, my shoulder is weeping blood, I think you just called me the closest thing you have to a friend, and I believe you're talking about a paradox," I said. "There's a cause and effect problem here. I remember none of this, yet we just witnessed a kidnap attempt against me that looked like it would have been successful if I – me from the future – hadn't foiled it. Talk about a time loop."

"Yes," Akiyama said. "Exactly."

"You know, the family war in Revelen I just went through is starting to seem simple compared to what you've dropped me into," I said as he stepped off the curb into the street and someone honked their horn. I waved at them and yelled, "It's fine, I'm fine, don't worry," as Akiyama hobble-walked me across the street and the car rolled on without another thought to my safety. "That bastard wasn't honking because he was worried about me being hurt, he was honking because we were in his way. Damned inconsiderate Iowans."

"In fairness to him, I failed to use a crosswalk," Akiyama said. "To my shame."

"It's called jaywalking and it's not that big a deal in America," I said, fighting against a dizzy, black feeling pressing in against my consciousness. "How did this paradox happen?"

"I do not know," Akiyama said. "It could be a naturally-occurring phenomenon-"

"How the hell would me being saved as a child by my adult self be in any way 'naturally occurring'?"

Akiyama didn't miss a step. "I don't know. Time is mysterious in its permutations and flexible in its course – until it is neither."

"...The hell does that mean?"

"You will see," Akiyama said.

"Oh, goody."

He pulled me into an alleyway, and I managed to catch myself on a wall as he let me loose. It wasn't cruel or sudden, but he definitely communicated by body movement that he wasn't going to hold me up any longer. I thudded against a wall, back first, as I grimaced against the pain. "You will heal in hours. Once you have, you need to track down your mother."

I squinted at him, trying to manage the pain. Seething didn't help much, but it was better than nothing. "How am I supposed to do that?"

"You know her," he said, and a strange buzz of invisibility ran across his midsection as he seemed to dip out of existence. "With that knowledge, you should be able to find her."

"That makes no sense," I said, clutching at my arm. The

shoulder wasn't squirting blood, but only because I was creating an impromptu butterfly bandage just by the application of my own pressure. If I moved before it healed, it would rip open and I'd start bleeding all over again. "I'm in Iowa, in 1999, and you're asking me to find my mother. I just told you I don't ever remember living in Iowa. How the hell am I supposed to find her on unfamiliar ground, in an unfamiliar time?"

"Because regardless of time," he said, all serious and grave, another patch of invisibility running over his lower body as it seemed to phase out of sight, "she is still your mother."

And then he was gone.

I thudded my head against the brick wall. "Clearly..." I said, gritting my teeth against the pain as it swelled, again, to a crescendo, and I toppled over into a trash can, "...you know nothing about me...or my mother..."

Then I was out again.

I woke to a click, the sound of something mechanical, something familiar...

Something...

Serious.

A gun safety being flicked off.

I opened my eyes to find myself staring down a long barrel, one that swept back to a shotgun, pool of circular darkness right in the center where the shot would come flying out and blow my brains out the back of my head.

Looking past the gun, I saw pale hands gripping it steadily, and a blue eye staring at me over the open sights, a single overhead bulb granting me sight in the dark of the alley.

"This keeps getting better and better," I mumbled, testing my shoulder. Still hurt, but not as bad. I looked at the woman who held her shotgun on me, steadily, finger on the trigger. "Hi, mom."

6.

"I already have a round in the chamber," my mother said, keeping the shotgun steady at my face, "so I have no need to threaten you by racking one just for the scary sound it makes-"

"Yep, never go without a round ready to fire, that's just amateur hour," I said, looking at her through partially squinted eyes. "And don't even get me started on the kind of idiot that would eject a precious shell just to threaten. Losers."

"Make no mistake, I am threatening you," she said, and she brought the barrel a little closer. Not close enough I could snatch it and knock it away, but enough to menace. "Who are you?"

"My name is Sienna Catherine Nealon," I said, and watched my mother's jaw tighten. "The grown-up version, anyway. You should know. You hauled the miniature version of me away from the playground earlier."

"You could at least pick a more plausible lie," she said, keeping the gun leveled on me. "Rather than one that's transparently, stupidly obvious."

"If I was interested in lying, yes, I could have," I said, putting on a kind of hammy rural accent. "I could have come up with something like, 'I'm Jane, from Des Moines, and my meta powers are wrasslin' pigs'. Something like that." I locked eyes with her. "But I'm Sienna, from Minneapolis, and I'm a succubus. And I am in the very, very wrong year."

"Why would I believe you?" she asked, almost whispering.

"Because you raised me, nimrod," I said, feeling a nice ache along my flank where I'd collapsed on the trash can. "Because I just took a bullet for you – and me, technically. Because in your time at the agency, you had to have seen some weird shit. I don't think I've been active in the meta world as long as you have and the shit I have seen? Would frizz – well, actually straighten – even your hair."

Her hair was totally straight, but most people probably didn't realize that was the work of a flat iron, because my mother, like me, had some serious natural frizz. "I'll grant you there's some weird stuff out there," she said, not lowering the shotgun at all. "But you want to sell me on this bullroar about you being Sienna? Sell me. For real. Tell me something only the two of us would know, not stupid details about my hair that anyone could have figured out from following me."

"Listen, mom, your hair's natural curl was a closely guarded secret from the outside world when I was growing up," I said. "Explain to me why you spent all that damned time flat-ironing it – we're talking hours a week out of your life – if you didn't want to keep it quiet?" I shook my head. "All right, fine. You want the inside dirt only someone who grew up in your house would know? Here goes: you shed like a dog-"

"So do a lot of women. That's hardly convincing evidence."

"I mean it's everywhere. You don't even bother to clean it, you made me do it, so I was forever running a wet piece of toilet paper against the baseboards and coming away with a full fur-baby, like we had one of those long-haired dogs-"

"That's not specific enough."

"Fine," I said, seething. "You trim your nails with scissors and no damns given for where the clippings fall. Which is really gross, by the way. Walking out to watch TV in the morning and getting a big toe's splinter stuck in my foot? I'd dance the heebie jeebies out, wake you up, and you'd get so mad-"

She lowered the barrel an inch. "That's...possible."

"You believe me now?" I asked. "Because of toenails? Good to know." I gestured to my shoulder. "Mind helping me up? Gently? I don't want to tear this scab-stitch before it has a chance to fully heal."

"Hold it right there, missy," she said. "I need some questions answered first. The basics, at least – let's assume I go along with who you say you are-"

"Thanks for the benefit of the doubt. I took a bullet for you – and me – so that's really touching, ma."

"-but I still want to know the answers to the other questions – what, when, where, why and how."

I blinked. "Well, 'where' and 'when' are kinda obvious, aren't they? Clearly Des Moines, 1999. Actually, I should be asking you *why* the hell Iowa-"

"Fine," she waved the barrel just slightly, an inch or so. "'What, why, how'. Answer them."

"Uhm...I don't fully know?" I shrugged, it hurt my shoulder, I did a little cringe. "Okay, try this – I got dragged out of my life by this guy I know who messes with time. Told there's a problem with...well, time."

Her eyes narrowed in the shadows of the alley. "What's the name of your Doc Brown figure in this?"

"Oh, cool, we can use *Back to the Future* as a point of reference," I said. "That'll make things easier. His name's Akiyama."

She bristled, brought the gun back on target. "Akiyama has been on an isolated island in Japan for decades. No one sees him."

"Not in 1999, obviously," I said, "but in the future – your future, my past – I helped him solve his...issues. Anyway, he's out and about doing stuff again. Including messing with my life and ripping me out of time, apparently."

"Okay, that's 'how'. Why?" she asked. "And what's happening?"

"If you can get him to tell you, you'll be having better luck than I am," I said. "Speaking of, how are those bullet wounds treating you?"

"Superficial," she said. "Yours hit an artery?"

"Yes," I said. "But it was a through and through, so at least I didn't have to extract the bullet in a dirty alley with my fingers."

She lifted up the shotgun barrel, finally taking it off me. She watched me carefully, but there was inch of relaxation in her features. "You really are Sienna, aren't you? You said it exactly like I would have."

"Well, I learned from the best," I said, offering a hand. She took it and carefully pulled me up, and I tugged loose of her before my powers could start to work. "Careful. You don't want to end up in my head."

She blinked, trying to keep her composure. "So... you're a succubus, too?"

"Well, I'm not a windkeeper like dad," I said, and she flinched slightly. "Yeah. I'm a succubus. Like my mother and grandmother before me." That sent off a little chill down the back of my neck. If this was 1999, my mom had no idea her mother was alive. If there was any lesson I'd learned from *Back to the Future*, it was that telling people too much about the future and exposing them to knowledge they shouldn't know was only a good idea if they were going to be gunned down by Libyan terrorists.

"You know about your grandmother?" she asked, muted.

"I've been through...a hell of a lot," I said. "Almost all of which I can't even tell you about, because..."

"Timeline," she said, nodding slowly. "That'd be a convenient lie, if audaciously big. Making some nice gaps in your back story that you don't have to answer because it'd 'ruin my future'." She did not raise the shotgun, though.

"And yet," I said, "here we are. There are just things I flat-out can't tell you."

"You became like me?" she asked, looking me over. "Your job, you...?"

"I hunt criminal metas, yeah," I said, "though it's more of a calling than a job at this point, strictly speaking." How much did I want to explain to my mother that I'd spent the last two years on the run? Kinda like she was now?

Not at all. That was how much I wanted to share with my mother that little nugget.

And how had I not connected those dots before now? That yet again I'd followed in the footsteps of Sierra Nealon, hiding from the powers that be?

"That's...really something," she said, but didn't look me in the eye. "Are you any good at it?"

"I do all right," I said. "Saved the world a time or two."

She inclined her head, a very slight show of respect. "Not bad."

A thought occurred to me. "Uhm...where am I?"

She blinked. "Right here."

"No, I mean – where am *I*?"

"Des Moines, Iowa-" she said, a little slowly, about a second from taking a step back.

"Not *me*, here in the alley," I said, coming off the wall to a burst of pain in the shoulder. "Argh, ow. Not big me – little me, from earlier. The one the guys with guns were after. Where's she?"

"Sleeping," mom said, a little more guarded. "I had to leave her behind to...hunt you down. It's not like I could leave her in the car parked on the street. She's safe, though."

"You left me alone in a house? How could you – oh, never mind, this totally makes sense," I said. "It's like a preview of my future. Of course you left me alone. How'd you find me?"

She frowned, thinking it through. "Oh. Big you this time?"

"Let's go with 'adult me', to spare my feelings. Also, I'm down quite a bit over where I was a couple years ago, so let's not send me into a shame spiral."

Her frown deepened. "You left a blood trail from the scene. Picked it up outside the police perimeter, followed you right to it. You're lucky they didn't pick it up. They'd have found you before I did."

"Who are the bad guys?" I asked, steadying myself.

She seemed to make a decision, of sorts. "Come on," she said, and beckoned me forward, putting the shotgun aside, letting the barrel droop to mid-calf. "Let's get you out of here. Your wound may have scabbed up, but we should bandage it until it fully heals. Can you walk on your own?"

"I doubt it," I said, still huddled against the wall, leaning on it.

A moment of indecision flickered across her features, and she reached a hand out. "Well...let's go. Before I change my mind about this insanity."

"Yes, helping your adult daughter walk after a GSW is definitely insanity," I said, pushing off the wall slowly and letting her snug an arm around my waist as we limped down the alley together. She slipped the shotgun beneath her coat. "Actually it's more like a family teambuilding exercise. Ow. Ow. Let's not turn it into a trust fall, though. Because that would probably re-open my arterial bleed." With every step, a little jarring movement of pain scorched down my shoulder where I'd taken the bullet.

"My daughter is not currently an adult," mom said, terse, "so forgive me if this is a little outside my present realm of experience."

"You're forgiven," I said as we approached the mouth of the alley. There were street lights glowing a white-yellow, shining down on the quiet avenue. Red and blue police lights were still flashing in the distance on the other side of the park, where they were maintaining a perimeter or vigil. "But the question remains – who were those guys? Who were they with? And what did they want with me? Little me?"

My mother's jaw worked into a tight joint as we moved along the street, her helping me with every step. "I don't know," she said, as we hobbled on into the night. "And not knowing...well, it scares the hell out of me."

7.

"Seriously, why Iowa?" I asked, leaning my head against the cool, passenger-side glass pane of my mother's car. "You raised me better than Iowa. Hell, you raised me to rag on Iowa every chance I got."

My mother was at the wheel, the street lights shining in through the windshield, shadows playing across her face as we would pass one, the instrument illumination from the car a pittance of light comparatively. "So what you're saying is, we go back to Minneapolis for the majority of your upbringing?"

"Sorry to spoil the future for you – nah, I'm just kidding. Spoiling it would be telling you we stay in Iowa. And by spoil, I do mean 'utterly ruin, forever, desecrating any and all hope'. Because, Iowa."

"It's a nice place," she said, ghost of a smile disappearing as the shadows returned after we passed another street light. "Quiet, until now."

"So you have no idea who those guys with guns were?" I asked, pulling my head off the window. How many times had I ended up injured in cars, letting someone else drive me somewhere while I tried to heal and use the car window's coolness to soothe me from the pain? It felt like a lot. Hadn't I done that with Angel a week ago? Or...twenty years hence? Whatever it was. Time was so confusing.

"They could be...I don't know," my mother said. "I had no shortage of enemies when I left the biz. It could be that guy...that guy that just...that killed-"

"Dad?" I asked, flicking a gaze toward her. She registered a little surprise, then nodded, once. "Yeah. I know all about dad and how he came to his end."

"Do you know who that man was?" mom asked. "The one who killed him? The one who-"

"I know him," I said. Sovereign. That bastard. I knew him and I'd killed him. Story of my life. Meet bad guy, kill bad guy. That's the Sienna Nealon way.

"It could be him," she said. "But he's hardly the only person I've pissed off in my life."

"I can sympathize with that," I said, nodding along. "Like for example, I put all these people in meta jail. Took years. And then a Supreme Court decision set them all free-"

"Why was the Supreme Court ruling on a metahuman case...?"

"Doesn't matter," I said, trying to gloss over that. Metas had been outed en masse when I was eighteen; I'd forgotten that right now we were in a world where people having superpowers was a closely held secret. "Anyway, they all got released and, big surprise, decided to come after me." I chuckled, mostly to keep from crying, since that sequence of events had resulted in my entire life going down in flames and fugitivity. Which is a word I just made up. "Good times."

"Looks like you made it through okay," she said, a little cautiously, looking over at me.

"I did," I said. "They didn't do so well, though."

She only gave me another moment's consideration before nodding, curtly. "Good."

"So... how long have you been living in hell?" I asked, indicating the window and the greater Des Moines metropolitan area with a nod of my head.

"Not long," she said with an under-the-breath chuckle. "We just got here." Her smile disappeared. "Already feels like forever, though."

"Iowa will do that to you. It's 1999, and summer, so...I'm five," I said, working it through in my head.

"Do you remember any of this?" she asked, nodding at the buildings passing outside the car.

"No," I said, frowning.

"Most people don't remember much before they're five or six," she said, shrugging lightly as she guided the car into a turn down a residential street. "I guess it's not that uncommon, what you're experiencing." A little veil of suspicion remained on her face that she couldn't hide, though.

"I guess," I said. "You'd know more about child psychology and development than I would. My exposure to kids has been somewhat...limited."

"So I'm not a grandmother yet, that's what you're telling me in a roundabout way?" she asked, sizing me up again. "How old are you?"

"You should never ask a lady her age."

"I didn't, I asked you," my mother said impishly. "And after knowing you – adult you – for all of ten minutes, I can tell already that ladylike behavior just isn't in your wheelhouse."

"Why, I am shocked. Shocked and appalled that you would think that me – humble little me, could be capable of – aw, hell, I'm kidding. Ladylike behavior went out the window several hundred dead bodies ago."

"'Several hundred'...?" My mother's eyes widened subtly. "As in... victims of the murderers you've hunted...?"

"Ahhhh...let's go with that," I said, not doing a very convincing job of selling that particular lie. "Hey, trying to hunt down dangerous metas isn't exactly an afternoon tea. It gets messy. Messier when you throw in all the mercenaries that people keep tossing at me."

"But..." she shook her head and looked back at me for confirmation. *"'Hundreds'?"*

"That's just a guesstimate," I said. "It's probably high."

Narrator: It wasn't high. Not even for this week. I'd killed over a hundred mercenaries in the quarry when I'd gone to save Angel, another few people in the Cube during my stint in prison, and several hundred more during the war in Revelen.

Man. I was not exactly living my best life, was I? Unless you defined killing literally a thousand or more people before age thirty as part of living your best life, in which case I was doing *awesome*. There were probably a lot of serial killers out there who would find me a very tasty prospect, and not just in the cannibalistic sense.

"How many people have you killed, exactly?" she asked, and her tone was very 'mom'.

"I can't tell you that," I said, tightly, clamming up, "for reasons of timeline." And also because I still possessed a scintilla of shame at my profligate taking of human life. If you could define mercenaries who killed for money and murderous prisoners as human. And apparently I still sort of did.

"Uh huh," she said, but you could see the tension ratchet up a notch in her shoulders, her arms becoming more straight-lined to the steering wheel, like ropes that someone had tightened. "Timeline. Sure."

"Look…" I said. "I feel like we're getting off track here-"

"I'm not off track," she said. "I'm wondering why a woman who claims to be my daughter from the future has killed hundreds of people. That seems important."

"Would it help if I said I was joking?" I asked. Her face turned even more serious. "So... that'd be a no, then."

"Maybe I should have raised you in Iowa," she said, looking straight ahead. "Maybe it would have turned out better for you if I had. Slower pace, less murderousness."

I chucked a thumb behind us. "That thing in the park didn't seem like murderousness to you? Because it felt like it to me." I brushed my wounded shoulder.

She just shook her head in that utterly mom way, such disappointment flowing out of her. "I just...I can't..."

"There were...reasons for all the killing," I said, a little lamely. "Self-defense reasons. I'm in a lot of danger, a lot of the time. Come on. You know this field of endeavor isn't exactly a safe career path."

She gave me a sideways look that radiated anger. "You know how many people I've had to kill in my career?"

"A lot."

Her face fell a little. "Yes. A lot. But less than a hundred." She shifted uncertainly in her seat. "Probably."

I laughed. "I like how you mustered up the righteous indignation that lasted up until you realized you couldn't remember how many people you've actually killed."

"Laugh all you want," she said, voice turning hard, "but

forgive me for letting it worry me that a woman who claims she's my daughter is so cavalier about killing. It's not a good look for you. It kind of reminds me of-"

"Of your mom?" I asked, looking at her out of the corner of my eye. "Or of great-grandpa Hades?" Her head snapped around as soon as I said it. "Yeah, I know all about our lineage. We're descended from the God of Death. I guess I've just sort of made peace with what I am."

"Which is?"

"Literal death to those who wish to visit it upon others," I said. "I'm the sword of the innocent. Or something," I shook my head. "I dunno. I'm still workshopping it."

"I'd keep working on it, because that doesn't sound great," she said, turning back to the road and taking a sudden left turn without signaling it. She must have caught my look out of the corner of her eye. "What?"

"You have a blinker for a reason, you know. It's not just ornamentation on the car."

"You've killed hundreds and you're judging me for not using a turn signal?"

"Yes," I said, "mine were justified kills. There's no justification for not signaling your turn. Only monsters do that."

She started to take a breath to say something, but it leaked out in a weak laugh. "I can't tell when you're joking."

"It's almost all the time," I said.

"Your dad used to do that," she said, shaking her head. "It'd drive me nuts. We'd be in the middle of a serious mission and – boom, he drops a sarcastic quip that would have me snorting in spite of myself." She looked at me sideways, and there was a brief moment of grief written all over her face. "You sound...so much like him."

"I didn't remember you dropping quips all that often when I was a kid," I said, thinking it over. "I mean, you would, sometimes. You had that really dry delivery, and you talked over my head most of the time, so it was tough to tell until I got older and 'got it', but..." I drew a sharp breath. "It makes sense that I would have gotten it from dad, because..."

I stopped myself before I said, "Because it feels like Reed

and I share a brain sometimes." No need to let my mom in on the fact that I was well aware of my step-brother, especially since she was not a huge fan of him at this juncture. For whatever reason. Probably petty jealousy.

"Is this one of those 'timeline' things?" she asked, frowning. "One of those things I can't know?"

"You're probably better off not knowing it, yeah," I said, turning back to the windshield. She took us around another leisurely turn – signaling it this time – and then we pulled into a driveway.

The house was a one story built up slightly from the road, cute with white wood siding and a dark roof, the color of which I couldn't tell in the dark. Mom killed the ignition and opened the door, stepping out and circling around behind us before she opened my door for me.

"Thanks," I said, taking her hand as she dragged me free of the vehicle quickly, keeping my hand in hers once we were out. I looked her in the eye; she looked back at me.

She did not take back her hand.

"Ooookay," I said, loosening my grip. "If you want to do this, just make sure you pull away once you know the burn is happening to you."

She gripped me tighter, looking me right in the eyes. "I will. If I have to."

"You'll have to," I said, as I felt the faint stirrings of my power working along the surface of my palm.

She stared at me with full intensity bordering on anger as my succubus power began to tickle at her skin. She felt it, I knew from my own experience being on the drainee side of the power thanks to Rose, but in the early seconds it was tough to tell if it was your power or your opponent's. She was glaring at me, probably starting to feel the burn, but wanting to confirm it beyond all doubt.

I tried to keep a straight face, but it wasn't easy. I hated to play into the ugly, internet conversations about my abilities, but succubus powers did have an almost sexual sensation to them. That much the internet got right, no matter how much I wished it weren't the case. It was a power that let me look into the very soul of others, to carve off slices or rip the whole thing from their body, causing the not-*petit mort*. The big death, rather.

And when it was done...and I mean really done, the soul ripped free of them and in me...yeah, there was an unhealthy satisfaction there that I had never wanted to explore too deeply for fear of what it might bring out in me.

My mom tore her hand away as the power started to really ramp up the burn, and I felt the first stirrings of her soul, tiny tendrils of her self slip into my head, a faint shadow without substance or form or thought. I took a ragged breath as she staggered a step back. "Satisfied?" I asked, then cringed. "Sorry. Poor choice of words."

Disgust mingled with pain across her twisted lips and narrowed eyes. "Well, I believe you're a succubus now. And a stronger one, at that. But you could be a distant relation for all I know."

I looked down at myself, then back up at her. "Come on, mom. Except for my hobo-chic, post-war fashion look, we're practically twins."

"You could be a kid of my sister's," she said, sticking her chin out in defiance.

"Ewww," I said, "I didn't know Charlie had any kids. That's frightening."

"She doesn't, as far as I know," my mother said, softening slightly at the mention of her sister's name. "And which I thank God for." She thought for another second, dark hair glistening in the street lamp's glow. "Fine. You could be a skin changer. With double powers, the second being succubus-type."

"Paranoia, thy name is Nealon," I muttered, rolling my eyes. I felt a little quiver run through my legs, which had grown tired of holding me upright. "Would you make a damned decision about where we're going? The blood loss is starting to get to me, and I need to sit down. Again."

"Fine," my mother said, and grabbed me around the waist again, pulling me off the car and shutting the door quietly. "But know this – I don't entirely believe you-"

"This is so shocking. I had no idea based on your behavior."

"-And this goes against my best judgment," she said, pulling

34

me along up to the front porch, "Also, I'll most likely kill you in the morning."

"Well, okay then, Dread Pirate Roberts. Better catch me sleeping, though, because if you come at me awake, you're going to have a hell of a fight."

She softened a little as she dragged her keys out of her pocket and unlocked the front door. "You really are my daughter, aren't you." Not a question.

"As much as I might have wished I wasn't about a thousand times when I was a kid," I said, and she pulled me into the house and closed the door. "Yeah. I really am."

She pulled me across the room carefully, and in the low light I could see a couch. I drooped down onto it as she turned me loose, controlling my descent so I didn't crash and burn on the cushions. I ended up flat on my back, my shoulder mewling in pain as she pulled back my blouse to look at it. "It's not so bad. Bleeding a little now from moving. I'll bandage it for you."

"You do that," I said, light-headed, voice dragging with fatigue and pain. "I'm just gonna...take a little nap...rest my eyes...replenish my blood supply..."

"Go on," she said. "I'll be right back with..."

I missed whatever she said as I slipped into the total embrace of the darkness, passing out. When I woke, light filled the room, streaming in through curtains, a shadow loomed over me-

And I was face to face with someone I never expected to be. Myself.

8.

"Hi."

The word came out a lot higher pitched than was usual for me.

Which made sense, because the me that said it...was not me.

Okay, it was me, but littler. Twenty years littler.

Man, my eyes were a bright blue, reflecting the sun shining in through white curtains. The little face was shining, curious, open – all the opposite of my current state – dingy, annoyed, cynical, twenty years of getting my ass beat down by mom, life and the world knocking all that youthful optimism out of me and replacing it with well-worn snark and more than a little pain.

"Ow," I said mildly, moving my shoulder. It still ached a little, but the balance of the pain was gone, leaving only a trace behind to remind me I'd been shot yesterday. "Hi," I returned at last.

"You're not my mommy," she said, peering down at me, nose only a few inches from mine. "Who are you?"

"I'm..." I suffered sudden brain lock, surprising considering I'd been on the run for two years and had been coming up with fake names, often on the fly, that whole time. "...Uh...Sienna."

She blinked a couple times at me, little clearly-defined eyelashes fluttering. "Yes?"

She'd taken my dumbfounded speaking of my name as me calling her by hers, giving me a few more seconds to come up with something. "I'm...Debra."

She made a frowny face, scrunching her lips together. "That's a funny name."

I did a little frown of my own in return. "So's 'Sienna'. You know what it means? Brown. It means brown."

Her nose wrinkled further. "I don't like brown. It's not my favorite color."

"Brown's not anyone's favorite color," I said. "Well, maybe a scatophiliac."

Someone cleared their throat from across the room and I turned. My mom – our mom? Weird how that worked – was standing there with a very *mom* look upon her face, irritation and disappointment all rolled up into one. "Sienna-"

"Yeah?" we both answered. Little Sienna looked at me and furrowed her little brow. "Sorry," I said. "I'm Debra. For real. For really real."

"Go play," mom said, and little Sienna ran off to the far corner of the room, which I could see in the light was a living area, complete with couch and TV and a few toys. She retreated to the area where a dollhouse was clustered with a little Barbie convertible and a few dolls. They weren't fancy or huge, but it was a respectable little play area. She settled down with a couple of the girl dolls and was murmuring to herself within seconds, ensconced in her own little world. I could hear her, of course, as she called one of the dolls 'Debra' and started to take them on a trip somewhere in the car.

Mom eased closer to me, arms folded, one eye on the little girl now playing the corner, mother lioness between her cub and danger. "How are you feeling?"

I indicated my shoulder, pulling free the bandage she'd apparently put on it after I'd collapsed last night. The skin was nearly flawless, only a little red to indicate where I'd taken the bullet. "Good as new."

She nodded, keeping her head down. "Come with me," she said, making her voice low enough that little Sienna couldn't hear it.

I followed her from the room and into the kitchen, where she slipped over to the sink and flicked the faucet up. Within seconds, steaming water was pouring out as she stoppered the drain. There were dishes filling one side of the sink, and an empty plastic drying rack on the counter awaited clean ones. "Help me do these?" she asked.

"You wash, I dry," I said. She shook her head. "Bummer." I slipped into position on the side of the sink that was filling and grabbed the dish soap bottle, squeezing some in. "Day one back at home and I'm already getting stuck with chores."

"If you inherited my singing voice, you're going to have to do something other than sing for your supper." She fished a dish towel out of a low drawer and came back over to stand next to me as I took hold of the sponge and started working on a plate that looked like it had weeklong, crusted PB&J lingering on the surface.

"Yeah, it's a real shame metahuman ability boosts didn't extend to singing voices," I said. "You'd think that'd fall under our superior abilities, but no, I sing and it sounds like I'm forcing a cat into a garbage disposal."

Mine mom stiffened beside me. "But...you've never actually done that, have you?"

"What? No!" I bristled. "I may have racked up a high body count in the line of duty, but I'm not into animal cruelty. Unless you count that time a shifter posed as my dog to spy on me. Him I could have done some animal cruelty to."

"Why would a shifter spy on you?" my mother asked, pausing in the middle of drying the first dish.

"Long story," I said. "Why are men with guns after you and little me?"

"I don't know," she said, sighing. "Like I imagine you do, I have enemies."

"Boy, do I have enemies," I said. "Most of them are dead now, but still...enemies."

"Well, most of mine are still breathing," she said, looking over her shoulder, probably to make sure little Sienna hadn't crept into the room as we were discussing killing people. "Which leaves it an open question as to who sent those two after us. I didn't recognize either of them, though."

"So they were probably working for someone else," I said with a nod. "They seemed the lackey sort."

She took up another plate from me and dried it, setting it

into the drying rack. "Look, I don't want to alarm you, but...do you have any money?"

"No," I said, not even bothering to check my pockets because I knew I didn't. I'd gone from jail straight to Revelen, and from Revelen back to my little prison room in DC. I didn't have a wallet, car keys, a pen, nothing. I didn't even have a gun anymore, because the Navy corpsman had disarmed me (wisely) before they'd carried me out of Hades's castle.

My mother evinced a short, sharp reaction that looked like a muted curse. "How do you not even have a driver's license with you?" She looked me up and down. "And what happened to you? You look like you've been through hell."

"Let's just say I'd already had a rough week before I ended up here," I said. "Not gonna say it was the worst week ever, because I'm sure I've been through worse, but it's definitely high in the rankings. Anyway, all my cash is in banks. My ID is...uh...toast, I guess. I don't really have anything on me."

She cursed under her breath again. "We're out of food. And I don't have any cash on hand."

"Yikes," I muttered. "That's not good."

She didn't meet my eyes, instead focusing hard on drying the plate in her hands. "Like you said...it's been a rough week all around."

"What do you mean?" I asked, pausing in my dishwashing as I handed her a newly-rinsed fork. We were through the dishes and now on to the silverware.

"Someone froze one of my accounts," she said. "I found out yesterday when I tried to access it from a branch a few blocks away from the park." Her eyes were heavily lidded, and she was looking down.

"That's how they found you," I said. "They figured out you accessed the money and boom – they knew you were in the area after you attempted a withdrawal." I paused, my eyes flicking back and forth as I pondered that one. "They must have had people nearby, then, if they got to you within-"

"Twenty minutes, I think," she said, nodding along. "I'd promised Sienna all day that we could go to the park after mommy ran her errand. I figured..." She shook her head, blowing air between her lips. "I figured I'd have at least a few hours before anyone got into Des Moines, if this was an attempt to track me down. I used a branch bank twenty minutes from the house. Passed up two closer branches to get there. I thought we had time."

"If these people have agents stationed in Iowa," I said, working it through, "and got to you within twenty minutes...this is not a small organization after you. Had you made any withdrawals here before that?"

"We were in Wyoming until a few weeks ago. Staying with a friend. I made my withdrawals large, in cash, and the last one I did in Northern California over a year ago. I should have made another before we left Wyoming, but..." She shook her head. "I didn't want to drop any heat on my friend. Didn't want to leave a trace. And..." She looked down at the wet towel in her fingers. "I thought we were clear of all this. That...whoever these people are...that maybe everyone had finally stopped looking for me."

"Whoops," I said, handing her a spoon. "I mean...that sucks."

She rolled her eyes, drying the spoon and sticking it in the rack. "Yeah. To say the least. But it doesn't exactly help now that I know that." She looked right at me. "I need money, and we need food."

My stomach rumbled as if to emphasize that point. My flight from Revelen to the US hadn't exactly been filled with cuisine. I'd had an MRE at one point and that was about it. "Okay. Well. I can get groceries, obviously, but...there's nothing I can do about the money. I don't have a bank account in this era." I clicked my tongue against the roof of my mouth. "Do you have a backup bank account, maybe?"

She sighed. "No."

"Wow, all your eggs in one basket," I said. "That's very un-mom of you."

"I didn't have much in the way of eggs to begin with," she said quietly. "It wasn't like the government paid well, and my mom and dad didn't exactly leave me an inheritance."

I felt a little heat suffuse my cheeks. "Oh?" I asked. She didn't know her mom was still alive. Or a princess.

"No," she said, "they pretty much left me with nothing. This

40

was going to be the last withdrawal before I had to find some sort of work of my own to pay for...well, living."

"Okay, so...we're basically out of money," I said, ticking off the problems at hand, "and there's no easy way to get more unless we want to...I don't know, rob a bank-"

"That's not something I want to do," she said, glaring at me through slitted eyes. "Seriously, what the hell have you been doing in life?"

"Surviving. Would you rather starve?" I asked, then cocked my head toward the archway to the living room. "Or have her starve?"

"We have enough for a small grocery run," my mother said, looking behind her again to make sure little me hadn't crept into the room. "I think."

"How much do you have?" I asked.

"Twenty bucks."

"I don't know what the price of anything is in this time," I said, "but...we should be able to buy some milk and eggs and a ham and... I dunno, stuff...for that, right?"

She nodded, slowly. "Some. Not a ton, though. Enough for a week or two, but it's not a long-ranging plan. If those guys that showed up yesterday are what I think they are-"

"They're the first tendrils of a larger organization," I said, nodding along. I had the barest suspicion about which organization it could be; there were a few possibilities, unfortunately – Alpha, the Directorate, Century, or...

Omega.

That last one made me quiver a little in the belly, but I ignored it. There was also the possibility that this was some other group, some group that either had ceased to be in the twenty years between now and my own time, or one that was underground that I hadn't run across yet. For all Hades's blather about staying clear of trouble in the US, this could be his doing for all I knew.

"Too many secret clubs in the meta world," I said, and my mother nodded along. "Too many stupid little conspiracies."

"Hear, hear," my mother said, and took the last fork out of my hand and rinsed it herself, giving it a cursory dry before she let it clatter into the rack. "But there are too few of us to make a dent in that problem right now." She looked me dead in the eye, and it was almost like looking into my own again. "I need to get my daughter out of this town. If they know we're here, they're going to keep looking. And if they catch us-"

"Yeah, I get the stakes," I said, nodding. "They get her...time breaks, because I'm no longer following the normal course of events." I shook my head. "That's what Akiyama was talking about. This is why he brought me here."

"Great, so there's trouble for both of us if we don't get this done," she said.

"I'd say so."

"So... how do we do it?" she asked, and for maybe one of the first times ever, my mother fell silent and looked at me expectantly, as if I were the one with all the answers.

I took a deep breath and looked out the window beyond the sink. It was covered by veiled white sheers, and the morning sun was shining in on us. The house next door was visible as a shape through the cloth, but most of the detail was blurred by the fabric. "Well...I like to tackle my problems one at a time. You know, cut 'em into manageable pieces and then manage those pieces. Which means first things come first-"

"Mommy?" a little voice came, and my mother and I both turned to find mini-me standing at the archway, her little head down but her eyes up, beseechingly, pitifully, looking at us. "I'm hungry."

My mother looked at me and I nodded. "First things first," she said, and forced a smile, turning it back toward little Sienna. "Okay, sweetie. Let's go get you something to eat."

9.

"...The wheels on the bus go 'round and 'round, all through the town."

I tried to keep my voice low on the chorus, the three of us singing along as we drove. It was just us three, none of whom was particularly good at staying on key, and all of us lacked decent pitch. Two of us were aware of it, my mother keeping her voice lower as well, trying to color within the limited lines her voice provided.

Little me, though? She sang at the top of her lungs and gave no damns about how horrible it sounded.

And it sounded...so bad. So very happy...but soooooo bad.

"Well, we definitely inherited your singing voice," I said, meta-low, as little me moved into the next verse, blissfully unaware that mom and I had stopped singing along. My mother wore a pained expression. She seemed to be experiencing the same aural discomfort I was, our metahuman hearing coupled with little Sienna's loud, off-key singing making us both grimace in pain.

"Don't blame me for this, I quit howling last verse," my mother said, under her breath. "This is all you."

"I'm a child," I said. "I don't know any better."

"What about when you killed all those people?" my mother asked, looking sideways at me, taking us into another turn without signaling. "Did you not know any better then?"

"Well, you did train me to never hesitate," I said, offering a light shrug. The smaller me in the back seat hit a particularly

43

bad note and I shuddered. "Though I wish little me would hesitate instead of wading into each note like it's an enemy I have to kill."

My mother just cringed, and I couldn't tell if it was from the conversation or the singing. Both were worthy candidates.

"Walmart is just up here," my mother said. I could see from the sign it was a supercenter, the grocery and retail store combined in one glorious place where you could pick up a gallon of milk, a pair of underwear and a shotgun all under the same roof. I kind of felt like I needed all three right now, though I doubted they'd sell me the shotgun without an ID. Or the money to pay for it.

"How are you doing for ammo?" I asked.

My mom hesitated. "Not great." She patted her purse. "I have a 1911 in here. Two spare magazines. In case things get...hairy. Shotgun in the trunk, twenty rounds total, five in the magazine."

"I had a... something...yesterday," I said, trying to remember what I'd picked up from those guys in the park. Whatever it was, I'd lost it in the alley or before, and had no memory of what happened to it now. "Guess that's kinda useless at this point."

My mother nodded. "We'll make do."

"Improvise," I agreed. "It's what I'm best at anyway."

"Does that mean you get caught flatfooted due to lack of planning a lot?" she asked, throwing me one of her ubiquitous frowns.

"It means I deal with a lot of complex and difficult-to-plan-for situations," I said. "As one does. Besides, you know what von Moltke said about plans and how they don't survive contact with the enemy."

"That sounds like excuses for failure to plan."

"Imagine, if you will, an army of giant Stay-Puft marshmallow men coming after you."

"An army of them?"

"An army, yes. Of several-hundred-foot-tall marshmallow avatars of evil."

She was frowning again. "All right. What now?"

"Plan for that. Keeping in mind proton packs aren't a real

thing."

My mother stared out the windshield for a long moment, then sighed. "Point. I guess."

I pumped my fist in victory. "Yes."

"Sh – uh, crud," my mother said, attention suddenly fixed on the rearview mirror.

"What is it?" I asked and looked in the sideview mirror.

A cop car. Right behind us, trolling along.

I looked over at my mother's speed. 46 miles per hour. "What's the speed limit here?" I asked.

"45," she said.

"Jeez, grandma," I said, "no wonder the cop's looking at you. Probably thinks you're either drunk or heading off to do something criminal. No one drives one mile over the limit."

She gave me a blazing look. "Oh?"

"No. You go at least four over. Maybe as much as nine before you start getting real attention. But not one, unless you're eighty years old or above."

The cop finally pulled around, speeding up as my mother slowed down. We both took a deep breath. About a hundred yards later, she turned into the Walmart parking lot, and by then the police officer had sped out of sight.

10.

"We need to keep this tight," my mother said as she took mini-me's hand and slammed the back door of her car, a two-tone eighties model Buick that had seen better days. It had a slate grey paint scheme on the body, but the roof of the car and the parts that rose up from the window were all a deep brown that looked like leather. It also had a hood that went on for far too long and was a lot boxier than the cars I was used to in modernity.

"I was thinking about this," I said, looking around as my mom held mini-me by the wrist, wrapping her fingers around the sleeve. My younger self was skipping down the parking lot lane, extending her free hand to me so that I could take it, which I did, carefully, by the wrist and over the sleeve like my mother so as not to put a sudden end to my life's journey by accidentally killing myself in the past. As soon as I had a decent hold on her wrist – mirroring how mom was holding her – she brought her legs up to her chest and put all her weight on us, a little human cannonball that we were forced to keep from dropping. "Uhm. Anyway, I was thinking maybe I should follow you through the place rather than walk right with you. You know, provide overwatch?"

Little me hummed something as she got her feet beneath her again and then did the same damned dead-weight thing. It took me a second to realize she was turning us into her own personal swing, wobbling a weak back and forth under our natural forward momentum. My mother didn't even seem to notice. I might not have either, since little me weighed next to nothing, but the sudden pull of her dead weight was a little annoying.

"Anyone who sees us is going to know you're with us if you're hanging in close proximity." She looked me over once. "Also, we should have gotten you some different clothes."

"Yeah, it's the nineties, I feel like I should be wearing parachute pants."

"That's eighties clothing," Mom said.

"Oh, yeah. What's the distinctive nineties clothing item?"

"Hell if I know. I'm still living in the thick of them and don't really have the perspective it would take to judge."

"That's a good point," I said, nodding along as we reached the curb. "You know, I'm not sure the nineties has a distinct look. Nor the decade after. I think we might have reached our apex of cultural distinctiveness in the eighties."

My mom made a face, and it wasn't because little me used us both as a swing again – probably. "I have a hard time believing that MC Hammer and the NES were any sort of cultural apex."

"You knew about the NES?" I asked. Reed was forever playing some stupid emulator of it.

My mom flicked an annoyed gaze my way as we entered the store. "I needed a hobby at the agency, and your father got me one." She shrugged. "It was...fun."

"Yeah, sounds like a real blast," I said, taking up mini-me's weight and lifting her up into the shopping cart my mother had pulled out of the long rows of them in the entryway. Off to the side, a claw toy grabber machine filled with stuffed animals glowed brightly. "I mean, I don't know what you call it when you have real fun, but that sounds like-"

"Oh, shut it," my mother said, pushing the cart as squiggly little me pretended to faint dead away in the child seat, trying to catch my eye. She giggled when I looked at her, a thin slit of eyeball visible through her partially closed lids. She was faking dead, and a peal of laughter was my reward when I stared down at her, pretending like I was looking for signs of life.

"Fooled you!" mini-me said, still giggling.

"I don't ever remember being this joyful," I said.

"That's...sad," my mother said.

"I don't remember ever seeing you joyful, either."

"Well, I've got a few things on my mind right now," she said, steering us past the deli and bakery. None of the fancy Walmart breads for us, no sir. We were on a budget that was literally too cheap for even those. "I imagine that's a trend that continues for the rest of your childhood, based on your crabby disposition."

"Hey, man, don't be talking to me about crabby disposition," I said as we took a left into the bread aisle. "I've had a few things on my mind these last few years, too." Mini-me pretended to faint again, then laughed to the rafters as soon as I saw her looking out through that thin slit between eyelids.

My mother snagged the cheapest bread in the aisle and tossed it into the cart behind young Sienna, who whipped her dark hair around trying to see what her mom had just picked up. Mom had managed to get it right in the middle of the cart, which made it tough for her to really see, but as soon as she realized what it was she tried to reach back and grab it, which did not end in success, fortunately for the bread. Because she was probably not going to treat it with care.

"Okay, fine, we've both got reasons to be cranky," my mother said, scanning the aisle as an old man with heavy jowls and droopy eyelids entered it behind us, pushing his cart very slowly. He looked like an old bulldog and seemed to take no notice of us as he began to examine the bread.

"Well, we're busy and serious people," I said as we cleared the end of the aisle. A giant fridge unit of red meat waited ahead, and my mouth watered just looking at it. I knew that none of that was on the menu, not at our price range, so I shook my head and turned away. "I mean, you've been busy being a mom the last few years and I've been busy...uh...kicking ass and taking names." There. That was generic enough to keep her from discerning the truth of how my life had turned and twisted since Harmon's little kick in the ass.

"We need ramen," my mother said, veering down another aisle.

48

"Ugh," I said. She shot me a curious look. "Sorry," I said. "I just...can't eat ramen anymore at this stage of my life." Because I'd eaten it my entire upbringing. I was foundered on it, as this southern cop I'd met a few years ago said.

"Well, it's that or almost nothing, unless you want to materialize some more money out of thin air," my mother said, dumping a bunch of ramen in the cart. Mini-me got ahold of one, then another, and started to play with them like they were dolls, talking to one another. Who the hell was this kid?

Oh, right, me. Before ten years of aggressive physical training involving martial arts and every weapon known to man. Kinda beats the ability to play with dolls right out of you.

We passed a blond lady with a few wrinkles around her eyes and puckered lips as she tried to decide whether to go with Crispix or Basic 4 cereal, and my mother and I both watched her carefully for any sign she was looking at us. Her cart was almost empty, but she didn't even glance our way as she studied the nutritional information on the side of the box as though it contained the secret to removing all those unfortunate mouth wrinkles. Probably from smoking, I guessed. Smokers tended to develop those more heavily than others. Also she stunk of it as we passed, I had smelled her from five aisles away with my sensitive meta nose.

"I think we need meat," my mother said, and I nodded along until she got to the plastic-wrapped lunch meat fridge. She started scooping a couple containers of turkey and I sighed, apparently loudly enough she noticed, because she snapped around. "What?"

"Oh, nothing, I was just..." I felt a little dumbstruck, caught out in the middle of telling a lie, so I just broke and went for the truth. "That prepackaged meat tastes like plastic."

My mother raised an eyebrow. "Look who's all hoity-toity."

"I have a refined palate, okay? I'm a foodie."

She frowned.

"It's a thing," I said weakly. "In my day. We kinda had this 'food revolution' and now everything tastes better."

"How does that work?"

"I don't know," I said. "More spices, less boiling of stuff, organic produce. I'm not really acquainted with the finer details, I just know stuff tastes better in my day."

That did not soften my mother's frown one bit. "Sounds like you people are getting soft."

"Yes, drill sergeant, we're getting soft," I said, and meandered down the fridge case to a big ham that was only five dollars. "Can we get this? It'll be good right out of the oven, and the sandwiches we make from the leftovers will be epic-level compared to that plasticky crap you're about to spend perfectly good money on."

She rolled her eyes and tossed the assembly-line mass-produced lunch meat back into the display as I put the ham in the cart. My mother did the mental arithmetic between the bread, the ham, the ramen, and the two bags of super cheap generic knock-off cereal. "We need eggs and milk. Probably heavy on the eggs."

"That's fair," I said. "Maybe some cottage cheese to offset the, uhm...ham and carb weighted nature of the diet?"

My mom looked back down at the cart. "Not sure we can afford much, but...yeah, okay. A tub of cottage cheese. Lucky I stocked up on mustard, ketchup and mayo last week." She looked up at me. "I went to Wendy's and stole a bunch of their packets."

"That's some budget shopping right there," I said, as a guy with terrible, terrible teeth pushed his cart to a stop about ten feet in front of us, examining the dill pickle jars. He threw a cursory glance at us, but shifted his attention quickly, not letting it linger like he gave a damn about us at all. I looked at his mouth only as long as I had to; it was closed now, but his lips pooched out like he had an over and under bite, and from the brief look I'd gotten, it felt like he needed enough dentistry work to keep an entire dental school busy for years.

"I've learned to be cheap and not picky," my mother said, pushing past him as I followed. "Unlike someone." She glanced at me. "I guess your life has turned out all right if you can afford the finer foods."

I shrugged at her fishing attempt. "Like I said, food revolution. But yeah...I've done all right in my life." No need to mention that until a little less than a year ago, I'd had a net worth of a half billion. Sure, it was from thievery (from thieves), but dammit, it was my half-billion. I'd stolen it fair and square. Someday, when I had the time, I was going to get my money back, too, maybe live the high life at last, at least between kicking the ass off of whichever metahuman villain was asking for it that month.

My mother seemed to take that answer in stride, nodding once like it satisfied her. Which hopefully it did, because who didn't want their kid to have done well?

We came around the corner into the last aisle, picking up eggs as we went past them. Now we were in the long channel back to the main aisle that would lead us to the check-outs, and the glass fridge cases that kept the milk cold were to our left. My mother surveyed the aisle ahead carefully; there was no one here.

"Let's get this finished," I muttered, and we rolled forward, little me still playing with the ramen packets, muttering something about taking the prince to the ball. I listened, wondering where the hell my life had gone so off-the-rails, from this innocent little thing to being an action addict who was living for the thrill of hunting down wrongdoers. Clearly the little girl sitting in the cart beside me wasn't thinking about beating the shit out of her fellow humans who stepped out of line.

Somewhere I'd gone way, way off course, and I didn't know quite what to make of her. Other than she was adorable.

It was hard not to admire her innocence as she played, the happy little look on her face as she concentrated on the ramen packets in her hands so completely different from the full-scowl, weapons-grade RBF I saw when I looked in the mirror. I had a deadly look, the kind that sent men running in fear, the kind that had earned me the reputation of being death, itself.

How had I been this little, happy, innocent, singing person only twenty years earlier? I mean, twenty years was a long time for me, especially at twenty-six, but still...that level of metamorphosis was incredible.

"Heads up," my mother said, jarring me out of my reverie. There was movement ahead as Mr. Jowls rolled his cart, now dotted with a few items, into our aisle, looking down as he shuffled along.

"Saw him earlier," I said, meta-low. "On the bread aisle. Didn't give us a look."

She nodded, then turned slowly to look behind us.

I matched her move. The blond lady with the smoker's wrinkles rolled in behind us, also seemingly not paying a whit of attention to us. "Could be coincidence," I said.

"There aren't that many people in the store at this time of morning," my mother said. We were conducting the entire conversation meta-low. "Two of three people we've passed are now in our aisle."

"It's the dairy aisle," I said. "Everyone drinks milk in the nineties. It does a body good, and lactose-intolerance and soy milk aren't a thing yet, are they?"

She shot me a funny look. "They make milk out of soy? How the hell does that work? Where are the udders on a soy bean?"

"It's not actually milk," I said. "It's like a milk substitute. They have almond milk, too, and you don't see any breasts on almonds. Though I suppose they do look slightly boob-like, at least if you're carrying the torpedo kind."

"I'm not so sure your so-called 'food revolution' was much of a revolution," she said. "Maybe a Maoist revolution-"

Ahead, more movement. The guy with the terrible teeth rolled into the dairy aisle, drawing the attention of mother and I.

She swore under her breath. "Coincidence, still?"

"Not looking as likely, is it?" I asked. I felt a little bead of sweat break out on my forehead.

They were all looking at us now, the pretense of shopping cast aside, along with their carts. All three of them – the two in front and the one behind – were standing upright, unmistakable challenge in their postures.

"No," my mother said, "it's not looking likely at all."

And she was right.

We were trapped.

11.

"Plan?" she asked, looking at me as she pulled the cart containing little me closer to her. She kept one hand free, ready to draw her pistol.

"I like that you're letting me quarterback this," I said. Our foes were just standing in place, the three of them, guarding the ends of the aisles, preventing our retreat. Two were in front of us, Mr. Jowls and Bad Teeth, and Smoker Lips was behind us, her raggedy blond hair hanging stringy around her face. "We don't know if they're meta or not."

"Nope," she said. Little me burbled something about a ball as she twirled two ramen packets together. What a childhood I'd had.

"You shoot down the two in front while I engage with the target at our six o'clock," I said, still speaking meta-low. I doubted they could hear us at this distance.

"Copy that," my mother said. "On three?"

"On one," I said, and caught the nod out of the corner of my eye. "One!" I shouted and turned on Smoker Lips.

She moved in a whirl, hair shooting at me in a furious tangle. She was a Medusa, her locks taking on a life of their own as they launched toward me. One of the tendrils seemed to form a fist, sneaking in under my guard and punching me in the stomach.

It had some oomph behind it, the hair punch, and I doubled over. I managed to keep my fists up, though, blocking her second attempt, taking the hit on my right wrist. I batted it

53

away when it lingered after delivering the blow, and I grunted as she came at me again, aiming for the ribs on my right side. She split her hair into several parts and was attacking me with each of them like a damned octopus.

My only advantage, if you could call it that, was that she was a touch slower than I was.

"Hey!" The shout drew my attention for a second. My mother had her pistol out and pointed down the aisle toward the guys, who were advancing on us, but she'd stopped to get my attention. I blinked, catching a hit to the ribs while distracted, and noticed she had something shiny in her hand, which she tossed to me-

A knife.

I snatched it out of the air and brought it around in a hard swing, chopping off one of Smoker Lips's strands like I was hacking my way through the jungle with a machete. "There's a donation for Locks of Love," I said as Smoker Lips grimaced and backed off, retracting her octopus hair. "Come here and we'll make sure all the cancer patients in the world have a nice wig – if they can get that damned awful smoke stink shampooed out."

Gunshots rang out behind me as Smoker Lips picked up her assault. She came at me in a rush, screaming to distract me as she charged, hair leading the way. I hacked off the leading lock but she managed to score a glancing blow against my knife hand with her follow up, and I swatted it away, bringing the knife down as a follow up of my own, hacking the damned thing off. The knife was very sharp and cut through the stiff arms of hair like they were jelly. As soon as I cut through one, the hair would go limp and just fall where it lay, the severed part as dead as any normal person's cut hair. The uncut portion of the tendril would race back to Smoker Lips, apparently deterred or in fear of its life or something.

"You know, you can pick up some product over in the health and beauty section to deal with this split end problem you're suddenly having," I said, taking off two more tendrils as I swung the knife in a circular motion in front of me, trying to shield myself from her attack.

She didn't say anything, and the sound of gunshots

intensified behind me. My mother had apparently gone through the whole magazine and reloaded. Now she was being a little more judicious, because she'd run through all eight rounds in about five seconds. Now I was hearing several seconds between each shot, but I didn't have the time or inclination to check on how she was doing. The scared wailing of little me at the painful sound of all the shooting was like a dagger to the heart in any case.

I took a step back as Smoker Lips paused her assault. Her hair was looking pretty chopped, retracted almost back to her head as she stood a few feet away from me, glaring. The strands wavered a few inches off her head, cautious now that they'd been hacked half to hell by my defensive efforts. "Come at me, girl," I said, waving her on, "let's finish up this pixie cut. It's going to look terrible – but it'll be very 'you'."

She broke into a charge, hair shooting forward like a series of pistons. I couldn't count them, they were coming at me so quickly, and trying to chop them off seemed a futile effort given how many there were. I ducked as they shot over my shoulder, one of them skipping along my left trapezius. It cut me, breaking the skin just as cleanly as if she'd used a knife, and boy did that burn. I wondered if you needed a tetanus shot for a hair cut.

I'm sorry. Terrible pun. But I couldn't help myself.

I slid sideways a step and brought the knife down hard on the hair tendrils that she'd just shot past me. The blade caught half of them at full extension and sheared the damned things good. They drifted down in individual clumps as she brought the rest back in a hell of a hurry, the strands whipping back to her like individual snakes. "Hey, so that's why they thought Medusa had snake hair-"

Something hit me hard in the side, and I realized that she'd reserved enough hair to pull a sneak attack when I dodged. It penetrated under my ribs on the right side, like a knife sneaking in just over my hip.

I let out a gasp and brought my knife down, chopping off the tendril. Strands of bloody hair floated down, colored by the flow out of my fresh wound.

It was hard to tell how deep she'd struck, but it wasn't a

shallow hit. I dropped my arm defensively over the wound as Smoker Lips smiled in satisfaction, wrinkles emphasized as she puckered in glee.

"Okay, then," I said, locking eyes with her and dropping my shoulder.

She must have caught my determination, because the smile evaporated as I charged at her. She threw her hair at me in another desperate, bladed attempt to take off my head as I came at her, but I dropped, sliding across the waxed tile floor and coming in under her defense.

I buried my blade in her belly and launched back to my feet, bringing the knife up, up, up, from her guts to her breastbone, and I didn't stop when I heard the cracking as the metal made contact with bone. I kept it going, using my meta strength to tear through any resistance.

Smoker Lips's eyes went wide as she lifted off the ground from the momentum of my upward thrust. She hung there, feet dangling about a foot off the floor as my attack came to its end, my stroke reaching its rest in the middle of her face.

"Hey!" my mother shouted, and I turned. Mr. Jowls had advanced, and Funky Teeth was a step behind him, using him as a human shield. I saw some spots that looked like bullet impressions, holes in Jowls's clothing. He was still moving forward, though, undeterred by the shots. My mom was changing mags and had stepped out in front of the cart where little me wailed, hands over her ears, face red from screaming at the top of her lungs at all the scary shit going on around her. The improvised ramen packet dolls had fallen to the floor, forgotten.

I glanced back at Smoker Lips. She was dead, twitching, and I kicked her off the knife blade and turned, sprinting at Mr. Jowls. My mother knocked the cart back a step with her hip, partially spinning it around with mini me still screaming in the seat, all the louder because of the sudden violence of being jarred sideways unexpectedly.

"What the hell are you?" I asked as I came at Jowls with the blade bared. I slowed as I got closer, because if the bullets hadn't cut his flabby ass down, I had my doubts that my knife was going to do any better. "A Blob-type?"

56

His eyes flitted, watching the knife, and he smiled around those pudgy cheeks. I hadn't been making a fat joke with the 'Blob' wisecrack. That had been the name of a comic book villain Reed had acquainted me with during one of our dreamwalk chats. He'd gone on and on and on and – you get the point. The Blob was an amorphous, uh, blob of a human being whose power was seemingly impenetrable skin. Shoot him, stab him, run him over with a train – nothing would happen, it'd all just bounce off.

I had a bad feeling this guy had a similar thing going. It was hard to tell whether he was an Achilles who had just let himself go, or whether he was something entirely different. Based on my mother hanging back, I had a feeling I was going to be the one to do the hard experimenting to get to the truth.

He came at me, a glint of joy in his eye at the prospect of doing – well, something surely unpleasant – to me. He giggled under his breath, and raised his hand, Funky Teeth a couple steps behind, still using him as shield.

I came at him with a low thrust of my blade, and it cut through his shirt with ease. I buried it into his belly and he guffawed as it bounced right back out, turned aside as easily as if it had been me blocking Smoker Lips's hair thrusts.

"Great," I muttered, and tossed the knife over my shoulder to my mother. Mr. Jowls watched me do it, still chortling, and then reached for me.

Damn, he was slow.

I pushed his hand out of the way and grabbed him by the throat. His skin was incredibly malleable beneath my grip, sliding and sloshing. He definitely wasn't an Achilles with some extra body fat distributed around, this was its own thing, and I didn't much care for it. "Keep Funky Teeth off my back a sec, will you?" I called to my mother as I pushed past Mr. Jowls's blubberous throat and left my wrist right there at his neck.

"On it," my mother said and took a couple steps to my right, trying to get a clear shot.

I used my superior speed to leap around Mr. Jowls's shoulder. He tried to alter his direction to bump me, but he was too slow for that. I got in behind him and he tried to lower his shoulder and turn into me, but my left arm was still at his throat.

Using a move I'd picked up from General Spider-Monkey Boy Bander Krall, of Revelen, I threw my right arm over Mr. Jowls's throat, meeting my left wrist, which was wedged against his windpipe, locking it in place with my right hand. I gripped myself as tightly as I could, then wrenched Mr. Jowls backward, dragging him off balance and making him gasp as I locked in the choke hold.

"Yeah," I said, dragging him so he couldn't use his slightly superior height to break free. He kicked his legs and bucked as he tried to gain footing and failed, because I was pulling him so quickly he couldn't. There were advantages to being super strong, and one of them was that I could haul a few hundred pounds of jowly douchebag like they were a mere inconvenience. "You're getting choked the eff out, ugly." I tightened my grip, putting my chin against the top of his head as I increased my backward pace.

I couldn't let him get his footing or he'd lift me up and drop back, crushing me beneath his bulk. It probably wouldn't kill me, but it might stun me enough to get me to let go, and I definitely didn't want that. I snugged my grip tighter and tighter, working my wrist across his throat like I was sawing it. I wasn't; I was just pushing in through the layer of blubber he seemed to be trying to summon to his neck's defense. His chin pinched against my forearm, but I ignored the pain as he applied pressure, answering with pressure of my own.

There was no defending against what I was doing to him, though, and he didn't realize that, even as he passed out about ten seconds after I had locked in the hold. Because I wasn't actually choking him. That would have taken a minute or so, trying to get his brain to fight itself out, to lose all oxygen so he could drift into a breathless unconsciousness.

That was too slow, and the stakes of the moment were too high. I swung him around, checking on little Sienna, who was still crying at the top of her lungs, abandoned in a cart by herself as I dealt with Jowls and mom tangled with Funky Teeth. I heard some gunshots over my shoulder and had a feeling that minus his inhuman shield, Funky Teeth was not doing so well.

Mr. Jowls finished his struggle without even a whimper, and I stopped moving backward as his legs went dead, the threat of him overpowering me now ended. Lucky I still had a mostly intact long sleeve on this side, otherwise I would have had a chubby fellow bouncing around in my brain just now.

I kept up the pressure, my wrist against his jugular. I hadn't choked him out – I'd cut off the blood flow to his brain via the jugular vein and carotid artery. Nothing in, nothing out, my metahuman strength the guarantor of his lack of oxygen. I didn't let go, though, spinning around to make sure my mother was okay. If she wasn't, I had a several hundred-pound sack of crap to throw at her assailant.

She was fine, though. The 1911 in her hand was smoking, and Funky Teeth was in his death throes on the ground. His mouth was open and I finally figured out what he was.

An Iron Tooth. He'd made it about a foot from mom before she'd dropped him, and he'd probably been going for the throat. She was retreating backward a step at a time, carefully, gun still pointed at him as Funky Teeth breathed his last.

"Nice shooting," I said, wrenching Mr. Jowls's neck as I altered my grip to take hold of him on both sides of the head. I didn't want him coming after us again, and since I'd never run across him in my future, I had to guess he didn't have much of one in front of him.

I broke his neck cleanly and dropped him to the floor with a thud as my mother watched. Her face fell a little. Not much, but it was there – disappointment.

"Sorry," I said, "but we don't need them coming back on us later."

She nodded, breaking past me and going for little Sienna as I scanned the aisle ahead. There was no sign of anyone else, no sound of screaming in the distance. "I think our grocery run just got cut short," I said, turning to find my mother pulling little me out of the cart to rest on her hip. "We should probably-"

"Shhh," my mother said, putting her forehead against mini me's, using her hair as a shield to her succubus powers. "Shhhhh." She looked right at me. "Shhhh," and I realized she was shushing me. "Do you hear that?" she asked.

"Hear wh-"

Then I heard it.

It was a crashing like thunder, but the skies had been clear when we came in.

A roaring like a tornado, but there hadn't been a cloud in sight.

The sound of crunching metal and destruction, and I turned-

Just in time to see a figure all in black come smashing through the freezer case behind me as cleanly as if he were a runaway train destroying anything in his path.

And my brain clicked, and I knew – everything.

What was happening.

Who was after us.

Because standing in front of me was a man clothed head to foot in metal armor that was anchored to his very skin by dint of his metahuman sticky powers. He'd stepped through the wreckage at a run and stopped in the middle of the aisle, freezer lights flickering all down the row from the damage he'd just done, the hiss of the ruined machinery crackling behind him as he stared at us through his thin eye slits.

I stared back at him, a man I'd killed years ago...or would kill, years from now.

"David Henderschott," I said, and he stared at me, cocking his head in curiosity. Because when I'd met him before – years hence – I'd called him Full Metal Jackass, and he'd worked for...

My jaw tightened.

I lowered my head in anger.

Because yes...now I knew beyond doubt who was after us.

It was the same assholes who had been after me the day I left my house.

I said in a whisper that felt like a hurricane of emotion, anger that I hadn't felt – hadn't even realized I still carried, a bitterness that had stuck with me through all the years since I'd last faced these assholes.

"Omega."

12.

Henderschott didn't waste a minute before he lunged at me, every inch of his skin covered in steel plating. "Get out of here!" I shouted to my mother as he swatted at me, trying knock me aside so he could get after her and, by extension, little me.

I dodged out of his way on the first hit, grabbed his arm, then flung him against the fridge units against the wall. Glass shattered and milk jugs exploded as I slammed him into the display. He landed after only about a foot of swing, feet flipping up as he went over onto his back, weighed down by his armor and off balance from my attack.

Swinging around, I found my mother already charging away, down the outside aisle behind us. She'd turned the corner, back the way Smoker Lips had come, and was sprinting along the coolers lining the outside edge of the building. We'd passed an Emergency Exit somewhere around the meat department, and hopefully she'd head for that because it'd be a hell of a lot easier to reach than the front entrance.

I glanced back at Henderschott, who was clawing to get out of the fridge, trying to get upright again, but was like a turtle on his back. I gave a fleeting thought to killing him by caving in his metal chest while he was down but realized that would probably terminally screw up the timeline since he and I had a date with destiny in about fifteen years. Instead I sprang off my back foot and leapt into the air, reaching the top of the aisle behind me and leaping for the next immediately, a controlled jump that carried me over the space between them with ease.

From up here I could see the entry to the store, and sure enough, it was swarming with official-looking people who were starting to head this way. I dismounted rather than jump again, coming down about twenty yards behind my mother, who was hauling ass up that outside aisle along the side of the building, heading for that emergency exit by the meat department.

"Let's go out that door," I said as I landed and kept sprinting. She'd ditched the cart and had little me clutched against her side, pounding furiously ahead, breathing heavy with every step as she leapt a center-aisle fridge display filled with sausage and bacon.

I altered my course and slowed for a second as I passed the ham, grabbing a big one. We'd totally botched this grocery trip and we desperately needed something to eat, so a little shoplifting seemed like a minor thing compared to the devastation and dead bodies we'd already left in this store. I tucked the ham under my arm and headed for the exit-

Something heavy slammed into my back between the shoulders, producing a cracking noise and pain, pain, oh the pain. I sprawled onto the ground, the ham flying from my hands and rolling away as I landed in a heap, spraining a wrist when I slammed into a floor cooler display on the way down.

I caught a fading vision of my mother battering her way through the emergency exit ahead as I raised my head. The pain was really exquisite, at least a 7 on a 1-10 scale. Broken bone for sure, and probably a serious one, a little off the spine and to the right, between it and the shoulder blade. I thought maybe that was a rib, a high one, but whatever it was, it felt as though I'd been speared in the back in the thick cluster of muscles around my shoulder blade.

A heavy thump sounded behind me, Henderschott cracking the floor tiles as he landed from his jump. Apparently he'd followed my leaping strategy, at least for an aisle or so, using the height of the freezer units to track me and then coming down after he'd nailed the shit out of me with his...

I looked around for what had hit me. There was a section of

black armor wedged under the fridge display, just sitting there as casually as if he'd slipped it off. It was a metal plate about a foot long and kind of sharp on either side, flat in the middle where he used his powers to bond it to his skin. It looked a little like a shield, slightly curving, small at the bottom of the plate and widening as it came to the elbow joint.

He advanced on me, and I tried to ignore the pain screaming in my back. However bad it was – and it was bad – it was only going to be so much worse if he got his hands on me. I swiped the plate with my left hand since my right side was on fire, numb tingles running down my arm to my fingertips, and rolled to my knees as Henderschott came at me.

I raised my makeshift shield and took a major hammering as he brought down his arm. It rang out like a shot, an explosive sound of thunder echoing through the whole store. It was probably drawing Omega personnel our way even now, which didn't leave me an abundance of time to fight him off before they'd be here. And as much as I'd displayed an aptitude for slaughtering Omega personnel, now that I was injured, my combat effectiveness would fade, and one of them would score another hit to bring that number down further. It'd be a grind of attrition, a steady attack of hyenas upon the lioness until I ended up falling, which would be...so very bad for me, especially here.

The shock of his blow rang through my whole body, rattling my already wounded back. Henderschott raised his hand again, ready to rain another attack on me.

Fighting him from the ground as he tried to pound me like a sledgehammer was not going to be a winning formula, not with my time running short. My mother would reach the car and burn out, leaving me behind.

And she should. Little me was a lot more important than big me at this point. Killing me here would be bad, mostly for me. Killing her would break time forever, at least according to Akiyama.

I rolled as Henderschott swung again, dodging his attack by inches and coming to my feet on the backward roll.

He didn't let up, though. He came at me again, and I swung my shield defensively, batting aside his blow.

Henderschott was damned strong, probably close to my level of strength. I had an edge on him for speed, though that was diminished by my back injury.

He swung at me again, this time using the left hand, the one he'd shed the upper portion of his wrist guard to javelin me with. He used his open palm to strike, which worked because he was wearing a black steel gauntlet.

Henderschott swung it high, coming at me with fury I could see through the slits in his black face mask. He wasn't playing nice. Wasn't restraining himself. I'd humiliated him by smashing him into the fridge units.

I met his attack with his shield and a devastating clang rang out. I knocked his hand aside a foot or so, and it hit the fridge unit that hemmed us in on our left. It bounced back and he grimaced. He'd struck his exposed wrist against metal.

I saw the opening and attacked. I brought my improvised shield down on his arm, driving the hard edge into the exposed flesh. I hit him mid-forearm and he screamed as I pressed the attack, driving the edge into his flesh like a knife. A really dull knife, but still.

He wasn't going to take that lying down, and I knew it before I sensed his reaction. A mosquito bites you, you swing for it, unthinking. Simple defense mechanism.

I drove his wrist plate into his exposed flesh. He tried to swat me.

Simple. Simple enough I knew it was coming before he did it.

I dropped like someone had cut my puppet strings, and he brought his other hand around in a hard smack that would have annihilated me if I'd stayed in place for it.

Instead, he found nothing there, all that windup and swing for nothing. I was already on the ground, and he was staggering from his unbalanced attack.

I pulled my knees to my chin, then double kicked forward. Henderschott caught it in the chest, but it wasn't a striking move so much as a good shove. I braced my hands against the hard floor for more leverage and heaved into him with a leg press.

Henderschott flew.

And not a short distance, either. He hit the far back wall of the store several hundred feet away, though it took a few seconds for him to get there.

Pain surged through my shoulder as I vaulted back to my feet. Spinning on the ball of my foot, I broke and ran, ham forgotten in my determination to get the hell out of here before any other Omega lackeys got hold of me.

I shouldered through the emergency exit my mother had knocked off its hinges, a wild wail I hadn't even noticed in my flight emitting from a box on the door. I skirted the outside of the building at a flat sprint, cradling my right arm, which was starting to go numb. Spots were flickering in my vision.

Reaching the front curb, I looked left to the entrance. It was swarming with people, and cop cars, and I straightened my posture and acted like a normal person, stepping off the curb and walking like I hadn't just been involved in a fracas inside that had resulted in the cops being called. I whistled a little tune under my breath to try and pretend like everything was cool, everything was casual, and everything hadn't just gone straight to hell. Just another customer shopping at the Walmart in Des Moines in 1999, nothing to see here, folks.

I caught sight of my mother's car across the parking lot. She, too, had slowed her pace, casting looks over her shoulder, trying to be as casual as she could in her flight. No one was following her, which I considered a plus, all the attention at the front of the store and the Omega assholes all inside.

That wouldn't last.

I picked up the pace a little once I'd cleared the main avenue through the lot and started working my way back to my mom's car. I couldn't see her anymore because she'd disappeared to the other side to strap little me in, but I knew I had seconds before she'd be getting the eff out of here. With one eye on the entry, I stooped and broke into a low run, hustling like hell.

The car started up as I reached its back bumper, and I practically dove to get out of the way, rising up as she skidded out of the space, missing me by about a foot. I could hear the muted wails of little Sienna in the back, still terrified. I reached for the passenger side door knob as I rose up.

My mom hit the brakes, a squeal of the tires my reward for startling her. Also, she was pointing her gun at me.

I rapped on the window, trying to keep one eye on the store entry behind her for activity. No one had noticed us. Yet.

She hit the unlock button and I slipped in, shutting the door as I entered the Buick. Little me's crying had diminished in volume, now including the occasional hiccuped sob as she ran out of steam.

"Wondered if you'd make it out," my mother said, finishing her reverse and slamming the car into drive.

"It's good that you were going to leave me," I said, chucking a thumb over my shoulder. "She's definitely priority. They get me, I'm a big girl. Shit happens. They get her, it's game over for time. Let's not let that happen."

"Working on it," my mother muttered as she rammed her foot onto the accelerator. The car revved up-

And went nowhere.

I caught the startled look from my mother as nothing happened. It was probably mirrored on my own face.

I spun in my seat as the car angled up slightly-

Henderschott.

He had us by the bumper.

"Shit-" I started as he began to lift.

Something strange happened just then. The world seemed to skip a beat, the whine of the engine revving way up as the motion of the car's rear tires just...stopped.

I could see the crowd at the entry to the store. Not a soul was moving.

My mom saw it, too, out her side window. "What the hell...?" she muttered, dropping the pedal to the metal.

The car revved higher, almost blotting out little Sienna's sudden scream. Henderschott had paused in his deadlift of the Buick, unmoving in the back window until-

Everything seemed to break loose at once. Henderschott was left in the dust as the car broke free of him in a sudden blast of forward momentum. We sprang ahead and he stayed still, comically so, as though-

"Frozen," I said, looking over my seat at him, "in time."

My mother cast a worried look in the rearview and must

have seen the same thing I did. She hit the curb as she skidded around, out of the parking lot and onto the street, where traffic was momentarily halted, cars in motion just stopped, a strange blurring action around their wheels.

Life resumed as my mother swung us out into the lane, bringing the Buick up to speed, nearly sideswiping a little Dodge in the process. It honked, but it didn't matter. We were already out of his way.

"You saw that?" I asked, looking back at the Walmart parking lot as it faded from view. My mother pushed the speedometer up past sixty, then seventy.

"Time freezing so we could get away?" She kept her eyes forward, ignoring the crying from the back seat. "Yeah. I saw it. That was Akiyama, I take it?"

"I assume so," I said. "That was...way too close."

She just nodded as she sped up, eyes glued to the road in front of us.

We left it all behind us as we rolled at high speed away from the devastation. Away from Omega.

For now.

13.

I watched out the back window, figuring my mother had the front covered. Suburban Des Moines blew past at high speed, and my mother showed no sign of stopping for any traffic lights, her grandma driving instincts safely left in the Walmart parking lot. I kept my eyes on the road behind us for the first few miles after we left the chaos at Walmart.

No sign of pursuit behind us, I finally decided, but kept partially turned to make sure, wary eye checking the rear window every few seconds just in case. "How are you doing?" I asked little me.

She sniffled and didn't produce a coherent answer. Instead she broke into a new round of crying, eventually getting the word, "Hungry," out between sobs. Her face was red as a tomato, and her cheeks were saturated with tears, as was her cute little frilly dress.

"Damn," I said, looking to mom. "I tried to grab a ham on the way out, but it didn't go so well."

"How did they find us?" she asked, white-knuckling the wheel.

"If I had to guess," I said, voicing a notion I'd had a couple miles back and worked through mentally to an unsatisfactory conclusion, "That cop that slipped behind us just before we turned into the Walmart ran your plates. Omega must have some sort of...I dunno. Mole, wiretap, something...in the DMV, or the local police."

"If they've got the police penetrated, that's a scary thought," she said. "How do you know Omega?"

"We've had...dealings," I said, once again wondering how much I could tell her. Like that I'd essentially destroyed the organization in question? Probably too much information. Vague was good. "You?"

"Same," she said. "Seems like they're always causing trouble in the meta world."

"Yeah, they're good at that," I said, trying to mentally run through where Omega would be in this. They had, after all, captured my mother – via Wolfe – and come after me at my house. Again, via Wolfe. After he'd failed, they'd sent in Henderschott and James Fries and vampires and the list went on, all the way up to Janus and Bjorn, or even Bastet and the ministers. Probably wouldn't include Rick, the Primus of Omega that I'd killed by beating him to death with his own chair. He'd be a baby at this point. "They've got a strong bench. Lots of powerful metas on their team." Most of whom I'd killed or had a hand in killing.

"Why are they after us?" my mother asked.

It didn't take much thinking to get to the bottom of that. "They're hunting for succubi," I said. "To run experiments on, I think." I remembered Andromeda – well, Adelaide. "And... other stuff."

They'd been looking for a bride for Sovereign when they'd come after me. Kind of a dirty plan B, but dirty was Omega's watchword.

My mother seemed to miss the last part. "We need food."

"Stop at a gas station on the way home," I said. "I'll run in and get some stuff while you two wait in the car."

She glanced at the dashboard display. "I'm going to need gas soon, too, and I'm down to my last twenty." Her voice held an edge of worry I was not used to getting from my mom.

"Yeah, I know," I said. "We'll figure something out."

"How?" she asked, still staring straight ahead, her shoulders stiff.

A little twinge of pain ran through my back where I'd tweaked it when Full Metal Jackass had thrown his plate into me. "That's a fantastic question and I wish I had an immediate answer to it. But I don't, so I guess we'll improvise."

She furrowed her brow, concentrating ahead. "Let me lay this out for you as I see it – we have no money. No food after we eat whatever overpriced crap you're about to buy at the convenience store. No way to get more of either, short of stealing-"

"Which is an option that should be on the table, Valjean."

"-and now Omega is going to flood the zone in this town," she said. "They have an army."

"We have a Hulk," I said, and she took her eyes off the road to stare at me blankly. "Never mind."

"They're looking for us," she said, turning back to the road. "And they know what to look for now. They have a description of this car, which means we have to ditch it, which is going to leave us without transport-"

"Again, I'm coming back to stealing. It seems the time, and we've got a powerful need."

"-Okay, fine, you're into thievery. But this is still a laundry list of problems." She shook her head. "We have to get out of this town."

"I'm with you on fleeing Iowa. As with you as I could possibly be."

"But where the hell do we go?" she asked, shaking her head. "And how do we get there? No money, no car – come on. No resources left to draw on." The first crack of worry appeared in mom's seemingly impenetrable facade. "What...what the hell am I supposed to do?"

My forehead wrinkled as her face opened up in a way I hadn't seen from her before. She seemed to awaken, at last, to the steady, muted sobs coming from the back seat. "It's okay, sweetie," she said, draping her right hand over the seat. Little me reached forward to take it, and she adjusted little Sienna's grip so she could hold onto mom's wrist, which was covered by her sleeve. "It's okay. It's going to be okay."

But she spoke breathlessly, and I knew in the moment she didn't believe it. It caused a strange shock to run through me – how many times had I heard her say things like that when I was a child and not realized that this was how my mother sounded when she lied?

"Look," I said, feeling just a little rattled at watching my mom come apart more than I'd ever seen before. "There has to be someone we can call for help."

She snorted. "Like who?"

"Alpha fights Omega," I said. "Dad was part of Alpha."

She shook her head. "I don't trust them."

"Dad did."

"Fine," she said, taking a breath, "how do we get ahold of them?" She looked sideways at me, and a gleam of triumph replaced the despair, just for a second. "Yeah. Exactly. Your dad was their only operator in this area, right?"

"Yeah," I said. And Reed would be the next one that I'd know, and right now he'd be only a little older than little me in the backseat. And thus, not of much use unless one required a blankie and a bottle. Or whatever kids that age were into. He-Man, maybe. "Okay, so I don't know that many people in this era, but..." I strained, my neck muscles pulling tight as one idea occurred.

"What?" she asked, catching my discomfort.

My sudden flex and clench had again aggravated that pain in my back. "Nothing. The name 'Erich Winter' floated to mind, but I don't think that's a great idea."

"Yeah, that'd be a wonderful call," she said, shaking her head. "He's after me, too, and has been since the night I stumbled away from the burning ruin of the agency. I hear he's putting together some new operation now."

"He is," I said. "But yeah...best not call him. Save him as an...'in case of emergency, nuke everything' card." I drummed my fingers on the door's arm rest. "Okay, fine. How about..." I closed my eyes, my voice trailing off.

"Don't say 'Charlie'."

"I'm not going to say it, but I did think it – briefly," I said, opening my eyes again, bright sunshine threatening to blind me through the windshield. "She's crazy but kinda useful in a fight. Nominally believes in family. Or something."

"And is a psychotic, thieving murderer. How about 'no'? Also, I don't see how she helps with the money or escape problems. In fact, I can see at least ten ways my sister would compound both those problems."

"Okay," I said. "I can't argue with that. But we're running

pretty thin on ideas."

"No kidding," my mother said, employing her famed talents for understatement and dryness all in one. "Maybe that's why I'm feeling this lingering malaise. Because I don't have any friends, really, or family I can call."

"Not even that person in Wyoming?" I asked. I started to put two and two together; after my mother had left me way back when Wolfe had captured her, she'd fled to Wyoming, too. Whoever was out there, maybe they were an ally we could use.

She shook her head slowly. "That's not a road I want to go down right now. Call it a dry hole. I only want to go that way if I have no other options."

"Shit," I muttered under my breath, thinking of my own prospects. Who could I call on in 1999? No one would know me. If I could find Harry, maybe he could look ahead and see the future-

But how the hell could I find Harry in 1999? And what good would that do? He didn't have any idea who I was at this stage of life. Hell, he was firmly ensconced in the 'drinking and gambling himself to oblivion' phase of his life and would be for another fifteen or more years.

So who else was there? All my friends were still too young – Reed, Augustus, Scott, Jamal. I blinked. Veronika Acheron probably had some miles on her by now, but I didn't know where to find her, and I didn't really class her as a friend the way I would the rest of those guys. Same with Friday, though he was probably an adult...ish...at this point. As much an adult as Friday ever was. Either way, he didn't know me from Eve. Which brought me around to Winter again, and his little quartet of trouble – Kappler, Bastian, Parks and Clary would be alive and probably adult. But again, none of them would know me.

None of these people would have any damned reason to answer my call for help.

None of the people I knew in my life in the present would come running for me now. I was in a time prior to their loyalties to me, and way before they had any cause to give a damn about me.

"Shit," I said under my breath, "I'm in the temporal version of no man's land."

My mom nodded slowly, whether she understood what I was saying or not. "Yeah. No friends. No family. No one to call-"

You can call me anytime.

Anytime.

"We're on our own." My mother tightened her hands around the wheel as she turned us, slowly, down a side street. There was a convenience store ahead on the right.

"Maybe," I said.

You are family to me.

Anytime.

"Or maybe not," I said as my mother guided us into the convenience store parking lot.

She pulled into a parking space then favored me with a puzzled look, pursing her lips together. "What do you mean?"

I'll see you soon, Lethe had told me as she left me behind in the Revelen war room. I hadn't known what she'd meant then.

I had a feeling I knew now.

The car idled as we sat there, and I glanced at the store front. There, right next to the pile of firewood for sale was an artifact of the times, something that had once been on every corner and in my day was now rarer than diamonds, a curiosity that had been replaced by technology's mad march:

A pay phone.

"I mean..." I said, staring at the phone, and remember what she'd said when she made me memorize the number:

It's been the same since the 1950's...

You can call me anytime.

Any.

Time.

"I mean..." I said, staring at the phone, little chills causing goosebumps to pop out all over my body, "...I might know *someone* I can call..."

14.

"Collect call from: Sierra Nealon."

The words were a jumble of computer voice for the first part and my own recorded speaking of my mother's name for the second, another strange throwback to the way phones used to work. I'd called the operator in Revelen collect, and now they'd put me through to whoever was answering the phone in the castle today.

There was a long pause. I heard the voice when it answered, but it was short, clipped, barely recognizable as female.

Hopefully it wasn't General Krall. She was probably still hanging out with 98 Degrees at this stage of her life rather than answering phones in Revelen, but it didn't give me a lot of hope hearing that voice answer. It definitely wasn't my grandmother.

"I will accept the charges," the voice said, still clipped, but English. A noise indicated the calling being connected, and through the frizz of electronic background noise, the woman asked, "Who is this?"

"Sierra Nealon," I said again. "I need to speak with Lethe. Immediately."

"Who are you?"

"Sierra. Nealon." I put a steady emphasis on each word.

There was another long pause. "Please hold," she said, and without waiting for me to agree, she put me on hold.

"Sonofa," I said as smooth jazz filtered out of the earpiece.

My mother slammed the car door behind me and I turned

as she opened the back door. "I'm going to get the food. You going to be a while?"

"I have no idea," I said. "They put me on hold. With Kenny G as company."

My mother pursed her lips in abject disgust. "Who are you calling and why would you put up with that?"

"Because we're pretty much boned if I don't wade through the mellow saxophone and get what I need out of this call, that's why."

"Transferring," came a robotic voice on the other end of the line, then a long, long pause before the phone started beeping in my ear like it was ringing somewhere else in the world.

"Hello," came a voice on the other end of the line. Less clipped, but no more patient.

Lethe.

My grandmother.

"Hey, it's-" I started to say.

"Call from Sierra Nealon," came the operator's voice stepping all over mine. "Unsecured, from a pay phone in Des Moines, Iowa."

There was a pause. "I'll accept the call," my grandmother said.

"Connecting," the Euro lady said, and then there was a beep.

"Who is this?" my grandmother asked, voice surprisingly calm considering.

"It's not Sierra," I said, "though she is right here." I waved at my mother, who was just getting little me out of the car and threw a frown my direction.

"Who are you, then?" my grandmother asked. "You sound familiar."

"I'm Sienna," I said. "Nealon. I'm-"

"I know who Sienna Nealon is," Lethe said, and now the tension was ratcheting up in her voice. "But clearly you don't, because Sienna is all of five and you sound a lot older."

"Well, I'm not the 1999 Sienna, that's for sure," I said. "But I am Sienna."

Another pause. This was a woman who'd lived thousands of years and seen some serious shit in her time. Calmly, she asked, "How?"

"Akiyama," I said. "There's a... time crisis. It's hard to explain."

"Akiyama is not in play at present."

"He's in play in *my* present," I said. "Playing like a toddler, wrecking everything. No, that's unfair. He's trying to save time from crazy paradoxical nuttiness going on. He brought me here to...fix...stuff. Related to Sierra. And... other Sienna. The little one."

My mother had made it up to the sidewalk and was standing a foot or two from me, looking at me like I was a particularly bizarre circus sideshow. "Who are you talking to?"

"You are with Sierra," my grandmother said on the other end of the line. Her voice sounded like the temp had fallen twenty degrees instantly, she was so chill.

"Yeah, and little Sienna, too," I said. "We're in Iowa, and we just had a close encounter with Omega assholes in the local Walmart. We're skint as the Brits would say, and a little outgunned. Meaning we need guns. Also, cash. Because I don't really have any that works in this time period."

"Just a minute," she said, and I heard her put down the phone, a rattling going on at the other end of the line. I heard her talking, muffled, to someone else, but I couldn't make out any of the conversation.

"Who is that?" my mother asked.

I took a breath, held it to a five count, then answered as diplomatically as I could, bearing in mind that at this stage of her life, my mother thought grandma was dead. "You wouldn't believe me if I told you."

That made her frown all the more. "I don't think being a hundred percent honest about where you come from is going to work out all that well for you here."

"Because it sounds crazy?" I asked, still holding the black receiver up to my face, waiting. How had people managed, dealing with these damned things? I mean, it had a cord. I couldn't even pace around while I was standing here.

"Yes. I'm still not even sure I believe you, and I watched Akiyama stop time back there," my mother said.

My grandmother's voice came back on. "How did you know how to reach me?"

"Long story, but you gave me the number for the castle," I said. "In the future, obviously. And told me to call...any time. So I took you literally."

"Very literally, if you're not lying," she said.

"I'm not," I said. "Nor am I crazy, though I am fully aware that I sound like I am."

Another long pause, and my mother was looking at me with just the same suspect level of, "What is wrong with you?" as I'm sure my grandmother was evincing on the other end of the phone.

"You told me you'd do anything for family," I said, after she didn't speak for a long while. "Well...I need help. And there is literally no one else I can call." I locked eyes with my mother, and her curiosity was getting deeper by the second. "*We*...need help. All of us. We got bushwhacked by Henderschott. You know who he is?"

"The Man in the Iron *Everything*," Lethe said.

"I put him through a freezer case," I said. "We took out three other Omega metas, but...they've got more. They're swarming into Des Moines and we've got no way out. Sierra's down to her last twenty bucks, and we're about to have to ditch the car because I'm pretty sure that's how they found us."

Another long pause. Like she was trying to figure out what to make of all the cards I'd just thrown on the table.

"You took my invitation very literally indeed," Lethe said.

"I have no one else to call," I said. "Or at least no one I could find. No one else who's seen what you've seen. Who could absorb the story I'm giving you without dismissing it out of hand as impossible madness."

"It does sound like impossible madness."

"Well, if you don't believe me I'm really screwed," I said, "because there's not a chance in hell anyone other than maybe your dad has seen any more than you have and would believe a word I'm saying."

A pause. "You know about my father?"

"'Vlad'?" I asked. "Yeah. We've met. He's a heckuva a guy. Kind of a smartass and lives up to his reputation. Reputations, I should say, since he has several."

"Just a second," Lethe said, and put the phone down again. I heard soft murmurs of another conversation, but again couldn't hear a word of it.

I held tight to the phone, and my mother stared on at me. I didn't dare spare a look for little Sienna, who was huddling against my mother's leg, snug against it like she'd never let go again.

My mother didn't ask again, though. Which was good, because I didn't know how to tell her...yet.

"I'll be there in five hours," Lethe said when her voice came back on the line.

"Five – what? How?" I asked.

"I'm already in the US," she said, brusque and on mission. "There's a flight in one hour from Abilene and I'm going to race to catch it. Be at the airport at 3pm. You'll know me when you see me, I assume?"

"Yeah," I said, feeling the thrill of my heart race. "And you'll know me when you see me, too. You're..." my voice seemed to catch. "You're really coming?"

This pause may have been the longest of all, and when she answered, it was just as cool as anything else she'd said before. "I'll be there." And she hung up without another word.

15.

We got milk and eggs from the convenience store, and two boxes of cereal, and went back to my mom's house to enjoy a cold breakfast. We'd blown through almost the last of the cash, paying nearly double what we would have for the same supplies from Walmart, and we ate in silence, all three of us, as though we knew this was the last supper.

"I'll take the car and ditch it at the airport," I said, staring at my bowl.

"Who are you picking up?" my mother asked, not for the first time since we'd gotten back to the house.

"I don't think I can explain it," I said, concentrating hard on the Cheerios drifting around on my spoon.

"Is it someone I know?" she asked, pressing harder.

"Kind of," I said, not looking up from the cereal.

I glanced at mini me, who hadn't said much since the Walmart adventure. My mother had pried her off when we got done with our shopping trip in the convenience store, and we'd driven home in silence. I could feel the worry radiating off of mom. She was thinking I was calling down the thunder on her, and I kind of was. Being evasive about who was coming probably didn't help.

"I need to know," she said, letting her spoon fall with a clatter. "I've trusted you up until now-"

"I am aware," I said, muted. My enthusiasm for this conversation was...well, not at all. "I'm sorry I don't have a good answer for you." And also that I was being a coward, because part of me almost hoped Lethe was bullshitting me, that she'd no show, and I'd never have to explain to mom that her mother was alive. Because how was that going to go? *So... you remember grandma? Yeah, she faked her own death without telling you. But she's totally going to help us now. For reasons I can't explain.*

And they really were reasons I couldn't explain. If Lethe cared so damned much about her family, why fake her death and not tell mom in the first place? She certainly seemed aware that I was alive, and five, which meant she was at least keeping tabs on what was going on.

So... why hide? Why not involve herself in my life?

All I had to go on in answering this mystery was a roughly twenty-year-hence conversation in which she'd told me that family was important enough to her that I could call her anytime for help. Which apparently included from the past, a strange, paradoxical fact that was still kind of weirding me out.

Thanks, Akiyama, for taking me away from one bizarrely bad situation and bringing me to another. Hopefully at some point my life would begin to make sense once again.

But I wasn't laying any money down on that prospect given that my last week had encompassed a cartel battle, a prison riot, a war and now a time-travel adventure culminating in a blast-from-the-past battle with Full Metal Jackass in an Iowa Walmart.

"I don't like this," my mother said, almost a growl.

"Being chased by Omega?" I asked. "Yeah. It's not a lot of fun as I recall. Hell, I don't even have to recall since I'm in the soup with you now and – yeah, it's no fun."

"You have less to lose than I do." Her eyes were burning now.

"Uh, no," I said. "You lose that, we both lose." I slid my gaze over to little me. "Unless you've forgotten who I am."

"I haven't forgotten who you say you are," my mother said, slitting her eyes into a glare.

"Oh, man, mom, you are eternally suspicious," I said, slumping back from the table. "I feel like a teenager again."

"How far off of being a teenager are you?" she asked.

I shook my head. "I can't answer that."

"I want to know," my mother said. She'd put aside her fork

and was now about the serious business of glaring me down. "If this is in your past, shouldn't you be able to talk about it in the future? When you get back from this little excursion?"

I could feel the danger, like a shark fin swimming by when you're up to your neck in the ocean. "I cannot tell you about the future. You get that, right? You've seen the movies, know what the consequences of screwing up a timeline-"

"You don't think your mere presence here is 'screwing up the timeline'?" my mother asked, going meta-low. She glanced at little me, who had her head down and was eating breakfast very slowly, and without much care for the two of us and our adult conversation. "How do you think this is going to show up in your memory? Since you can't seem to remember it?"

"I'm assuming I repressed it, given how damned traumatic watching us brawl with scary people in a Walmart aisle probably was," I said, stealing a glance of my own at little Sienna. She seemed to be operating in a haze, zoned out and moving at 1/100th speed. If she wasn't in the middle of a bad round of PTSD, I'd eat my plate one shard of ceramic at a time. Which I might have to do anyway given that we hadn't bought much food and I was already ravenous again. I swear, my lifetime meal plan was the ultimate in intermittent fasting. At least I was still relatively trim these days.

My mother shook her head. "This isn't a joke to me. It's not a game-"

"You think it is to me?"

"We live here," she said. "This is where we were supposed to be safe."

"Well I hate to torpedo your little Iowa cornfield dreams, but that ain't happening," I said. "And I didn't grow up here, anyway."

"Well, there's nowhere else I can go right now," my mother said, and lapsed into a silence, looking at me sullenly over her now-empty plate.

I thought about that for a second, too. How had we gotten the house in Minneapolis if mom was completely broke? I stole another glance at little me, who was fully awake but just seemed catatonic, a very un-Sienna state. Hopefully damage to the timeline hadn't already occurred, though I suppose I'd only know about it if Akiyama popped up and told me, and if things had gone to hell he might be too busy trying to keep the flow of time running to warn me.

None of this made any sense except for me calling Lethe. That was literally the only part of this that clicked for me, and only because she'd been so weirdly leading in her attempt to get me to memorize her phone number back in Revelen. Everything else felt like the usual bizarre brand of Sienna making shit up as she went, with a time-travel twist I couldn't have imagined.

I put my palm against my forehead and rested my eyes. "I don't like any of this. None of this is right."

"Tell me about it," my mother said.

"If there's something I'm not telling you," I said, "it's for a reason. It's because it's something I don't think you know in the future." I looked back up at her. "The identity of our helper is one of those things. I'm trying to figure out how to run this whole...disaster, frankly...without ruining the world."

"Do you like being kept in the dark?" my mother asked.

"No, I hate it," I said, "yet I frequently operate there, obviously." And I threw my hands up to indicate the world around me. "Witness this train wreck of a mission."

"It feels more like a DeLorean wreck," my mother said. "One that carries a special sort of literal time bomb with it."

I let a half-smile slide across my lip. "If what I say is true, you mean?"

"I saw time skip," she said, shaking her head, "I believe you're not from here. You're probably my daughter, though I guess you could be another relation who's a succubus." She looked up at the ceiling. "How did you end up finding out what you were?" She looked back down, right at me. "I've been preparing a speech for years on the assumption you'd be like me and not your father."

I swallowed heavily but tried to keep it to myself. How had I found out about my powers? Draining the life out of Wolfe. "It's...one of those stories," I said. "The kind I can't tell you."

"This just flat-out stinks," she said, shaking her head again. "Every part of it."

"C'est la vie," I said. "Or at least such is my life."

82

"I know that feeling well," my mother said. "So... you really can't tell me who you called?"

"I don't think so," I said, settling back in my chair. "If I could...I would. I'm not trying to keep you in the dark for kicks. It'd be a lot easier on me if I could just tell you everything and be done with it."

She nodded, slowly. "Fine. I guess I trust you after Walmart." She tossed the keys across the table.

I caught them out of the air, the glimmering, shiny little things. I forced a smile, and it was tough. "I won't let you down," I said. "Either of you." And I meant it.

16.

The Des Moines airport drop-off seemed different than the airport drop-offs in my day, being pre-9/11. No bollards to keep out the car bombs, no thick security presence that was starting to seem ubiquitous at MSP the last few times I'd been there, airport police toting submachine guns or assault rifles. No cops threatening to ticket you if you parked in one place for longer than the span of a butterfly's wing flutter.

I pulled up in front of the Arrivals terminal and just waited there in my newly purloined car, windows down, against the curb, and watched the door. Heat crept in as the sun rose higher and the day got hotter. I could tell it was summer by the sweat rolling down the small of my back, and somewhere outside the city the corn was surely growing tall and strong by now.

People were passing through, getting in cars, dragging their luggage along. The old-fashioned carry suitcase still seemed very popular, apparently the wheeled model – and common sense – not arriving in wider usage yet.

I was wearing a couple items from my mother's wardrobe, having finally discarded the shredded clothes from Revelen that had been through a literal war. And looked like it. Dark sweat marks already stained my "new" blouse. Which looked like it was from the seventies, a fact which I'd remarked on to my mother only to get a derisive snort in response.

My mom. Not exactly fashion forward, even in 1999.

I drummed my fingers nervously against the door frame,

keeping my eyes nailed to the reflective glass arrival doors. They kept swooshing open every few minutes to disgorge some traveling family or some business guy coming to Des Moines to deliver a PowerPoint on how this company could sell more corn if only they'd buy his thingamajig. Clearly, I had no idea what went on in corporate boardrooms, but that was my image of it. "They'll buy more corn if you have my super-duper deluxe thingamajig!"

The sweat was working its way down my forehead now, trying to slide in under my sunglasses. Every few minutes I'd remove the dark lenses and mop my brow with my sleeve. I was starting to see the appeal of a pocket handkerchief.

I'd messed up and stolen a car with less than a quarter tank of gas and uncertain mileage. It was a decent enough car, but because of the dearth of gas – and cash – I was afraid to run it while I waited for Lethe, lest we be stranded on the side of the highway after pickup. Fuel efficiency standards probably weren't grand on these old minivans, after all.

Someone came walking out in front of my car on their way into the arrival gate, and I took notice of the movement against the flow of traffic. It was a tall man in a suit, impeccably dressed, and who looked like he could be one of those corn thingamajig salesmen. He even had a silk pocket square, which I was suddenly envious of, because I bet it'd feel great to mop my sweaty forehead with silk instead of a soaked sleeve, as I was currently doing.

I tried to stretch in the car seat and tweaked that back injury that Henderschott had laid on me earlier in Walmart. "Usually the injuries in Walmart happen on Black Friday," I muttered. I stretched, feeling the pain spike. It wasn't a break, at least not anymore, but it was still a serious pain.

I couldn't assume that a guy crossing against traffic, who hadn't given me a single look, was immediately a servant of Omega, but I couldn't really afford not to think that, either, not after this morning's incident in the dairy aisle.

"Come on, come on, stick together," a woman's voice said, drawing my attention from the businessman for a second. She was clicking her way through the crosswalk ahead, pushing a stroller, three kids in tow behind her. One was older, a girl with enough years on her to have that sullen teen thing going on while she followed just far enough behind her mom to look like she was actively distancing herself. The next two kids to follow were younger, a pre-teen boy who was bopping along happily, and another boy about little Sienna's age who was scrambling to keep up with mommy and kept trying to hold her hand even though she was plainly fully occupied pushing the stroller. "Come on," she said, sparing him a glance backward, and he ran-walked to keep up with her rather than fall behind to his older, cooler siblings.

Bringing up the rear seemed to be her husband, a dark-haired, middle-aged man in a Polo shirt and cargo shorts, with pale, hairy legs that made me pucker in slight distaste. He wasn't unattractive, in fact he had kind of a hot dad thing going on, but those cargo shorts and pale legs with the bushy, squiggly hairs? Yikes. He either needed jeans or manscaping of the legs, and I didn't care which. It would also be fine if he just marched on, but I felt strangely compelled to watch as he walked by.

I spared a glance for the mom at the head of the procession. She was pretty, blond hair in a ponytail, loving eyes on her brood as she hustled them across the street. "Come on," she cajoled again, just as she reached the curb in front of the arrival door. "Don't slow down now. We're almost there."

What a cute little family, I thought. Some days it was easy to forget that people like this were the reason I was out here, fighting my ass off to keep the bad guys from messing up everything.

I did the craziness I did so that ladies like this could raise their kids without metas going nuts in the streets. So that she could go work her ass off doing...whatever she did during the day and then climb into bed at night with Mr. Cargo Shorts and breathe a sigh of relief, maybe make love before drifting off to sleep secure in the knowledge that her world would turn on and the sun would rise tomorrow.

I breathed a little sigh of my own and raised my sunglasses as I went to mop my brow again, sweat trying to find its way into my eyes to give them a little sting for the crime of being open and trying to watch stuff. I flicked my gaze back toward the door, looking for the corn thingamajig salesmen, and caught a brief glimpse of his back as he disappeared inside. "Maybe you were a real salesman after all," I muttered as I replaced my sunglasses, eye burn momentarily averted.

The little family had stopped at the curb, the mother rifled through her purse looking for something. She waved at the dad to take up the stroller, and he did, wheeling it a few feet before entreating the sullen teenage daughter to do something about it. She almost snarled at him, something in the vein of, "Come on, dad!" before he turned to the over-eager boy child, who was jumping up and down about getting to push the stroller. Dad, wisely, passed on that gem of an idea that would probably end in a baby being dumped out on the concourse floor after a collision with a random pillar or a bad turn, and let junior the pre-teen take up the task. The boy rolled his sibling in the stroller onward, through the arrival doors, and the overly excited preschooler followed.

What a cute spectacle, I thought, as the mother pulled a .44 Magnum out of her purse and pointed it right at me, meta-speed.

"Shit!" I said, diving down behind the dash, hoping that the engine block would protect me from slugs the size of my pinkie finger. The Magnum boomed, bullet embedding itself in the hood of my car as I reached for the keys to start the ignition and failed, striking them. They dangled and clattered – I'd found them above the visor, of all places – way to be trusting, Iowa – and slipped out, falling to the floor. "Shit!" I shouted again as the Magnum boomed once more, this time breaking through engine and making the radio explode, little shards of metal showering me as I realized...

Damn.

I had not seen that one coming at all.

17.

Okay, so the first task was to get the hell out of here before I caught a Magnum bullet, and to that end I tried to reach across the passenger side and throw the door open, hoping these fine, masquerading people would think I'd lunge out in the direction I'd opened the door in. This would, of course, be a terrible idea for several reasons, least of which there'd be zero cover between me and the lady wielding the big damned gun.

A third boom sent a shredding projectile through the passenger door, opening a hole the size of my fist in the door-mounted armrest.

Yay. That could have been my torso.

Wasting no time, I snaked sideways and low through the gap between driver and passenger seat, thudding into the back seat just ahead of the bench. There was only one sliding door out of this van, it being a model before they'd started commonly engineering the doors on both sides, but that was fine. I wasn't planning on going out that way anyhow.

The floor here was flat, and the middle and back benches were mounted into it like an actual bench, on metal supports, presumably for easy removal to turn the cargo space into a... cargo space.

That left me a relatively wide-open path to crawl back to the rear hatch. And crawl I did. Meta-speed.

Once I reached the back, I found a small problem.

No handle to get out.

Cursing under my breath, I looked for spider-web cracks in

the back window. They were certainly there; one of the rounds had plowed all the way through the vehicle and done a nice number on the back window, leaving it kind of a mess.

Putting my palm against the glass, I applied a steady, ramping-up amount of force as the Magnum rang out again, and something behind me exploded. Mommy Dearest must have thought I was in the back seat and had fired a round in to test. Stuffing poofed out of one of the seats where the round impacted, and my ears rang in the confined space as I pushed against the back glass.

My fingers broke through after a second or two of increasing the pressure, and then I forced my whole hand through the safety glass as it pebbled off. On the balls of my feet, I only rose as much as necessary to reach out of the back of the window and grasp for the handle that would open the damned back hatch.

I found it almost immediately and yanked up.

Nothing happened.

"Oh, come on," I muttered. Of course. The owner had left the damned driver's door unlocked, but naturally they'd lock the damned hatchback.

Another boom and the bench behind me exploded in a tuft of stuffing, like yellow snow flittering through the air. If she was running with a traditional revolver, she was down to one shot left. If she was running with an untraditional one...she might have two remaining.

Either way, she was closing on my position and would be here in seconds, at least one bullet ready to punch a giant hole in me.

I was trapped, on my knees in the rear cargo area of the van, my breathing hard and fast, waiting for the last bullet, the hatchback like an impenetrable wall between me and survival.

18.

Nothing focuses my mind like certain death. If I had one advantage over most other people, it was that in situations of life or death, I didn't tend to get quite as cloudy or adrenaline-fueled, locked into stupid or reflexive action. Don't get me wrong; in the middle of a situation like this I was still thinking fast, mind racing like a squirrel on meth trapped in a shoebox. But there was always a certain detachment that came over me when the adrenaline kicked in, years of my mother's training drilled into me like a program, keeping me calmer than I should have been.

It was a strange disconnect, like I could see through my own eyes, but not worry as much about things I really should worry about, such as getting killed. Where others might panic and lose their heads and start shooting wildly in a battle, the chaos and threat of death seemed to pull me out of myself and allow me to see the clearest way forward, or at least the logical progression. The panic of crazy situations tended to come down on me later, in the form of a pulse that elevated after the nutso shit was done.

Coming down off those highs, after a mission, after a case? Yowch. Sometimes it made getting to sobriety seem like an easy thing. I'd crashed after the war in Revelen had drawn to a conclusion, just as much from non-stop adrenaline finally stopping after an extended hard pump through my veins as from injury.

Being trapped in the hatchback raised my pulse only a few

beats per minute, pushed my mind into a faster circle, running the track of logical possibilities with great speed and only a little unease bleeding through. That would all come later, after the crash, and I had a feeling – given that I hadn't yet processed at least the prison break or the war and probably not even the cartel thing, I was in for a nice, long emotional crack-up once this was all done.

Still, ways forward: two side windows, one that would bring me out right in front of the lady with the Magnum, one that would bring me out on the opposite side. Either way, breaking it would make noise and draw attention to me, and they were so small I'd have to wriggle out and almost certainly get shot in the process. Non-optimal.

Go back under the seats. Also not-optimal, because I'd cross under Magnum mom's steady, searching field of view, probably, and she'd plug me. Even if she didn't, I'd be stuck in the middle of the van, no exit, little cover. Nope.

Then there was the hatchback. The window was partially busted where I'd forced a hand through to try and open it. Forcing myself through was a possibility, but not a great one. I'd get my ass – literally – caught as I was squeezing through, hips snugging on the glass as I made my way out if I did it quietly. If noisily, I'd be launching myself through the air and the element of surprise would be wasted.

Nope, nope, nope. All bad options.

That left me with one: go out the hatchback without opening the window.

Ding ding ding. We had a winner, and I came to a conclusion on that one pretty quickly, as I tended to do during battle.

Added bonus: I might be able to do some damage in the process.

I thumped onto the small of my back, tweaking that shoulder blade pain that had been nagging at me since Walmart. I gritted my teeth and ignored it, pulling my knees to my chest. I was only going to get one chance at this, and I needed to focus until I heard-

A footstep through the shredded glass as Magnum mom stepped in front of the hatchback. Guess she'd missed me at the side window. Yay for heavy tinting.

I tightened my legs to my chest and then unleashed an unholy double kick into the hatchback. Both feet slammed into the plastic lining and destroyed the interior covering. I pushed through in a millisecond and hit the metal beneath, transferring all the force of my mule kick into the hatchback.

Steel buckled and whined as the force of my strike ran through to the three primary points at which the hatchback was sealed – two hinges and a lock. Two at the top, one at the bottom.

Every last damned one of them gave under the strength of my super-meta mule kick.

The door exploded off the rear of the minivan, catching Magnum Mom as it flew like Henderschott had been launched across the Walmart. I saw her surprise for a flicker before it caught her in the chest and sheared her legs and head cleanly off, carrying her torso with it thirty feet to crash into the car behind me.

I rolled out of the van and landed on my feet. "Whew," I said. "It was getting a little stuffy in there."

A cry of muffled outrage burst out to my left, and I looked. Cargo Shorts Dad was standing his mouth open, hands burning bright with blue plasma. Over his shoulder, Sullen Teen Daughter already had an early tear streaking down her face, and her eyes were glowing. Cyclops type.

"Oh, so she actually was the matriarch of the family? That was legit? You aren't just a traveling assassin group posing as a family?" I asked as they both ripped their attention off the hatchback, which had finally come to rest, a smear of blood beneath it. "I guess I shouldn't speak ill of the dead, but – seriously, who brings their family on an assassination mission?"

I didn't have a chance to dwell much on the effect of my inflammatory words, because Cargo Shorts Dad lost his shit and let out a scream of grief that would have been worthy of a Klingon funeral. He came at me fast, and I dodged around the van, hitting it with a spin kick as he tried to skirt the back corner-

It clipped him as the van's back tire jumped the curb from the force of my hit, and he went flying, blue plasma fading to bare hands as he went. He crashed through the floor-to-ceiling glass windows that separated the Arrivals terminal and baggage claim from the hot, sticky Iowa summer. Or used to. They might have to cool the outdoors, now, but it was nothing but an improvement, for sure.

"I didn't come looking for trouble from you people, little girl," I said, ducking behind the van. I'd been on the receiving end of cyclops beams before. Just this week, in fact. Or...twenty years hence? Whatever, it was like yesterday, when I'd gone up against Adoncia, the pissed-off cartel former moll/current leader. "And you've picked a fight with the wrong person."

She just screamed and blasted, shredding through the minivan. I'd anticipated this, teenagers not being renowned for their reason at the best of times, and definitely not after they'd watched their parents get murdered by some random stranger.

I went low in a roll, came up behind the van's tire as she cut it in two. Cars were honking behind me, tires were squealing in front of me as people hurried to get the hell out of whatever was going on here. I had a feeling the Des Moines PD would be explaining this one as a gas leak or something similarly lame, since word of metas hadn't made it out into the world yet. Kinda like the time western Kansas had burned and the government had blamed brushfires or something stupid like that.

"Well, damn," I said, looking around for an easy answer to my pissed-off teenager problem. Kicking the van up over the curb was not going to be a simple solution. She stopped her eye beams for a second, loosed another inchoate roar of anger, and then started slicing the back section of the van to ribbons. It didn't take a genius to figure out that the front of the van was next, and that it'd only take her a matter of seconds to finish her work on the rear of it.

There was no cover behind me, no cars left for me to duck behind once my current vehicle was finished being annihilated. No pillars within easy sprint, nothing to hide behind, and I was running low on things to throw.

My only option left?

Charge.

I steeled myself and rounded the bumper just as she was finishing up her slice-and-dice on the rear of the car. The odds were very, very good she was going to whip around and blast me into my component atoms when I came at her, but since I was dry of other options, I readied myself for the sprint. If I could make it to her before she turned, I might be able to...well...pummel the shit out of her. It'd be hard to slice me up with her eye beams if she couldn't open her eyes.

As plans went, it was not my most confidence-inspiring, but it was what I had, so I lunged off the bumper and over the curb. I'd reach her in about three long steps at meta-speed, a matter of seconds or less.

She could turn her head in a fraction of a second, though. And I doubted my flesh and bone would survive a beam that cut through a car body.

Her eye beams stopped for just a beat, and she turned and looked at me, steam rising off her cheeks where the eye beams were heating her ceaseless tears.

Then she set her jaw, and the glow began in her pupils as she prepared to destroy me.

A thunderous punch knocked her sideways, putting her lights out and closing her eyes for me as she tumbled ass over teakettle into the wreckage of the van where she stayed, still and unmoving.

My grandmother stood just behind her, fist cocked, as her eyes fell to me.

"So," she said, "you must be Sienna."

19.

"I can't tell you how good it is to see you," I said, feeling a little muscle tension slacken in my neck and back, that radiating pain from beneath my shoulder blade starting up again. "I'd offer a welcome-to-Iowa hug but...it's Iowa, and you've already been in battle after being here for all of twenty minutes, so..." Sirens rang in the distance, the clarion call of Sienna Nealon. sounding through the arrivals area. "Maybe we should skedaddle in case Omega has any more trouble heading our way."

She stared at me for a second, assessing, then loosened up, un-cocking her fist. She had a suitcase in her hand, and her posture returned – mostly – to normal, just a thread of alert stress still keeping her stiff. "Okay. Where to?"

"I don't know – exactly."

She paused in contemplation. "Okay. How do we get out of here?"

"Not sure yet," I said, looking around for an answer. "How'd you know I was in trouble?"

"Saw a guy in cargo shorts go flying through the window inside. Figured it might be you."

"Good guess," I said. "Can you believe his wife let him go out in those? With those legs?" I stole a look at where I'd caught her with the hatchback. Her lower body was still there, twitching, separated about mid-thigh and bleeding out onto the pavement.

And beyond that were cars and witnesses, staring, paralyzed.

These were people who hadn't run because they'd been too afraid.

"I don't like the look of cargo shorts, either," my grandmother said, stepping off the curb to join me. Her hair wasn't as curly as it had been in Revelen, more straight like my mother's. I hadn't really thought about it, but now that I did, it sort of reflected an evolutionary pattern – mom still cared that her hair wasn't straight, so she flat ironed it like a fiend to keep it in order. My grandmother, by the time I met her in Revelen, didn't give a shit anymore, and thus let the curl come out so she looked like, well, Sigourney Weaver in certain movies.

Me? I didn't have time for hairstyling, so mine was always either up or dealt with, to avoid frizzy strands falling into my eyes at inopportune moments.

"What now?" my grandmother asked.

"Let's do some GTA," I said, and nodded at the cars down the way.

"...GTA?" she asked.

"It's a popular game in my day. Grand Theft Auto. Named for the criminal charge of the same name."

"Hmm." She didn't seem convinced.

"Come on," I said, and broke into a run toward the waiting cars.

When they saw me coming, most of the people who'd done the freeze thing instead of flight changed their minds and ran. It was like startled pigeons bursting out of a thicket. There were only a few cars to choose from, and I listened for the sweet sound of a running engine.

I found one in a small Nissan Sentra. I waved to my grandmother to follow me, but when I turned to look back she was barely a step behind, keeping up, sweat already beading on her forehead.

"I hope this thing has AC," I said, slipping around the open door. Keys were in, it was running, over a half tank of gas. Annnnnnd...a cool breath of air blew out of the vents. "Hallelujah! Finally a lucky break."

My grandmother slid in next to me, depositing her suitcase in the back seat. "Oh?"

"Yeah, I've kinda had a run of crappy luck lately," I said, "maybe it's finally turning around though, since-"

Something heavy and black landed on the front of the car, smashing the engine and killing it instantly. The crunching of metal sounded like the world's worst auto accident, and I was thrown forward into the steering wheel, which popped me in the nose, no airbag to save me from a blow to the head.

"Nope," my grandmother said, bleeding from the forehead as she raised her head.

I was bleeding some, too, warm, sticky liquid rolling down my upper lip. "Yeah," I said, puckering my lip and spitting out a tooth. "I should have kept my mouth shut."

Waiting there on the hood, back in his complete armor and looking at me with pure fire through the eye holes...

Was Full Metal Jackass.

20.

"Someone has really got to give me a vacay after this," I said, leaning back, ripping the steering wheel free and hurling it into Full Metal Jackass's chest through the open air between us. The windshield had mostly been shattered by Henderschott's landing, offering us a perfect view of him leering down, with only spiderweb-cracked remnants of glass filling the edges.

"Vay...cay?" my grandmother asked, ripping the door off the glove box and hurling it through the windshield. It rang out against Henderschott's head, causing him to wobble slightly.

"Don't ask," I said, "the English language is a mess in the future. I blame cell phones and texting."

If she wondered what those were, she didn't ask, probably because she was too busy slamming her shoulder into the door and throwing herself out of it. I followed her fine example, ripping mine free to use as a shield. I noticed her do the same, planting a foot against the frame of the car and tearing it from the hinges with a simple pull.

I nodded at her, she nodded at me. Then we both turned our attention to Henderschott, who was alternating between looking at each of us in turn, waiting to see what we'd do.

"I hear you have a pretty face, Henderschott," I said, circling to my left as he stood in the center of the crushed hood. My grandmother moved behind him. The strategy was simple, if unspoken. Flank him, charge him, tear him apart. Easy stuff, even for two near-strangers like us, and communicated with but a look.

He started to wheel when he heard my grandmother move behind him, but I lurched into motion, door held high in a ramming motion, planning to Captain America's shield him if he turned and making my move flashy enough to distract him so he didn't.

Henderschott picked the worst of both worlds – he made a half turn and then hesitated when he saw my aggressive motion, trying to decide whether he should deal with me or deal with grandma.

Big mistake.

I made a hard feint at him, turning it into a real charge once I realized he was hesitating to commit. His focus was split, trying to keep an arm at each side, in position to deal with us both at the same time.

Circling a little more behind him, forcing him to commit, I finally got him to turn his back on my grandmother so he could deal fully with me-

Grandma did not hesitate.

Lethe threw herself at him in a headlong charge, pouring on the speed in a leap that turned her into a blur.

Henderschott was decided at that point, though, because I was about five feet from him, and both his arms were angled to deal with me. There was no way he was going to be able to pivot or reach behind himself to get to her in time.

She slammed into him, and the hard crunch of metal meeting metal rang like an artillery shell bursting. The remaining glass in her door-shield shattered as she crashed into Henderschott and sent him forward off the hood of the car and falling toward me.

Not to be outdone (or crushed), I took advantage of his sudden momentum shift to keep moving, get under him, and spring up-

I slammed my shield into his chest while he was stunned, arms pinwheeling from his failure to keep his balance. I drove into him with all my force-

Henderschott flew into the sky like he'd been launched from one of those Punkin' Chunkin' catapults, a black-limbed projectile. He sailed over the terminal, and a crash in the distance heralded his landing.

"Looks like Team Rocket's blasting off again," I said, lowering my door shield, "Unidentified flying jackass, this is tower. You are cleared for crash landing."

"He didn't even get any peanuts," Lethe said, completely serious, as she hopped off the wrecked hood of the Sentra.

"Worst flight ever," I said. "Though to be honest, that's happening a lot in the future." My grandmother cocked her head in curiosity. "No peanuts on flights. People are highly allergic, so they're kinda going the way of the eight track."

"Or vinyl," my grandmother said.

"That's actually making a comeback," I said, and she frowned. "I know. The future is weird." I looked into the distance, where Full Metal Jackass had disappeared on his long, tumbling arc. "Though, honestly, the present here isn't much different." The sirens were getting closer, and a dozen or so paces back I spied an unattended Cadillac with the engine still running. "Come on, let's get out of here before the cops show up, because past, present or future, I know neither of us want to get pinched right now."

21.

"So...is this your first time traveling through...time?" my grandmother finished, a bit awkwardly, frowning as she tripped over the last word.

I was behind the wheel of the Cadillac, trying to keep us on the back roads. I figured we'd get where we were going eventually if I just kept heading in the same direction. "Not really," I said. "When I helped Akiyama get uncorked from his...uh...exile, sorry to mix the metaphor, I got some snapback time travel effects there."

My grandmother arched an eyebrow. "Did you see anything interesting?"

I nodded, following the slight curve of the road. "I got a vision of my future, I think. A few of the things I saw then have already played out in the present. My present. Still your future, I guess."

"Hm. Care to share?" I couldn't tell if she was assessing me for baseline honesty, like a polygraph would, or if she was just curious to see how much info she could get out of me.

"I'm going to probably be a little bit cagey about it as it relates to the future, but...sure," I said. "One of the things I saw involved a lady named Angel I work with and me getting into an... I don't know how to describe it – chase scene? In a car."

"Angel?" Lethe's eyebrow maintained its perfect arch, a query behind it. Always, it seemed.

"Angel Gutierrez," I said. "We kinda got into a scrape with

a cartel, it ended in... well, violence, as most things with me tend to. Anyway, I also saw your pops saying, in a very dramatic voice, 'This was always to be your fate'. Which he has said to me several times since."

"That's a perennial favorite of his," she said. "Though I'm surprised you've met him. He's not the social sort."

"Neither am I," I said. "But we got along well enough." Considering I'd wrecked his country and beat the shit out of him.

Hey, for me, just letting him live meant we'd gotten along all right. It was a sliding scale, and you had to take my extreme anti-social tendencies into account when judging.

"He doesn't usually do that, either," she said, frown deepening.

I shrugged. "What can I say? I'm a real ray of sunshine."

She shook her head as if trying to dispense with the effects of a particularly dazing thought. "So...my daughter. Your mother."

I pursed my lips. "Yeah. I haven't told her about you yet. As far as I know, she's still unaware you're alive in my day." Because she was dead. But her failure to mention her mother being still living up to then? Strong indicator she didn't know, or else was playing things so ridiculously close to the vest as to defy-

Actually...it was well within the realm of possibility that my mother could have known and not said anything. After all, she hadn't uttered a peep about me developing superpowers until after I'd done so at age 17. I'd had to find that one out from the people at the Directorate. It was a little like learning about your cycle from random strangers you'd just met. Except maybe a little less awkward.

"Though she's not exactly the warmest person and it's entirely possible she knew and just didn't bother to tell me," I said.

Lethe nodded slowly. "Mother-daughter relations in our family are not of the highest quality."

I snorted. "Mine locked me in a metal box to keep me confined in childhood. You can say that again." I frowned. "Or...she will be doing that sometime in the near future." I ran a hand through my hair, pushing it back. I needed a hair tie for it because somehow it had all gotten free during my fight with Omega back at the airport. "Time travel makes grammar annoying."

"Yes, it's all very tense," Lethe said, utterly deadpan. Only the trace of a smile told me she was making a pun. "So... who's after you? And how did you know to call me?"

"Those dipshits Omega," I said. "And when we met, you did this weird thing where you made me memorize the castle number and told me it had been around forever and emphasized that I could call you *anytime*."

"Mm," she said, taking it in, presumably to perpetuate this loop in about twenty years. "Omega? That'd be Gerasimos's criminal syndicate."

"I guess," I said. "I never met the guy. Though I did have a lethal encounter with his son."

She looked at me sideways. "Rick?"

"You should probably try and forget I said that. That's future info and all that."

"Was it a tough fight?" she asked.

I cleared my throat, mostly out of awkwardness. "Not particularly, no." Rick had turned out to be human, so it had basically been a slaughter. Not exactly my proudest moment.

"Nothing like his father, then." Lethe looked out the window as the Des Moines city landscape passed us by. "What does Omega want from your mother?"

I frowned. "Little me, I think. They're seeking succubi."

Lethe's eyebrows climbed up her forehead. "You think they know, then? That you're one?"

"Well, I'm five, so they can't know for sure," I said. "And from what I know, mom was pretty low-key about being one-"

"'Low...key'?"

"She didn't advertise she was a succubus," I said.

"Why would anyone advertise being a succubus?" Lethe asked. "It's a fast way to get yourself exiled from any meta community." She slapped her knee. "Damn. Forgot my luggage."

"Yeah, I'm running a bit low on fresh undies, too," I said.

"I had my purse in there," she said. "Including my driver's license and... everything."

"Ooh," I said, cringing. "Is that going to be a problem when the police show up at whatever address you have listed?"

"No," she said, "but it's going to be annoying the next time I go to buy a bottle of White Zin." She must have caught my funny look. "What? I still get carded all the time." She looked out the windshield innocently. "Makes my day."

"Okay, well-"

"This does present a problem," she said, "or at least a narrowing of options."

"How's that?"

"I can't rent a hotel room without any cash," she said. "So unless you have some..."

"Nah, I'm tapped. Left my wallet in the future, which would be a convenient excuse if we went out to dinner and anyone else I was with had a buck to their names. But mom's broke."

"When it rains it pours, doesn't it?" she asked. "I might be able to help with that, but...it's not going to be as simple as going to Western Union and picking up some cash. Since I don't have an ID any longer."

"That's a secondary problem anyway," I said. "Bigger issue – what do we do with you in the absence of sticking you in a hotel?"

"Sticking me in a hotel was a bad idea anyway. How am I supposed to help you if I'm not near enough to fight?"

I slumped in the driver's seat. "Damn. You have a point, there. And it's like a sword point, right to the heart."

"You don't like the idea of me staying with you to help you?" she asked.

"I don't like the idea of mom's reaction when she learns you're not dead," I said. "And I like even less the idea that she's going to keep that from me for the next...uh...however many years."

"And yet," Lethe said, "apparently that is what we must do, to protect the timeline so that you can go on living."

"Great," I said. "Well, here comes a super awkward conversation for the ages. Almost as awkward as the one that's going to follow."

Lethe's brow furrowed. "What's the one that follows?"

I took a slow breath. "How we stop Omega from getting what they want without tearing up the organization root and branch."

"That...is a bit more complicated," Lethe said, nodding along as we made our way, slowly, through the afternoon traffic. At least, unlike the problem in front of me, the traffic seemed to have holes. The Omega issue?

That one...I didn't see any easy way out of.

22.

London, United Kingdom

The office was wood-paneled, its occupant of the oldest tastes when it came to style. It could have been pulled out of the 1600's, the full bookshelves lining one wall a remnant of an age when books were so expensive that reading was seen as the most powerful pastime, one only able to be pursued by those who were truly wealthy.

And Gerasimos was a man of wealth. Oh yes, he was. He stared out the window over London's changing skyline. That atrocious Millennium Dome project made the ancient city's august skyline look...stupid. There were other architectural decisions he felt did similar damage, but that one...it rose like half a metallic fruit on the south bank of the Thames, surrounded with construction cranes, and his lips puckered in distaste just looking at it. He would not get used to it anytime soon.

"...Revenues for continental Europe are up this month over the same month last year," Janus said, shuffling through papers from the visitor chair across Gerasimos's desk. "The outlook continues to be excellent, mostly attributable to the people we have in place. They are all experienced, and we have managed to waylay some of the interlopers from Alpha who interfered in our business last year, causing the second quarter revenue to throw off the entire year."

"Hera," Gerasimos murmured. "From the grave, Poseidon

106

still haunts me, using her as his implement. She loved him, you know. More than ever she did her husband. Disloyal creature."

"I would not care to speculate on Hera's motives," Janus said, closing his folder. "She never required Poseidon's lead before sticking her nose into the business of the day."

"They never understood our purpose," Gerasimos said, thick eyebrows arched into heavy lines above his inset eyes. "We are above humanity, Janus. You know this. We were made to rule. Once, we did it from above them, as gods. Now, we do it from the shadows. The world does not work without a hierarchy. It descends, becomes low, is chaos, unbridled."

"I expect she sees it differently," Janus said.

"She sees it as a child would. Or a woman. Her compassion runs away with her."

"She is several thousand years old," Janus said with a smile. "And compassion is hardly the worst weakness."

"That is also the thinking of a child," Gerasimos said, rising from his chair. It clicked as he stood, pulling his powerful frame from it, wood creaking as he did so. "Don't let her Women's Auxiliary interfere with our business. Bloody their noses if you have to. Stop short of killing them, if possible." He buttoned his jacket.

"May I ask a question?" Janus stood as well. He probably sensed by Gerasimos's motion that their meeting was at a close.

"You may," Gerasimos said. "Come, Janus. We are old friends. Older than oldest friends. Why so formal?"

"What is going on in America right now?" Janus asked.

"Ah," Gerasimos said, coming around the desk and putting an arm around Janus's shoulder. "I should have thought that would be the question you'd ask. It is a small matter, unworthy of your notice. I have Bastet tending to it."

"Yes, I know," Janus said. "Rumors have reached my ears that you were running something sensitive over there. Des Moines, I believe?"

"Yes, Iowa," Gerasimos nodded. "Dreadful place. I hope to have our people cleared out of there immediately. Just a small errand, that's all."

"And unrelated to the project you have brewing in Eagle

River, Wisconsin?" Janus's smile was small, the tiniest admission of victory.

"I would ask you how you know about that, but secrets hidden from you seem to be impossible to keep," Gerasimos said with a smile of his own. "Yes. They are related. I think."

Janus nodded slowly. "Very well, then. I will leave you to manage your secret project in peace."

"Janus," Gerasimos said. "I did not keep it a secret out of lack of trust. Or spite."

Janus raised a greying eyebrow. "Oh?"

"I know your limits, my friend," Gerasimos said. "The edges of what you are comfortable with. This...is beyond that frontier."

Janus took off his glasses and took a cloth out of his tweed jacket's pocket, rubbing the lenses. "It deals with a child, then?"

Gerasimos nodded slowly, once. "Indeed. So I handed this to Bastet. She is, of course, quite comfortable with such things."

"She is quite comfortable with almost anything," Janus said, a trace of accusatory tone there.

"We are who we are, Janus," Gerasimos said. "You just read me a revenue report about our criminal operations. We hurt people. We take money. It is all rightfully ours to take, because strength is on our side, but...this is who we are. We live outside the laws of men, because we are beyond them."

"But...a child?" Janus asked. "Truly?"

"The child will be unhurt," Gerasimos said, waving him off. "I need her alive."

"Somehow I doubt very much you are seeking her, whoever she is, to make her your new ward," Janus said. "So... how is she to be...'all right'?"

"Because she will be in our hands soon enough," Gerasimos said. "And our hands are the safest." He smiled broadly. "Safer than in the arms of her mother."

A beep from his desk drew the attention of both of them. "Bastet here to see you," his secretary's voice chirped over the intercom.

"Send her in," Gerasimos said, and the door opened

immediately. "Ah. We were just talking about–"

An august, ebon-skinned woman walked in, catlike in the smoothness of her movements, shutting the door behind her at meta speed. "Our Des Moines operation has run into a problem," Bastet plunged in immediately, without waiting for leave to speak.

"What sort of problem?" Gerasimos asked, eyes narrowing.

Bastet flicked a gaze at Janus, who watched her with something akin to amusement. Probably mildly gleeful that he wasn't the one bringing bad news. "We have an unidentified subject interfering in our efforts." She pulled a manila folder from beneath her arm and flipped it open. Black and white security camera photographs waited within.

"If you'll excuse me," Janus said, and opened the door. "I expect I am not wanted in this...endeavor."

"Janus," Gerasimos said, taking the photographs in hand, "your help is always wanted. But forgive me, my friend, for wanting to protect your spirit from aspects of what we do that you might find...distasteful."

Janus just smiled. "I do appreciate it. In fact...I think I shall go and wash the distaste from my mouth even now." And he nodded, closing the door behind him as he departed.

Gerasimos shook his head. "A shame he draws his lines so carefully around matters such as these." He snapped his gaze down to the picture. "This is Sierra Nealon, yes?"

Bast shook her head. "No. It is not." She produced another photograph, of a similarly dark-haired woman carrying a child. "*This* is Sierra Nealon." She pointed at the photo in Gerasimos's hand. "This woman...same height, same build, but not Sierra. She is with Nealon, though, and helped her, killing two of our agents at the Walmart."

"Wal...mart?" Gerasimos asked.

"An American store," Bast said. "Surely you have heard of it? We believe she killed several more later in the day at the airport in Des Moines. We'd picked up a tip of a high-value metahuman moving into the area–" She flipped up another photograph.

Gerasimos's eyebrow raised. "Lethe...?" He stared. "I thought she was dead."

"So did we all," Bast said. "But she is here, now, with her daughter and this woman."

Gerasimos tapped the photograph of the unknown, dark-haired woman. "Is it Charlie?"

Bast shook her head. "We have eyes on Charlie. She's in Las Vegas."

"Curious," Gerasimos said, puckering his lips. "No one knows that Lethe is involved in this? Other than you and I?"

Bast again shook her head. "Henderschott clashed with her, but he reported her as another unidentified subject. Few would know her name."

"This confirms something we long suspected but could not verify," Gerasimos said, taking the picture of the young woman and walking back toward his desk. "Lethe was indeed Lisa Nealon. And Sierra is her daughter, as is Charlie." He looked up at Bast and saw her questioning gaze. "I know, I know. It's still supposition, you would say, but I ask you – why would Lethe come back now, from death, to this – Iowa, if not to help one of her daughters?"

"Perhaps she wanted to visit the corn museum," Bast said, voice dripping with irony. "I don't know her motives. I don't care. The linkage is undefined." She brought over another photograph, this one showing Lethe and the new girl confronting Henderschott. "This unidentified subject killed two out of the three operatives of the Gustafson family. The mother and father. Quite brutally, I might add. The daughter is expected to recover, and the younger children survived-"

"See they're taken care of," Gerasimos said, frowning as he dropped his considerable bulk into the chair. "Scholarships, whatever they need. That family has done good work for us. We owe them, especially if they met their end as-" Bast lifted autopsy photographs of the Gustafsons in front of him. "Stars, that is brutal." He felt a smile break across his face. "Who is this girl?"

"No idea," Bast said. "But she looks like a Nealon, doesn't she?"

Gerasimos made a harrumphing deep in his throat. "Sierra Nealon, for all her reckless use of force, was never that casually brutal. What type of meta is she?"

"Uncertain," Bast said. "Energy projection seems unlikely. She's had opportunities where those abilities would be very handy and she has not employed them. Her strength is top of the charts. She broke big boy's neck with her bare hands. Excellent marksman. Could be a Reflex-Type-"

"A Diana?" Gerasimos looked up from the photograph. "She looks a little like her. The angry eyes."

"They remind me of Sierra Nealon's," Bast said. "Everything about this girl reminds me of Sierra Nealon. Standing next to each other. Helping each other. They could be sisters."

"Does Lethe have another daughter?" Gerasimos asked. "One we don't know about?"

Bast shook her head. "There's much we don't know about Lethe. Or Sierra. Or Charlie, for that matter."

"I like her already," Gerasimos said, putting down the photograph, centering it on his desk. "I want her. Want to know who she is, where she comes from. Get her, get the mother. And the child, of course."

"Of course." Bast nodded, short and sharp, filled with displeasure. "It will be as you say, but don't expect it to come easily. Five dead already. And now with Lethe in the mix-"

"Lethe is old," Gerasimos said, taking up the casualty list. It featured the manner of death and injury, and he found himself nodding in respect as he read it. "Her days draw to a close. And we have means to counter her." He looked up. "You know who to send?"

Bast nodded once. Smiled. "I know who to send."

"Send him, then." Gerasimos found himself looking back down at the security footage of the dark-haired girl, and smiling. "Send...whoever you have to. See it done, Bast. I want this girl. Both these girls. And to hell with anyone who gets in your way." He looked up. "Even Lethe."

23.

Sienna

We pulled up to the house about an hour later, having taken a circuitous route back and having switched out the car with a freshly stolen model lifted from a parking garage near the bus station. With luck, whoever had left it there wouldn't notice it gone for a while, because I'd had about my fill of stealing cars. Hell, I was beginning to feel like a one-woman crime wave hitting Des Moines.

"Just be cool," I said, slamming the door and looking around. The neighborhood was quiet, mid-afternoon laziness having settled on the place and all the residents presumably inside to hide from the stifling summer heat.

Lethe raised an eyebrow at me. "You think my coolness is going to be a problem? You're the one who was looking around furtively while you stole this car."

"I'm not really used to being a criminal," I said, doing a little more furtive looking around, seeing if anyone was staring out of windows at us. The last thing we needed right now was some troublesome do-gooder reporting us for a noise violation and rolling us up for grand theft auto while we were on the run from Omega. "I'm kinda more used to...smashing them."

"You really followed in your mother footsteps, didn't you?" she asked as we made our way up the front walk.

"Well, I'd have followed in yours, but being a pillaging

Valkyrie isn't really a viable career path these days."

Lethe raised an eyebrow at that but said nothing. We were already to the front door, and it swung open to reveal my mother standing behind the storm door, peering out at us with a hard squint.

I braced myself. This was bound to be a hell of a thing.

It wasn't. My mother took Lethe in with a casual look, then opened the door for us. "Mother," she said.

"Sierra," Lethe said, and walked past me into the house.

I was left standing on the front steps, waiting for something more to happen. An explosion, a yelling contest, a gentle breeze to knock me over.

Something other than, "Mother," and them both to just disappear inside.

I followed, expecting some sort of furious fight to be going on, meta-low, in the living room, but I just found Lethe looking around in mild curiosity and my mother standing a few feet away from her, looking pretty casual overall. I waited a minute, then two. Nobody said anything.

Finally, I'd had enough. "Okay," I said, "get it out."

They both turned to look at me, and did so in exactly the same way, with the same expression on their faces. "Get what out?" my mother asked.

"Whatever awkwardness there is between you two," I said.

They exchanged a look. "I'm fine," my mother said.

"Same," Lethe said.

I opened my mouth, then closed it. "You...did not know your mother was alive," I said to my mom.

She shrugged. "I didn't rule it out as a possibility." She traded a look with Lethe, who nodded. "It was a closed casket funeral, after all."

I felt like I wanted to scream, so I stuck my right index finger in my mouth and bit down. Not too hard, because I could take that finger off easily if I wasn't careful, but enough that a warm trickle of blood ran down into my mouth, a long-familiar sensation and taste of copper. "Okay," I said, "that's...fair. But-"

There was motion at the far end of the room. Little me stood there, clutching a teddy bear and rubbing her eyes.

"Sienna," my mother said, making her way over and kneeling next to little me. She looked up at Lethe, and mini me's attention followed. "I want you to meet your grandma."

I felt like my head was going to explode. I didn't remember any of this at all. Had I already broken time and didn't know it yet?

"Hello, Sienna," Lethe said, way more sweetly than anything she'd said to me yet. She dropped to a knee. "It's so nice to finally meet you."

Little me just sort of stared for a minute, like she was trying to make sense of everything, trying to figure out who this new person was.

That lasted about a second, and she shouted, "Grandma!" and boom, she was off and in grandma's arms.

I just stared. It seemed a little strange to me that she'd know what a grandma was and be that affectionate out of the gate, but apparently. I didn't really know myself.

"Huh," I said, watching the scene unfold, "this is...quite something."

Lethe was being very careful not to touch skin to skin, her hands placed strategically on little me's t-shirt. "What's that?"

"This is kind of a big moment," I said, dropping my voice to meta-low. "Feels like I would remember this. I'm starting to worry we're breaking the timeline."

My mother looked around. "Wouldn't breaking time result in actual breakage of the sort we could see?"

I shrugged. "What do I know about breaking time? We could have created a completely different future for me in the last five minutes." I touched my forehead gently. "I hope this doesn't erase me from existence."

"You seem fine," Lethe said, still hugging little me. "You're not fading away or anything. Got a picture of yourself we can use as a frame of reference?"

"I like that everyone's seen *Back to the Future* and thus we're all on the same page about the perils of time travel," I said, "but I'm not sure it works exactly like that. I will say, though, having a flying DeLorean feels like it would solve a lot of our current problems vis-a-vis Omega."

That took some of the wind out of mom's sails. "What are

we going to do about Omega?"

"No idea," I said. "It's not like we're presented with an abundance of options. We still don't have any money thanks to grandma leaving her suitcase at the airport during the attack-"

"You were attacked again?" my mother asked.

"She was, mostly," Lethe said. "I only did a little, and mostly against the man in the black armor."

My mother's eyes seemed to glow with rage. "You should have killed him at Walmart. Like the others."

I shook my head. "Can't. I fight him in the future."

She rolled her eyes. "Stupid time. How did they find you at the airport?"

"I'm going to hazard a guess here," Lethe said, now bouncing little me up and down slightly, producing a little series of giggles in the process, "Omega's thick on the ground in Des Moines. They've infiltrated the police and other institutions in the course of this operation, and they're looking at everything they can get their hot little hands on. Flight records, traffic reports – anything that will generate a lead to you. They've probably inserted their agents posing as federal ones with local law enforcement, maybe even the civil government, and they're using all these assets to turn up anything related to you. That's their MO when they move into a town. Usually they exploit these connections for criminal purposes, but they're doing something different here."

"Not so different from my experience with them," I said. "But if you've seen this from them before…what comes next?"

Lethe just shook her head. "Hard to say, but they seem quite determined to find this little one." She pulled her face back so she could smile at little me, who let out a peal of laughter at the play. It was kinda sweet, melted my stone-cold heart by a few degrees. "I would guess more of the same, and maybe worse to come if they feel like redoubling their efforts. If the death of this many of their operatives discourages them, maybe we'll see a reduction in our troubles. Either way," she said, squeezing little me tight to her shoulder again, "we need to lay as low as possible. If they don't find anything for a while, if the trail goes cold, they'll start to pull out of the area. Once the noose loosens enough, then we can slip out of town."

My mother and I exchanged a look. "There is another problem," I said. "We're light on money and low on food."

"We have enough to last a couple days if we stretch it," my mother said. "But that's about it."

"I would have been able to help with that if I still had my luggage," Lethe said. "Unfortunately, now it appears we're all in the same boat."

"And it's a leaking boat," I said. "With no treasure chests. Ahoy, mateys. I think we might need to do some plundering, unless you can orchestrate a bank transfer." I looked at Lethe.

She shook her head. "That would be a bad idea. Omega has a very definite toehold in the banking world. I promise you they're watching transactions in this town right now, and possibly for several hundred miles around. That would be a quick way to call the lightning down on our heads."

"Great," I said, looking at the white ceiling, which was starting to show its age in the form of lines indicating the seams of the plaster. "So we're broke and we have no way to get more money short of one of us getting a job. Or thievery."

"I saw the way you stripped that ignition," Lethe said. "I wouldn't rule out the thievery option so quickly."

I sighed. "The things I do to save my past self, I swear." Another long sigh made me feel a hint of sleepiness creep in. "So... what now?"

My mother looked to Lethe, who pulled mini-me off her shoulder again and made a face, drawing a giggle out of the little girl in her arms, one that was so very...un-Sienna. "Well, I can't speak for you two, but...I think I'm going to play with my granddaughter for a little bit if we have nothing else planned." She raised her voice out of meta-low. "I see some dolls and a doll house in the corner over there. Those must be your mother's."

Little me giggled. "Noooo, grandma. Those are mine."

"Yours?" Lethe mimed absolute shock. "Why, I love playing with dolls. I should go play with them right now. Do you mind if I play with your dolls all by myself?" She put little me down.

"No," little me said, "you can't play with those by yourself. Those are *mine*." So serious.

"Well, can we play with them together?" she asked, and got a nod for her troubles. With a glittering of eyes, she made her way past us to the dollhouse in the corner, holding little Sienna's wrist all the while. "Oh, my, this is a precious little doll. What's her name?"

"It was Bertha," little me said, "but now I call her 'Debra'."

I straightened as little me looked at big me. Just a quick glance, then away.

Oh, right. Debra was what I'd called myself to her. I blinked a few times.

"She doesn't know that many people," my mother said, back to meta-low. "It's been a rough few years." She had her arms folded in front of her. "I'm going to make some tea to try and hold off these hunger pangs. You want some?"

"Yeah," I said, feeling a rumbling in my stomach unrelated to hunger. "Please." I looked at Lethe, and she nodded at my mother. Three teas. Sierra disappeared into the kitchen.

"'A rough few years'," I repeated, under my breath. Running and hiding from Omega, from whatever other troubles there might be out there. Sovereign, for instance.

What my mother didn't know...what she couldn't know...was that the next years, the ones filled with me locked in a house while she worked to support us, the years of training, of my youth...

...of the box...

Those years weren't going to be any better.

And I stared at the little me, in the corner with her grandmother, happily explaining why the driver of the car couldn't possibly be Debra the doll, silly grandma! And my stomach rumble did not get any better.

24.

Mom had turned on the stereo at low volume, tuned to a classics station, bluesy, beautiful saxophone blaring the opening bars of Etta James's "Sunday Kind of Love," as I sat on the couch, my belly full of the last of the ham and eggs, a mostly-drunk glass of milk on the end table next to me. The last strains of day cast an orange glow outside the living room window.

The dishes were done, and my mother, my grandmother and I all sat arrayed around the living room, little me playing quietly in the corner, her entreaties to grandma to, "Come play with me," sweetly rebuffed by Lethe, her, "I played with you all afternoon!" filled with a sort of kind exasperation. Eventually, little me had given up and retreated to her toys, leaving the three of us to sit in silence as night crept in behind us.

It felt surreal, sitting here on a summer's eve in Des Moines, watching myself as a child play in the corner while my now-dead mother and my until-recently-thought-dead grandmother sat around me, all of us embracing the surreal feel of the moment and the silence it brought.

"This is the weirdest day ever," I finally said, prompting nods from both of them.

"Tell me about it," my mother said. "I find out my daughter grows up just fine and that my mother's not dead, all within about twenty-four hours."

I cringed. "I wouldn't go assuming that we make it out of

118

this just fine. Akiyama brought me here for a reason, and he's already had to intervene once, that's how close we got to messing things up."

"Well, I'm guessing he'll intervene again if things get too serious," my mother said. She seemed a lot more relaxed now than she had been earlier. "I mean...I know we're not out of it yet, but the fact that it looks like we will get out of it-"

"Mom," I said, shaking my head, "don't go thinking that way. If this was certain, I don't think Akiyama would have-"

"She has a point," Lethe said. "There is an element of destiny to this, it seems." She leaned forward. "Think about it. You knew to call me in this time because I tipped you off to it. That suggests that I – well, future me – has already lived this moment, and survived it." She nodded at my mother. "The fact you grew up with her also suggests that she survives."

"Nothing suggests *I'll* survive," I said, looking at each of them in turn. "This could be the end of my journey, right here, and no one would know it."

"I don't think so," Lethe said, settling back. "I would have known it in the future, when I gave my number and told you to call me. Do you really think I would perpetuate a loop that ends in your death?"

"Probably not," I said, "but I guess I don't know you that well."

She quirked her eyebrow up. "The answer is no, I wouldn't."

"Fine," I said, "you both seem assured that we're going to make it through this. Here's my take: that's dangerous thinking."

My mother sighed. "How so?"

"We're facing Omega here," I said. "And again, Akiyama brought me here for a reason, and it's not because you're up against a threat that's so gentle we can just walk through it like a summer day in the park, okay?"

"We had a summer day in the park yesterday," my mother said. "As I recall it was filled with gunshots."

"Great, so keep that in mind," I said. "We cannot play this like it's a sure thing. Because that is a definite way to lose this fight."

Lethe let slip a little smile. "That sounds...familiar."

My mother rolled her eyes. "It sounds like something you'd say, mom."

"And I learned it from you," I said to Sierra. "Looks like it made its way down the line."

"Your point is taken," Lethe said. "By me, at least."

My mother wore a sour look. "It's not lost on me, either. But forgive me if I hang on to a shining ray of hope in the darkness of this moment when we're broke and lacking direction. I just wanted to think we might be able to get out of this without excess difficulty."

"Nothing good comes easy in my experience," I said.

"Nor mine," my mother and grandmother said as one. They looked at each other, then my mother looked away. Lethe just smiled, and my mother matched it a moment later.

"This is so weird," I said again. Because it really was.

"I should put Sienna to bed," my mother said, rising from the couch. "After that, I'm thinking...wine. Anyone else in?"

"Me," Lethe said.

"I'll stick to water," I said, shifting uncomfortably on the couch. "I don't want to...muddle my head. Not now, anyway. Not with all this trouble lurking over us."

My mother nodded as she picked her way over to the corner. "Sienna..." she said sweetly, "...it's time for bed."

"I don't want to," little me said, not looking up from her dolls. She was clearly right in the middle of something and was not brooking any interruptions.

"If you go now, I'll read you a book," she said, "and grandma will tuck you in."

Little me straightened, looking up at her with bright eyes. "And Debra, too?" She glanced over her shoulder at me and smiled.

"Uh, sure," I said, "I can tuck you in."

Little me sprinted off, disappearing into the back hallway before I could even fully process what I'd just agreed to.

My mother must have sensed my apprehension. "Just sit on the bed and talk to her for a couple minutes. Tell her a story, maybe."

"It's easy," Lethe said. She shared a look with my mom. "I

guess this tells us where we stand in relation to grandchildren and great-grandchildren, though."

"Hey, I've been busy living my life and saving the world...and stuff," I said. "It's complicated."

"It always is," my mother said, and disappeared down the hall after little me. I heard them in the back, water running and some muttered arguing about best practices for brushing teeth.

"Do you want children?" my grandmother asked after a few minutes of silence.

"I'm not violently opposed to them or anything," I said, still watching the dark hallway where my mother and little me had disappeared with something akin to quiet dread. Tuck-in at bedtime? I'd done this job for Eddie Vansen while babysitting, and it was always a combo of weird and hilarious, because kids tended to come up with the most bizarre ideas, ones that seemed to be good for a laugh, always.

"That's good," my grandmother said, "because they tend to put people who violently oppose children into prison."

I puckered my lips. "Well, that's not me." Boy, would she get a charge out of the irony of that statement if she remembered it in twenty years. Since she had, in fact, busted me out of prison.

We settled into an easy silence, just listening to my mother's entreaties to little me. There was a little back and forth, every word of which we could hear.

"How long are Debra and grandma staying with us?"

"I don't know, sweetie. I think we need to move again soon. They'll probably stay with us until we finish doing that."

"We have to move again?"

"Yes." My mother made a shhh-ing sound. "It'll be okay."

I exchanged a look with Lethe, who kept her voice low when she asked, "Was it like this for you growing up?"

"Arguably worse," I said. "She has to lock me at home all day, every day, while she goes to her job."

Lethe frowned. "How did that work? You don't seem like the type to just sit at home and wait."

I looked at the window behind me, the orange sky fading at the close of day. "Well...she set up a pretty compelling punishment system, so...it did more or less work."

Lethe shook her head. "Sounds terrible."

"I can't complain," I said. "I mean look what we've dealt with in the last couple days. Two meta attacks and an unpowered couple of human agents trying to get me. Imagine trying to fight through that every day for the next ten years."

"I can't imagine it would be easy," she said. "But neither can I imagine that living confined for a decade is going to be, either."

"Well, it made me who I am today," I said, smiling wanly. "How can I complain about that? I had a training regimen, a school course load...it may have been tough, but it made me tough. And I certainly needed that after I got out."

"It just seems...so unfair that you should have to go through that during your upbringing." She leaned forward, clasping her hands together in her lap. "There are alternatives, you know. Other places you could go where you might be welcome."

A little alarm bell rang in my head. "Except that's not how I was raised."

"Maybe this is your chance to choose differently," she said. "To be different. Like Marty, teaching his father to slug Biff and waking up in a different world when he got back to the present. Maybe your life could be different – in a good way."

"Yeah," I said, "or I could ruin everything. Akiyama seems to believe that time bends only so far and then it breaks. He gave me this whole lecture one time about river rocks and currents and – never mind. Look, the man once tried to change time for himself. Tried everything, near as I can tell. It didn't work for him, and it nearly destroyed the world, maybe even the universe." I shook my head. "I don't want to mess with existence. It's way more important than my upbringing, which I survived, and which made the ass-kicking machine you see in front of you."

My grandmother's brow jumped an inch in amusement. "'Ass-kicking machine'?"

I shrugged. "Everyone's gotta have a hobby."

My mother appeared at the door to the back hallway, looking way more tired than she had when she'd gone in. "She's ready. She wants 'Debra' first, then grandma."

"Oooookay," I said, rising to my feet. "Guess I've been summoned by the big boss. I better not keep her waiting."

"Damned right," Lethe said.

My mother let out a laugh as she exhaled and collapsed onto the couch. "You're not far off. Five-year-olds, I swear." She shook her head. "Bet she has a nightmare tonight."

"Oh?" Lethe asked as I headed for the hallway.

"That Walmart thing...I think it's going to stick with her, what she saw there," my mother said as I walked down the darkened hall. There was a night light outside an open door, shining into the room, which was also lighted by a bedside lamp.

I'd been shown little me's room by the girl herself sometime during the day. She proudly gave me the tour, insisting that I saw her room. It was definitely worth seeing, especially since it had once been mine and I had no memory of it at all.

I paused at the door. Her little shape was completely covered over in blankets, and I hesitated.

She threw the blankets off in an eruption of cloth and was smiling at me underneath. "Hi," she said, backlit by the faint twilight outside the curtained window behind her.

"Hey," I said, and crossed the threshold, like a vampire being invited in, except more uncomfortable. "I hear it's my turn to do tuck-in." She nodded, plopping back onto her pillow, dark hair spilling out across the white cloth. "So... what does one do during tuck-in? You gotta help me, I've never really done this kind of thing for you before, I need some expectations so I don't f – errr, mess it up."

"Not teaching her any swear words would be a good start," my mother growled, meta-low, from the living room. I cringed.

"On it," I said.

"On what?" little me's brow puckered.

"Never mind," I said, sinking onto the edge of the bed. "What do we do at tuck-in time? I'm so lost. It's been a long time since I was little like you, and I don't remember tuck-in."

"Did your mommy not do tuck-in time with you?" Her little face was just amazed by that idea, it was so foreign to her.

"My mommy was really busy with other stuff," I said, trying

to remember any tuck-ins. Nope, never happened that I could recall.

"Oh," she said. "My mommy's not busy."

I snorted. "That's because she's not doing radiology yet."

Little me's face quirked in curiosity, but she dropped that and moved on to talking about more important things, namely whatever was on her mind: "Can we play dolls again tomorrow?"

"Sure," I said. "Absolutely."

"Good," she said, then seemed to rise and flop on the bed again in a single motion. "Tell me a story?"

"Oh, uh...sure," I said, trying to think of something. "What...kind of story do you like?"

"I don't know," she said. "Tell me a story."

"Uh, okay," I said, trying again, in vain, to come up with something. "Uhm...uh..."

She watched me hem and haw for a few seconds, then said, "You're not very good at telling stories, are you?"

"Not for G-rated audiences, no," I said. "Dirty jokes – got 'em by the ton. Even a few limericks of the ribald sort. But for a five-year-old audience, yeah, I'm a bit light on age-appropriate content. Give me a second." And I concentrated. "Okay, I think I have something."

She clapped her hands together. "Yay!"

"Once upon a time," I started, because, dammit, that was the only way I knew how to start a story to a five-year-old, "there was a fierce, angry woman in charge of stopping bad guys-"

"So she was a police woman?"

"Basically, yeah," I said. "And this, uh, police woman, was sent to Boulder, Colorado – do you know where that is?"

"Where it snows?"

"There's a lot of mountains there, and yeah, it sometimes snows. In contrast to Iowa, here, where it snows but you couldn't find a hill with a telescope and prayer. Anyway, I was in Boulder, Colorado-"

"I thought this was about a police woman?"

"Oh, right, this police woman was in Boulder, Colorado-"

"What was her name?"

124

I cleared my throat. "Oh, I don't know. What would you name her?"

"Sienna."

I nearly choked. "Well, what a coincidence. Because that was actually her name. So Sienna went to Boulder, Colorado, the land of mountains and snow and no flat-butt cornfields, to catch a very, very bad man whose name was Gordy Fletcher. And Gordy was so bad that his mommy had called the police and said, 'My son is a total tool, and you should arrest him'-"

Her little mouth dropped open. "What did he do to his mommy that was so bad?"

"It was less about what he did to his mom and more about him robbing banks on the sly – though I guess he was partying until like three, four in the morning and still lived with her, which made her mad enough to search his room while he was out and boom – she found all the money from his bank robberies. So I guess you could say if Gordy hadn't been a jerk and gone to bed when his mommy told him to go to bed instead of smarting off, drinking beer, and generally flipping her the bird at bedtime-"

"What's 'flipping the bird'-"

My mother grunted in the other room.

"It's being mean to, uhm, flick a bird," I said, making a flicking motion with my fingers.

Her mouth fell open again. "That is so mean. Why would he be so mean to a bird?"

"You think that's bad, you should see what he did to the bank tellers that ticked him off. Anyway, I get out to Boulder on this anonymous tip about Gordy, and – errr, ooops, I mean Sienna does that – and as soon as she gets there, she finds Gordy behind his favorite bar, passed out from, uhmmmm...too much chocolate milk and skipping his nap. Yeah. That's it. You ever get tired when you don't get your nap?"

She nodded. "And sometimes I sit in here without taking my nap and just talk and play, and sometimes-"

"Okay, let's get back on track. So, anyhoo, Sienna finds him sacked out in the alley behind the bar, which, is again, an instructive lesson on why you shouldn't skip your nap or talk back to your parents. Or rob banks, but y'know, that one's sort of implied as a good rule of everyday life. So Gordy's out, face down on an alley floor, and I'm thinking – err, Sienna's thinking, this is bound to be the easiest collar ever-"

I paused. Outside the window, a shadow passed behind the curtains. It was only there for a second, highlighted against the fading sky, but it was there – then gone.

I frowned. Had something just walked by out there? I stopped a second, listened-

Nothing. Must have been nothing. Maybe a car passing on the road? But I hadn't heard anything...

"Debra?"

I frowned. "Sorry. Where was I?"

"I don't know," little me said, frowning in concentration. "Bank robber? Nap?"

"Oh, right," I said. "He was asleep in the alley when I – she – got there. And so she starts walking toward him, tiptoeing gently-"

I paused again. Had I heard the crunch of someone walking on grass outside? There was yelling in the distance, someone shouting to the heavens in glee about a football game or something, but closer-

I listened. Nothing.

I shook it off again and launched back into my story. "Well, anyway, long story short, Gordy might have been asleep, but he was not going to just let me, uh, her, slap the cuffs on him and take him to jail without a fight-"

The shadow moved across the window again, big and grand, taller than the glass pane, casting darkness through the curtain as it blotted out the last light bleeding through the cloth. The crunch of a large foot on grass, too, told me that it was close-

"Someone's coming," I whispered, meta-low, and heard an explosion of motion in the living room.

I scooped up little Sienna around the waist, her pastel nightgown flapping as I yanked her free of the covers before she could even squawk. She let out a little noise as I reached the door with her, shoving her out behind me, putting myself between her and the window as it exploded inward in a shower of glass-

Putting my arm up, I caught a shard in the wrist, and it stung. Warm blood trickled down my wrist as something huge landed on the bed. The frame took the weight and shattered as the hulking specimen rode it to the ground.

I took a sharp breath.

It. Was. Huge.

And... oh so familiar.

Long, mangy hair was strung around his shoulders, a dirty white t-shirt covering his massive chest. Old jeans stained with blood and bile covered his legs, like tree trunks they were so huge. His muscular arms ended in fingernails filed to points, and in the darkness I could see canine teeth shining behind a cruel smile-

It had been years since I'd seen him in the flesh.

And nine months since he'd left my mind.

Six months since he'd died, trapped in the brain of another.

I took another breath, barely, and my skin went cold, as though someone had run chilly water from the crown of my head down the back of my neck, over my flesh all the way to the soles of my feet, and every inch broke out in goosebumps as the name popped from my lips, unbidden-

His name.

"Wolfe."

25.

"You know the name of the Wolfe," he breathed, throaty, coiled on the collapsed ruin of the bed like he was ready to vault off of it. "Ahhh...so flattered. But the Wolfe doesn't know you...little doll."

"I bet you call all the girls that," I said, pushing little Sienna behind me, into the arms of our mother, who'd just made it to the door. Without looking back, I felt her get scooped out of my hands.

"No, little doll," Wolfe said, still grinning, "you're special. Just like every other little doll, meant to be played with. Aching to be."

"I already played dolls once today," I said, flexing my hands one at a time, cracking my knuckles. For show, entirely. His skin was practically impervious to traditional attacks. "But for you, I suppose, I could play again. You like to be Ken, right?" I pointed at his kneeling posture. "Because he reminds you of yourself? You know...down there?"

Wolfe's smile disappeared. I guess like most men, he wasn't impervious to cracks about the size of his manhood. "Do you want to see, little doll? See how wrong you are?"

I put my fingers to my lips and puffed my cheeks out. "Ooh – oop – sorry. Just threw up in my mouth a little. Probably unrelated. Go on, you were saying something about how you have to compensate for your small penis by driving a Volkswagen?"

Wolfe's eyes flared. "The little doll greets the Wolfe with

128

insults."

"Well, I wasn't going to greet you with a big, sloppy kiss. I mean, look at those teeth. Do you even brush them, or do you just go straight for the milk bones?" I tapped the door frame. "Back up," I whispered. I was sure Wolfe caught it, but I didn't care. I needed to make sure mom was clear before he lunged at me, which was probably coming any second. Wolfe was not one to get caught up in distractions for long. Not when there was the prospect of meat and play at hand.

He growled, a sound long perfected as an intimidation tactic. One advantage of having had him in my head for years was that knowing this took most of the dread out of it.

Most of it. But not all.

"Listen to you – you're just a big puppy, aren't you?" My strategy was to take the piss out of him until he lunged at me. Admittedly not exactly genius-level brainstorming, there, but when you were faced with an unstoppable, near-invincible force like Wolfe...well, you had to do what you had to do. "Don't expect me to pet you, though. God only knows where you've been. I mean, really, the gutter would be such an improvement over where you probably end up most nights-"

That did it. He lunged, finally, springing off the remains of the bed and launching it into the wall behind him with the force of his jump. It shattered against the dresser, but I barely noticed because there was a giant Wolfe flying at me, his mouth open.

How do you stop a runaway train?

Punching it wouldn't help. I mean, it might, if you could theoretically punch hard enough to knock it off its track, but the strength and momentum behind it were far, far stronger than a human – even metahuman hand – so even if you delivered a perfect blow, and knocked it aside, you'd still probably break every bone up to your wrist.

Pushing it definitely wouldn't work. That'd be a fast way to see yourself dragged underneath, if not shredded and splattered completely.

Running certainly wouldn't do it. Turning was a time-consuming process, and the train would be on you – and over you, splat splat, before you even managed to spring back.

No, the only way to stop a runaway train was to not stop it at all.

I dropped backward, like I was falling in a trust exercise, kicking my legs up off the ground at the same time. Wolfe sailed toward me, claws extended, his grungy t-shirt right there as I dropped. He swung his hands for me, comically, trying to readjust to my insane and possibly desperate move of letting him roll over me-

I brought my feet up and put them in his belly as he swung his hands down to strike at my legs. I hit the ground back-first, in a slight backwards roll, my legs chambered, my knees almost against my chest.

Then I pushed hard for the third time today. Geez. What a versatile move.

It was a perfect counter for a runaway train, getting underneath it and then shoving it upward, off its intended track. Wolfe pinwheeled his arms, dark eyes wide and frightened as his gut realized that his intended course had just been lost and he was now flipping through the air.

He didn't make it far, crashing into the hallway and through the wall opposite. The kitchen was back there, and the stove, and I heard him hit them all as the momentum from his lunge carried him through plaster and drywall and into steel. If he'd been human and not Wolfe, I would have heard some bones breaking and the righteous squeals of pain, but as it was-

I mostly heard grunts. And swearing.

"Oops," I said, to my mom as I sprang back to my feet, "You do your best to keep these kids off of drinking and swearing, but then they go and meet the local bad boy, and all your good work just goes right up shit creek."

"Not helping!" my mother shouted, clutching little me as she ran down the hall.

"Car!" I shouted back at her. "Keys on the counter." I threw a look at Lethe, who was standing, shadowed, just behind me. "Go with her. There may be more here than just Wolfe."

I couldn't see her expression in the dark, but her voice held the edge of worry. "I don't know if that's wise. He's not so easy to handle."

"Trust me," I said. "I've handled him before." And I turned

back to face Wolfe.

He snarled as he stuck his face through the Wolfe-sized hole in the wall, and I greeted him with a kick when I heard him coming. It didn't stop him, probably didn't even hurt him, at least not at the skin level, but it did knock him back a step. That was the thing most people didn't realize about Wolfe, if they lived long enough in a fight to stagger him. His skin was damned near invulnerable because he'd damaged it so many times over the years, and in so many different ways, it had grown impervious to most physical damage.

But his head? His brain? That still responded to blunt force trauma, even if it didn't break the skin.

I reared back as he hit the side of the hole in the wall, aiming at his temple and putting my foot into it with a kick that would have gone right through a normal human skull. With him, it just stopped, all that force returned to me, and I adapted by hitting the ground and rolling back out of my own kick.

Still, Wolfe splayed out against the wall, his head probably ringing, on his knees. "That...wasn't a sweet trick, little doll."

"Sweet is for treats, dickless." I launched up and kicked him in the head again, knocking him back to his knees just as he was starting to rise. It was hard to see in the dark, but I swear I could see stars in his eyes. I bounced off again, off course, but he swiped a paw at me as I flew back, missing me by about an inch. He tried to get up and fell back down instantly. Apparently I'd rung his bell.

"Who is this...little doll?" he asked, turning his head to look at me.

It was dark, shadowed, and I had to hope he wouldn't recognize me when next we met. I turned my voice huskier, like the female equivalent of Christian Bale in the Dark Knight. "I'm...Batgirl."

He cocked his head in confusion. "...What?"

I came at him again in a running charge, and a blatantly obvious one at that. Hilariously, Wolfe panicked, utterly unused to people damaging him or charging at him. He swung a hand, blindly, trying to club me away, but I jumped high and over him, coming down above his guard.

I landed on his head with another mighty kick, driving his

neck against the huge hole in the wall I'd made. It was like a guillotine, my kick carrying with it the full force of a metahuman blow, my power not exactly runaway-train-like, but at least speeding-car-like. He was driven down, throat greeting the remnants of the wood beams in the wall, head bouncing off the floor once he'd crushed his way down about as far as he could be. His jaw ricocheted off the wood, leaving a Wolfe-sized impression in the subfloor, and a trickle of blood from his nose or neck, I couldn't tell which in the dark.

He burbled and gargled and generally made very un-Wolfe-like noises, and I knew this state of affairs wasn't going to last. He'd be on his feet in seconds, and that'd be a problem. It was possible to kill him, but it would also be highly detrimental to my future given that my battle with him had defined me, and his presence in my head had saved my life more times than I could even count.

So I grabbed, lifted him up above my head in a military press, one hand anchored to the scruff of his neck and the other firmly clenching the back of his jeans, which were just way too tight considering these pre-hipster days. With a hearty shove, I pushed his back up into the air, bouncing it a couple feet off my palm, and in a move right out of the WWE-

I brought his head down in a piledriver, smashing it into the subfloor so hard it buried him through all the way up to his shoulders.

He dangled there, head buried in the concrete and wood. His body was almost certainly already healing itself, and I figured I had seconds at best. I bolted out of the hallway as his left leg spasmed, his body at a bizarre angle, bridging over so his whole body was arched, his lower back probably uncomfortable. Not that I gave a single damn for his comfort.

I heard the Wolfe's roar behind me as I burst out the front door. Lethe already had the car going, rolling out of the driveway. I could see my mother's shadow in the back seat, and she was rolling down the window.

Leaping, I sailed into the car feet first as Lethe accelerated. I toothpicked through the window, hands at my sides, and almost nailed little me as I sailed in and through, smacking into the far door with an almighty thump as we took off.

"Nice moves," my mother said as I peeled myself off the door and dropped onto the seat. I could see Wolfe running behind us in the street lights, a hulking shadow whose rage-filled face was illuminated each time he passed under one. "What did you do to him?"

"Showed him the limits of his fighting style," I said, looking out the back window. "Pushed him to the limits of his survival."

My mother frowned. "What does that even mean?"

"It means I kicked his a – well, you know," I said, booping little me on the nose with my index finger as Wolfe receded behind us and my grandmother took a curve with a squeal of tires.

"Congratulations," Lethe said, "that's not a thing that happens very often."

"I'm not sure it's a thing that's going to happen again," I said. "I caught him by surprise this time. Made him mad, kept him angry and unthinking. He's not stupid, though. Next time he comes at us, he'll be cooler." I looked behind me, but Wolfe was gone.

Didn't matter. I'd be looking over my shoulder the whole rest of this little trip, because he had a bad habit of showing when you least expected him to.

"Next time," Lethe said, finishing my thought for me, "he won't underestimate you. And... he'll be looking for blood."

26.

"What do we do now?" my grandmother asked after we'd taken another dozen turns. It was dark outside the car, street lights passing outside the windows, dusky sky growing dimmer by the minute.

My mother was staring off into space, little me squeezed between us in the back seat. Mini Sienna was incredibly still, eyes still open, pressed against her mother on one side, head leaned against my right bicep. She looked up at me as though expecting me to answer the question.

"Well, we don't have an immediate fallback position," I said. "And we just lost our food and base of operation, so..." I shrugged.

"If you want to go to West Texas, I can promise asylum down there," Lethe said, looking at us both in the rearview.

I glanced at my mother, who looked wearier than little me. "I don't care where we go," she said, and she sounded even worse than she looked, if that was possible.

I tried to think about how I'd felt all the times I'd been pursued by enemies or the government. It was wearying in a way that was hard to describe. It wasn't any one thing, necessarily; it was the combo platter of everything that wore you down. Hearing sirens and turning on instinct, sure that they're coming your way. Your adrenaline spikes, you listen, and they pass, but you can't shake the feeling that they're still coming after you, that this was just a feint.

Then, for the rest of the day, you're tired and edgy, like

someone drained all your energy out of a hose hooked up to your bloodstream.

Imagine that feeling persisting for days, weeks, months, years. It was miserable, and my mother was five years into it, always looking over her shoulder.

Add a daughter to the mix, one that she was perpetually fearful of losing? One that couldn't pull her weight, couldn't even properly run from trouble?

I just shook my head. I didn't even want to imagine what that was like. Hell on earth, I supposed, or as near to it as the human brain could conceive. It certainly made me empathize with her decision to lock me down in one location. Keep that location secure and you had one less thing to worry about.

"Whatever you've got going on in Texas, that might work as a long-term solution," I said, not actually thinking it was. After all, I didn't grow up in Texas, I grew up in Minnesota, and that meant eventually my mother and little me would have to head that way – somehow. "But in the short term, we're in a stolen car and Omega's called in the big damned guns. Their biggest gun, in fact, I think. Trying to run from that is going to be...difficult."

"Standing and fighting him strikes me as a peculiar sort of suicide," Lethe said.

"Well, maybe you could charm him into leaving us the hell alone," I said, looking at her in the rearview.

She blinked in surprise but recovered quickly. "I don't think Wolfe is very susceptible to charm."

"How do you two know Wolfe so well?" my mother asked, and man she sounded haggard and put out.

"I don't," I said, and found myself chorusing with Lethe. Our eyes met again in the mirror, and we each knew the other was lying.

"Fine," my mother said. I guess all the adults knew we were lying.

"How do you know the bad man?" little me asked. Okay, so everyone in the car knew.

"I've fought him before," I said, trying to limit the flow of information. For timeline purposes. And maybe shame, because who wants to admit to having Wolfe in your head for years on end? "Many times."

"No one survives enough clashes with Wolfe to get to know him," Lethe said, still watching me in the rearview.

"Yeah, well, most people don't survive him crushing on them for millennia, either, but here you are," I said, going ahead and giving away her entire game.

She hit the brakes and the car slewed, threatening to fishtail until she worked the wheel enough to get it under control. She coasted us to the side of the interstate and turned on me. "How do you know that? There's no way in hell I'd ever have told you...that."

"Grandma said 'hell'," little me observed quietly. "That's a bad word. We don't say that."

"You wouldn't have told me all about Wolfe to save my life?" I asked, trying to take the conversation in a direction that would lead me away from having to make a painful admission about how I knew Wolfe so well. My mother and grandmother did not need to know Wolfe's ultimate fate. Hell, for all I knew, telling them would convince them to do something to alter it, and no good would come of that.

Her eyes were hard, assessing me, looking deep into mine. "I didn't tell you any of this to save your life."

"Well, I've told you all I can without messing things up in the future," I said, retreating to that rhetorical safe harbor. "We're going to have to leave it at that, and you can comfort yourself knowing that someday you'll find out the whole truth."

"Uh huh," she said, withdrawing back over the seat and putting both hands back on the wheel. She accelerated slowly off the shoulder, taking us back into the flow of traffic, which seemed light for this time of night. "I'm sure I will. You can count on it."

I rolled my eyes. She'd find out; her and the rest of the world, eventually. She and my mother weren't thinking in that paradigm, though. Metahumans and metahuman events had been a secret all their lives, for the most part, or at least somewhat shadowy, occluded by being part of myth and legend whatever other bullshit metas did to hide back in my grandmother's days of hanging out with Odin and Thor and whoever else. The fact that I was a modern-day celebrity in my own time was probably not a thought that had occurred to them, nor was a world in which my absorption of Wolfe was common knowledge to...oh, everyone, and much-discussed on the internet even now.

"So we need a short-term plan and a long-term plan," my mother said. "Short-term...we need to get out of Dodge. With no money and no food, and a stolen car. That's a few pretty major problems."

"Long-term we have to outmaneuver Omega," I said. And get my mother and little me hidden from their sight since we couldn't completely annihilate Omega in 1999. Couldn't say that, though, so instead, "And get a safe house where you can lay low."

"Right," Lethe said. "One problem at a time, I suppose. How do we solve the short-term issue?"

"Rob a bank," I said, because it was the first idea that came to mind.

That drew every eye in the car. Except little me's, because hers were finally closed. When had she gone out? Hell if I knew, but she was out, and she stirred, bumping her head against the side of my arm.

"Why a bank?" my mother asked ruefully. "Why not a jewelry store? Or an art museum? I mean, if we're going to turn to a life of crime, why not do it right?"

"Because," I said, trying to answer her silly question with absolute seriousness, "we need cash in order to get the hell out of town and solve our short-term problems. Grandma has no access to immediate cash because she lost her ID-"

"It's true," Lethe said. "If I had an ID, we could just do a bank transfer. Or if we had a stable base of operations, I could call for help and have them meet us with cash. Without either, though..."

"We need money," I said. "Not priceless art or jewelry that we'd have to fence. Cold, hard cash enough to buy a car that's not stolen and drawing police attention, then we drive like mad to get out of this flat, empty, forever-hell of a state."

That prompted a long silence. "So you want to rob a bank?" my mother asked, sounding like she was about to keel over right there. Also, that she was severely unimpressed with my planning skills.

"I don't *want* to," I said, "but I think we *need* to. We need enough money to get out of Iowa. That means a clean car that's not going to constantly be in danger of getting us flagged to the cops and by extension, Omega. It means money enough to fill said car and our bellies so that we can execute that combat move and get the eff out of here." I looked at the little face smushed against my arm. I'd said 'eff' and she was sleeping. Just being safe, I suppose.

"What if we get caught?" my mother asked. "What if we draw Omega right to us? We've lost them for now. We can ditch this car, get another-"

"Rinse and repeat as we starve our way north to the next nearest city?" I asked. "What then? We still won't have any money, or legal means of getting any. All we'll have done is maybe shake our troubles, but I question that. I think a string of stolen cars across Iowa is likely to lead Omega right to us. I've followed those kinds of trails a few times myself." I smacked my dry lips together, wishing I'd had something to drink before we'd fled the house, because man I was feeling parched, especially because my first time following one of those sorts of trails had been chasing my mother down across southern Minnesota and up through Wisconsin to an Omega facility in Eagle River.

My mother nodded, once, which was as much of a concession of defeat as she was probably capable of at present, and a hell of a lot more than I'd have gotten if she'd been well-rested and unworried. "You make a valid point, but...I still don't have to like it. And I don't agree that bank robbery is the hands-down solution."

"It's really more of a stick-up solution," I said. "Though honestly, we'd probably be better off doing it right now, while the bank is closed. No need to worry about witnesses or hostages, and if we're careful we might not even trigger the silent alarm."

"Robbed a lot of banks, have you?" Lethe asked, looking once more through the rearview mirror.

"Solved a few bank robberies," I said, looking right back.

138

She didn't need to know that yes, I had robbed a bank, literally in the last week, going by my concept of linear time. And it had been a smashing success...in the sense that we'd smashed through the wall and gotten what we came for before the cops got all over us.

"I don't like it," my mother said, chewing her lip.

"How do you like a starving baby girl?" I asked. "Or running out of gas? Or getting caught stealing another car?"

"Even less," she finally conceded, though it took a minute of silence for her to get there.

"How do you want to do this?" my grandmother asked.

"Ideally, we'd put a wrecking ball through the wall and just walk in," I said, "but since we don't seem to have a wrecking ball available...I dunno."

"We might be able to cut in through a ceiling for maximum ease," my grandmother said. "Or smash a window, though that's bound to set off the alarm. Getting through into the safe is going to be the big problem."

"Or...we could hit something else," my mother said, shifting uneasily in her seat. "Something less likely to draw law enforcement attention. Something we could better handle."

I shared a look with my grandmother. "Do tell," I said. "I'm definitely open to anything that keeps me out of trouble with the law, even in these wild, old days where they're not likely to come looking for me if they pick up a fingerprint." Seriously, who was going to charge a five-year-old with robbery?

"Oh, it's still thievery, so there's plenty of trouble to be had," my mother said, keeping her eyes front, straight ahead. "But we'd be stealing from a slightly less...legal...source. Which would keep the cops out of it, if we do it quietly."

"What are we talking about here?" I asked, trying to figure out a large, extralegal organization that would have lots of money on hand that we could sweep up in a robbery.

"There's a mob casino here in town," my mother said. "It's night right now. They're open. Lots of cash hanging around. We go in fast, knock 'em down, and grab every dollar we can." She looked over the seat at me. "A little more dangerous than a traditional bank, but you get that warm feeling of not stealing from the savings of decent people, and the mob won't be prepared for metahumans."

"Neither would an empty bank," I said, "but you've got a good point. A mob casino isn't going to be as physically hardened a target."

"And they won't call the cops," Lethe said. "They'll try and track us down themselves to break our legs – and worse."

"I am the one who breaks legs," I said, catching a blank look from my mother and grandmother. I sighed. "Urgh. I forgot *Breaking Bad* doesn't exist yet. No one understands me here. What a primitive age you live in."

"Do we all – including the surly, time-traveling teenager – agree this is a better option than robbing a traditional bank?" my mother asked. "Easier entry, we don't have to bust through a wall or a roof or figure out a way into a vault, less entanglement with law enforcement-"

"Plus I don't have to feel guilty if I bust up a mobster," I said. "Fighting cops does not make me happy."

"Exactly," my mother said.

"Seems reasonable to me," my grandmother said.

"All right," I said, shifting the little head against my arm so that I could regain blood flow to my hand, "let's do it." I paused, thinking hard about what I was saying. Well, it was certainly...different. "Let's go rip off the mob."

27.

What does it take to rob a mob casino?

At minimum, I'd suggest guns, planning and masks. Guns, because thugs of all kinds respect them as a symbol of instant death. Planning, because it's helpful to know your entry and exit points, where probable troubles will arise, where the money is, and masks because...

Well, who wants the mob on your ass after you steal their cheddar?

We had no guns, no masks, and no time to plan.

"I could put a sock over the bottom of my mouth," I said, pondering whether that was an idea worth even trying. "On the other hand, I've been wearing these socks for a while, and I don't think my meta sense of smell is going to respond well to them." I almost retched at the mere thought.

My mother and grandmother each gave me a pitying look.

"Yeah, I guess we're going maskless," I said. We were sitting in the parking lot outside the casino, which was really just an old building not far outside downtown, on one of the original two-lane highways out of Des Moines that had become a commercially built-out strip as the city expanded. The building we were looking at was blocky and square, and once upon a time it could have been just about anything – a diner, a small warehouse, a municipal water pumping station for all I knew. It was utterly nondescript and was lit with an orange neon sign that proclaimed it "Speakeasy."

"Does anyone else think it's a touch ironic that it's named

'Speakeasy'?" Lethe asked, staring up at the sign. "I mean, once upon a time Speakeasies were the illicit places where society practiced the frowned-upon and illegal underground activity of the day, drinking. Now, gambling."

"I'm not in the mood for irony," my mother said, staring over the steering wheel at the sign. It didn't dominate the front of the building, but it was the only feature of interest other than the lummox that stood in front of the door. They probably should have put him inside, but my gut told me he was the lookout, there to duck in and shout a warning should any cop cars or suspicious characters come pulling into the parking lot. "What's our plan?"

"You wait here, grandma and I go sully our hands with the dirty work," I said.

Lethe looked over her seat at me. "You want to take a third of our strength out of equation here?"

"No," I said, "but I don't want to leave mini-me alone in the car." I shifted little Sienna, gently, to lay her down across the back seat. She didn't even stir at the movement, just smacked her lips and kept sleeping. "Plus, if this goes as well as my usual plans, we'll probably need a wheelman – err, woman – for a quick getaway."

"So that's why you had me switch seats with mom when we stopped off at that convenience store." My mother's arms were draped over the steering wheel, but she looked back at me with jaded irritation.

"That, and concerns that a woman grandma's age shouldn't be driving." I caught an ireful look from Lethe. "What? I'm concerned you're still operating from horse-and-cart instincts, that's all. I mean, come on, you've been alive for several millennia, but cars have been around for all of a twentieth of that."

"I'd wager I've driven more in my life than the two of you combined have in yours," Lethe said. "I owned a Ford Model T, okay? I was an early adopter." She bristled in the passenger seat. "I'm...hip."

"Fine. I'll wait in the car," my mother said, looking sidelong at Lethe, who was still seething. "I didn't want to participate in your stupid casino robbery anyway. No point in getting my face on the mob's most wanted list."

"That's the spirit," I said. Lethe frowned at me. "What?" I asked. "What do you have to fear from the mob?"

"The busting of my kneecaps, like anyone else, I assume."

"Your kneecaps will be fine," I said, throwing open the door as a wash of humid night air came in. "Those of the enforcers they send after you will probably be forfeit, though, if I had to guess." I stood, stretching, and looked down at my sleeve. It hung, just above the elbow, partially shredded and crusted with dried blood. Wolfe had torn it somehow in our clash. Or I'd gotten it stuck on a nail at some point. Who knew, honestly, with me? I ripped it free and tossed it to Lethe as she got out of the car. "If it bothers you that much, wear this as a mask."

She caught it deftly, then tied it around her face. "Fine."

"Fine," I parroted, smirking as I turned to head for the door. "I'll take out the watchman, you follow behind in the shadows but don't show yourself until he's down. We don't want to warn them about what's coming."

She nodded and disappeared as she sunk down behind the car and started creeping her way through the lot, not making a sound.

I, on the other hand, tried to make a lot of noise. I whistled as I walked, trying to be a little off-key as I worked through the theme to *Back to the Future*. I tried to put a little wobble in my walk, pretending to be drunk, figuring the guard would be more than happy to admit a young, drunk woman who had money. He couldn't see that my outfit was torn all to pieces in the shadowy parking lot, after all, and maybe ripped clothing was in style in 1999.

The guard fixed his attention on me as I came staggering into the light hanging just above the door. It extended in a halo over the dirt parking lot for about twenty feet off the front step, and I zigzagged my path just slightly, enough to make him unclench as he mentally sorted me into the "not a threat" column.

"Hiii," I drawled and took a stumbling step.

"Hey," he said, and reached out to catch me as I recovered, heading for the lone step-up into the place. "Rough night?"

He was taking in the tattered appearance of my clothing, but the alarm bells weren't ringing for him yet.

"Yes," I said, full of feeling. "You would not believe the night I am having. First there was a bachelorette party – not mine," I shook my head loosely, still feigning drunk and throwing out an un-Sienna-like girlish giggle, "and there were shots – so – soooo many shots. Then I played a round of night golf. You ever play night golf? I think I broke somebody's window. Probably shouldn't have kept going when I chipped into that guy's yard. Not gonna get that ball back. Should have used the three wood, I think-"

"What are you doing here?" the guy asked, politely, but definitely trying to cut short my ramble.

"Right now?" I asked, focusing on his eyes. He was a big dude, probably six-five, three hundred pounds. "I'm hanging on your arm, duuuh." I lifted my hand, because his was on mine. "What are you doing here?"

"I'm-"

I twisted his hand into wrist-lock and before he could let out a cry, lifted my elbow into his jaw. The crack was familiar – I'd broken a lot of jaws in my time – and his eyes fluttered only once before he dropped insensate into the dirt parking lot.

"Get him out of the light," Lethe said, appearing at the edge of the illuminated halo effect. "Put him in the bushes over there."

"Yeah, yeah," I said, dragging him by the neck, using the opportunity to continue my skin-to-skin contact with him in an effort to learn the security and layout of the place. I managed to pull what I needed quickly and left him behind a shrub that didn't adequately cover him.

"Well?" Lethe asked as I emerged.

"Security cams," I said, ripping off my other sleeve. No point in leaving video evidence of me robbing a casino in 1999 to come washing up on some news program twenty years hence. It wasn't the sort of thing one could easily explain away, after all. "Guards are packing." I blinked. "Which reminds me." I hotfooted it back to the shrubs and pulled the guy's pistol, an old but serviceable snub-nosed revolver of the .38 Special variety. "You want this?"

Lethe waved me off. "I'm not a hard-nosed PI from the thirties."

"Come on, darlin'," I said, putting on the appropriate accent for that era, "we're about to hit a speakeasy, see. Gotta be prepared for the era, see."

"No one spoke like that in that era," she said, shaking her head at me. "Let's get this over with." She opened the door and held it for me.

"Oh, I see how it is," I said, taking the cue and entering with my gun held up. "So much for 'age before beauty'."

"You lead because you have the gun," she said, rolling her eyes.

"Suuuuuuuuuure."

I plunged into the building, finding myself in a fairly ordinary-looking bar. Using the memories carefully extracted from Mister Goombah out in the parking lot (I seriously hadn't even bothered stealing his name, I was so blasé about rifling through his brain), I charged the bar and leapt over, catching the bartender with a kick to the chest that sent him shattering into the mirror behind him and a dozen bottles rattling down in a shower of booze and glass.

Whipping the .38 around to the patrons, I said, "Everybody be cool. This is a robbery."

There were only three people at the bar, hell, in the entire upstairs, but the parking lot had been packed. One couple who looked pale and shocked, and another guy who was really, really deep in his cups. He, of course, was the one who spoke: "The guy in *Pulp Fiction* said it better." And he slurped his drink noisily.

"Shut up, or I'll bend you over this bar and pretend you're Honey Bunny," I said, and yanked his tie, smacking his face into the wood surface. He pitched back, legs flying up into the air as he keeled over. I pointed the .38 at the couple. "You two sit right there. Listen and you'll live through this just fine. Get brave or decide to do something stupid, your life expectancy is going to take a dramatic dive, understand?"

Nods signaled they got me. I motioned for the corner, where the fake door led to the casino. Lethe was already on her way, as though she had picked it out from the paneling.

"Oh, and if you try and go out that door or attempt to call the cops or the mob – well, let's just say it's going to get ugly for you," I said, leaping the bar to join Lethe. "You're on your honor, kids. Help yourself to anything behind the bar, but if you walk out that door, our guard outside is going to plug you full of lead." I mimed a gun firing with my free hand, and I could tell by the looks on their faces that they believed me.

"Nice," Lethe said as she reached the section of wall that opened into the casino. "What's your plan here?"

"There's a guy behind the wall," I said. "You can knock twice and he'll slide open the-"

Lethe kicked down the wall and it shattered open on a central hinge like she'd bulldozed it. I heard a scream from behind it as the guy on watch duty got crunched underneath it, and his cries of pain suggested it was not his most fun evening ever.

My grandmother walked over it as daintily as if she were climbing a small hill, evincing no reaction to the mobster screaming underfoot. A concrete staircase twisted down into the basement – and presumably casino – below. Once we were over the knocked-down section of wall, Lethe squatted and lifted the wall with one hand to reveal the mobster beneath. She cracked him across the jaw then felt his jacket until she came out with a Beretta 92.

I looked at the Beretta in her hand, then the .38 snub nose in mine. "No fair. Yours is way better."

"Yes," she said, and she was off, down the stairs.

"So much for wanting better for your progeny than you yourself have," I said, trailing after her and picking up the pace to keep up. She was hauling ass now, probably because we were in the midst of losing the element of surprise.

"I've worked hard for what I've got," she said, not even cracking a smile, though I could hear the thin traces of amusement in her tone. "That's the problem with you kids nowadays. You think you can just have it all when you start out, skipping over the lifetime of hard work that gets you to the heights of success." There was a glimmer of amusement in her eye as she snaked around the stairs and we reached another door, this one made out of metal and armored. She took up position on one side of it as I stacked up on the other.

"You look like you've done this a time or two," I said. She was holding the Beretta like a pro, at low rest, ready to come around the door frame.

"I had a brief career in the eighties as a cop," she said. "In this no-name backwater where shit was always going wrong, and they never had enough manpower, so I was always getting to help kick in doors and whatnot. Ready?"

I drew a long breath. "Yep. You want me to do the honors this time?"

She smiled, and it was slow and amused. "No." She came off the wall and kicked in the steel door, the metal buckling and bowing and crashing to the ground in front of us-

And the next thing that greeted us was a hail of gunfire.

28.

Little pieces of concrete and spackle showered me as bullets impacted all around the door frame where I was huddling. I hit my knees as the gunfire started, then went prone, figuring it'd be easier to duck under the shots than to try and catch one in my teeth.

Okay, it was more like I was following normal, sane operating procedures in the event of gunfire, but still...catching a bullet with your teeth? Probably not easy, unless you're Penn and Teller. And the last thing I needed was to get my damned brains blown out in 1999 in Des Moines, Iowa. Talk about a hell of a way to die.

"I think our plan just dissolved into chaos," my grandmother said under the endless volley of shots.

"Yeah," I said, "I don't know how you did things in your day, but this is pretty much standard operating procedure for me. Come up with a workable idea, watch it go to shit, innovate and destroy your foes. Rinse, repeat."

She nodded slowly, her hair turned white from the concrete dust flying all around. "That's pretty much how it worked in my day. Maybe with a little more yodeling, battle cries, that sort of thing."

"Battle cries?" I asked.

"Yeah, you know," she said. "To throw the enemy off balance."

"Got it," I said. "Should we do one now? A battle cry/yodel?"

"Yodel was probably the wrong word," she said, "but you can feel free. Not sure it's an advisable strategy now that enemies can deliver pinpoint fire to your position if they hear you."

"Pffffft," I said, nodding my head toward the open door. Bullets were still singing their way through at a pretty decent volume. "There's no way in hell the guys barraging us from in there are hearing shit at this point. They've fired a hundred rounds, easily. They're deaf as a modern music producer at this point."

She blinked. "Wait. Important question – does music continue to suck in the future?"

I felt the pinch of my expression. "If anything, it gets worse."

Lethe made a face. "Not sure I want to survive this, now."

"That's a reasonable reaction to homogenized, mass-produced tunes," I said. "But there are some glimmers of hope out there. Indies and whatnot. Anyway..." I paused listening. The volume of fire had slackened. "At some point, we're going to have to make it through this door."

"Wait a sec," she said, rising back to her knees, tight against the wall. She seemed to slide like a snake, coiling around certain prominent holes in the wall, so whoever was inside couldn't see her shadow. She grabbed a chunk of concrete the size of a finger and tossed it at the single lightbulb hanging above us. The bulb shattered, casting us in darkness.

I didn't say anything. I knew what she was doing.

"Stop shooting!" someone shouted from inside. "Knock it off, Phil! You, Larry – go check it out. Make sure they're dead."

"Huh?"

"Make sure they're dead!" came the answer, twice as loud, presumably to overcome Larry's newfound deafness.

Lethe's eyes gleamed in the dark. She indicated the door. Whoever had the clearest shot at Larry was to take it, and then...

Well, then we'd be going to work.

I waited in the dark, trying to listen over the ringing in my ears. This hadn't been a great day for my hearing, but hey, what day was? Certainly not yesterday, when I'd shot a grenade launcher until there was blood running down my cheeks or been in the center of an AC-130 bombardment and had myself nearly shredded by shrapnel and explosions.

"'The only easy day was yesterday' really should be my motto," I muttered under my breath as a shadow fell in the doorway. Larry was getting close. He seemed to be approaching from my side, which meant Lethe was going to get the clear shot at him. "I feel like the Navy SEALS should be willing to share, given all I've been through."

I shifted down and off the wall, trying to get a quick peek through some of the bullet holes without giving them a clear view of my eyeball peering in. I had an idea of the room layout thanks to what I'd absorbed from Mr. Lummox out in the parking lot, but I had a feeling things had changed if the guards had decided to turn loose on the freaking door with every bullet in their arsenal.

Five. There were five guards inside, and I could see four of them. Every single one of them was carrying an HK MP5, a submachine gun that was absolutely illegal under federal law, especially for these purposes. But honestly, if you're already running an illegal casino, who gives a damn about violations of the National Firearms Act of 1934? They were probably chump change in prison time compared to the other stuff going on here.

"I want one of their guns," I muttered, and my grandmother frowned, but nodded. For most people, automatic weapons were a terrible idea. Tough to control, accuracy goes all to hell, and overpowered for the purposes they were put to. In the hands of a meta, though, they were a lot more controllable and accurate. Give me one of those MP5's and I could shred the last four guys in seconds.

I'd do it, too. Anyone who decided to open an illegal gaming house and then responded to an attempted kickdown of the door with high-volume fire was an asshole worthy of being shot. We could have been cops for all they knew.

Larry was getting pretty tentative as he approached the door. His shadow grew longer in the frame, comically exaggerated by now so that he looked like the world's tallest man. He was really hesitating on these last few feet, reluctant to present us a clear shot. He shuffled from side to side as he approached, trying to cover both sides of the door frame and not doing a great job of either.

It was a good thing Lethe had smashed the light, because otherwise we'd be clearly shadowing through the bullet holes in the wall, giving the guys inside a perfect idea of where to shoot for maximum effect. As it was, we were both trying to stay a little off the wall to keep from allowing the light inside to highlight our clothing, which would give us away almost as well. The wall was reasonably thick, fortunately, and the lights inside the casino were low, providing us a nice double coverage against that method of detection.

Lethe gritted her teeth rather obviously, patience flagging as Larry made another cowardly sidestep. She shook her head, met my eyes, and nodded once.

I got what she was saying, and rose to my feet, five inches off the wall.

She went low. I went high.

I sliced the pie, putting my revolver barrel against the edge of the door frame and stepping out an inch at a time until I had a clear shot at the first hostile. I had the hammer back on the .38 and drew a bead on the center of his head as he registered surprise at my sudden appearance.

Pressing on the trigger gently, I felt the kick of the .38 and controlled it as the barrel jumped and the cylinder cycled. I fired again, going for the double tap, even as I registered that I'd caught my target mid-forehead with the first round and a geyser of red sprayed out the back of his skull, pink mist filling the air behind him even before my second shot had left the barrel.

I stepped out further, slicing the pie by another couple of inches. Larry's bulk was now in my way and I caught him looking down, moving his attention back up because of my muzzle blasting inches from his face. He must have seen Lethe go low, because he'd started to shift his aim down, my shots forcing his attention back up. As tends to happen when a gun goes off a foot from your head.

Bringing the snub nose around, I centered the target on the

middle of his forehead and lit him up. I double-tapped, two quick shots that prompted a spray of red in my direction and sent him stumbling back. I reached out and caught the barrel of his MP5, which was snugged around him by a sling. I ignored the burning feeling as it singed my palm and yanked the barrel up and over his head as I kicked him back into the room in hopes of causing a little chaos.

Sliding back around the edge of the door, I took a knee and dropped the .38 into my pants at the small of my back. Mom's jeans had a snug enough waistband that the .38 held there, at least for now. I didn't hold much hope that it'd remain in place if I started getting acrobatic in my motions, but the scalding barrel rested against the flesh at the base of my spine, forcing me to again grit my teeth against the burning sensation of hot metal against my skin. I only had one shot left anyway, so it was definitely getting relegated to backup gun status.

Lethe was in the doorway, firing between Larry's legs as he tumbled backward. She rolled, prone, sideways toward me as someone fired back through the door, chewing up the concrete where she'd been a second earlier with about thirty rounds in ten seconds. It was like being back on that tarmac again in Revelen as the AC-130 lit it up, except on a much smaller scale.

I stooped and looked through the bullet holes in the wall, picking out my target. I could see one guy standing, and thrust the MP5 into one of the bigger holes, trying to aim without use of the sights. I lined it up as best I could and pressed the trigger. The submachine barked, hammering a quick blast that chewed through the guy around the midsection and caused him to scream as he fell backward, blood already seeping out from between his fingers as he hit the ground.

I held up a single finger and Lethe nodded. I swept left, rolling through the long shaft of illumination at the door, seeking targets as I moved. An MP5 chattered at me from behind the far-left side of the door frame, out of my view.

Someone was trying to get in position to shoot at where I'd been huddling, and they were pretty close. Only my choice to move had gotten me out of the arc of their fire.

Once I was safely on the other side of the door, I looked at the Swiss-cheese-like bullet holes covering the wall. I was seeking the shadow, looking for where the guy was covering.

I found it about five feet back from the door frame and drew aim on the biggest hole in the wall I could find in that sector, letting it rip with a quick burst.

That drew a scream, and the shadow moved down the wall as my target fell to his knees. His head appeared in one of the holes, and I took aim, letting loose another burst, finishing him.

Lethe aimed through the door with her Beretta, covering the whole room as she cut the pie and finally emerged into the casino. She had her mask back up. It had fallen sometime in the fray, as had mine, and it reminded me to do the same. Once that was done, I stepped into the light behind her.

"Money, money, money," Lethe said, plainly practiced at this. There was a crowd of huddled patrons all scattered on the floor around gaming tables that were piled high with chips. "That's all we're here for, so if you be good boys and girls and stay down, you don't have to fear catching lead, lead, lead."

In the corner of the room was the money cage, a concrete structure built into the basement and probably usually protected by the guys we'd just killed. I spared a thought for how their deaths might affect the timeline and decided that probably – probably – the deaths of five or six mobsters from Des Moines weren't going to utterly change the world.

Also, was all this built into the timeline already? Since Lethe had clearly hinted to me in my time that this had happened?

I put the paradoxical, time-loop thoughts, which seemed destined to cause me a headache, out of my head as we stormed our way toward the casino cage. A metal door on the far side of the squat little structure kept it locked off from the gaming crowd, and the guy inside looked like he was panicking and looking for a way out.

There wasn't one, of course.

Lethe went right up to the cage and shoved her pistol under the metal bars. "Open the door."

The guy inside ducked down, under the sweep of her aim. "No," he said, voice muffled where he'd buried his face under the counter.

"Please?" she asked, nodding to me to take the door.

"Pretty please?" I offered. "With sugar on top?"

"No!"

"Suit yourself," I said, and came around the side of the cage. It was about as big as an outhouse and looked like an unnatural outgrowth of concrete from the basement wall. The door was steel and reinforced, which told me these mob guys took the security of their money very seriously.

Such a shame for them I needed it more and respected the ways they'd accumulated it not at all. This was the problem with operating outside the law. It left you open to all sorts of unsavory types – like me.

I kicked the door off its hinges and it crashed inward, prompting the guy behind the counter to scream. The oversized door got lodged tightly in the confined space, which was probably not all that much bigger than the box of legend my mother had used to punish me when I was a kid – though clearly, she hadn't resorted to that just yet, judging by the innocently sweet me sleeping out in the car.

With a sigh, I let my gun hang on the sling and reached in. The steel door was now wedged into the cage, and the guy behind the counter was screaming like I was actively murdering him. "If you don't cut that caterwauling out, I'm going to give you something to scream about for real when I get this door out of the way," I said, lifting it and turning it sideways to drag it from the cage.

Lethe appeared a step behind me, apparently having given up on trying to shoot the screaming moron through the cage window. "How's it coming?"

"Slowly," I said, having muscled the door over into position to drag it free of the cage opening. "Just a sec."

I heaved the door into the corner of the room, careful not to tweak my back by twisting it too unnaturally. Because of this overabundance of caution, I ended up doing a full turn from the cage-

And I caught a shotgun blast in the back for my troubles.

The boom of the shotgun was world-ending, like the sound of death and thunder and lightning actually striking me down, the AC-130 losing control of fire and walking 40mm shells over me on that tarmac. It was fire and hell and it stitched its way across my spine and down to my kidneys and burned in my lungs.

I pitched forward as Lethe fired mercilessly into the cage, my face finding the floor and the carpet, a thin-pile kind that lacked much in the way of cushion. That mattered little, because however much the landing hurt my jaw, it was a mere pittance of pain compared to the angry nuclear bomb that someone had detonated in my back.

"You okay?" My grandmother was at my side, hand on my arm. I'd fallen on my MP5, but it was the least of the discomforts afflicting me.

"I got shot-gunned in the back," I said, a little blood spraying from between my lips. "No. No, I am most definitely not okay."

"I have to get the money," she said, patting me on the shoulder. "Can you walk?"

"I don't know," I said, gritting my teeth. I tested my toes. They still moved, somehow. "Spine's intact, I think. But I'm about a quarter second from screaming my head off because this hurts. So. Much."

"Okay, just hang out for a second," she said.

"Yeah, yeah," I said, squeezing my eyes tight. "Stay on mission...and we'll..." I had to stop mid-sentence because blood ran out between my lips.

Lethe patted my arm and then she was gone, catapulting me into what felt like an hours-long battle against the pain. It felt like someone had taken an icepick – no, a rock drill – and was probing all the different corners of my back with it. And that they were using a blowtorch attachment to heat things up before each press. You know, for added fun.

My breaths were hard and every one of them hurt. They were coming in fierce gasps, and I tried to settle them down, make them slower and easier so they'd hurt less, but this did not work, much as I might have wanted it to. Blood was streaming out of my mouth at this point, pooling on the carpet below my lips. I tried to lift my head but failed, and ended up kissing the puddle, my lips making an impression in the thickening liquid.

"I said give me your purse!" Lethe shouted somewhere behind me.

"What...the hell...?" I called. "I thought we were taking the house, not the patrons?"

"We forgot to bring a bag," she said, returning to the cage, her footfalls loud enough I could hear them.

"Oh," I said, and my back spasmed, sending me into a blackout world of pain. When I came out of it, the blood puddle beneath my face was smeared all over the threadbare carpet.

"All right, I got the money," Lethe said, returning to my side. "Oh my."

"How much?" I muttered.

"Enough," she said. "Close to a hundred thousand, I think."

"Cool," I whispered, and pitched forward into my own blood again.

When I came to once more, my feet were dragging against the concrete stairs, my grandmother pulling me up, her arm under both of mine. I fumbled for my MP5 in case we ran into trouble on the way out, but she managed to get us to the top of the stairs and navigated the kicked-in section of wall daintily, only the minimum spikes of pain hammering me as she did so.

"Get the door for me, will you?" she asked the couple who was sitting at the bar, still, apparently cowed by my earlier threat. The man leapt up to do just that, holding it wide for her, wobbling a little as he did so. I noticed an empty bottle on the bar in front of his companion, and I guessed now that all three of the barflies were tanked, or would be very, very shortly, once the alcohol fully made its way into his bloodstream. "Thank you," Lethe said, pulling me through sideways.

"Have a good night," I mumbled, slurring my words a bit. I thought about asking him to toss me a bottle of something, because if a shotgun to the back wasn't a reason to break sobriety, especially when there were no painkillers readily available, I didn't know what was.

But I bit my tongue – literally – and let Lethe haul me out into the parking lot, and the moment of opportunity passed.

"Whew," I said, once we were halfway to the car. It started up, lights flaring ahead to blind me. My mother must have seen us coming.

"What?" Lethe asked.

"Nothing," I mumbled. It was damned dark out here, save for those headlights. Or was that my flagging consciousness? "Just...stayed strong, that's all."

If she shot me a befuddled look, I missed it in the blackout pain. Mom threw the car into gear and skidded across the dirt parking lot to come to a stop in front of us. "Get in," she said, putting the car in park and stretching over the back seat to gently lift little me, pulling her over the front seat and strapping her in.

"That...is a violation of child safety laws...involving car seats," I muttered as Lethe threw open the door and pushed me in. I let out a gasping scream and went out for a second, coming back into focus as the pain died down a few notches, from "death, horror and screaming," to merely, "horror and screaming."

"I think that might be the least of the laws we've broken tonight," my mother said, putting pedal to metal as my grandmother slammed the door behind her.

"Take off your mask," my grandmother ordered me, and I tried to, thought it wasn't so much a mask anymore. It'd become kind of a knotted cloth around my neck, like a bloody noose. I worked it free, wondering exactly how much of my face it had actually covered in the final stage of our heist. Probably not much, at least on the way out.

She was working on my back and had my shirt up. "Damn," she muttered.

"How bad is it?" my mother asked. Hopefully she was keeping her eyes on the road, because based on the level of vibrato running through the car, we were really hauling ass.

"Well, it's not good," Lethe said. "Double ought buck to the back seldom is."

"Lucky it wasn't to the head," my mother said. "There are some things you can't heal from, after all."

"This...might be one of them," Lethe said. "At least...not without some help."

"...What?" I muttered, trying to get into the conversation without actually having to speak much. Because...man, it hurt. Little lights were flashing in front of my eyes even as I was burying my face in the cloth back seat. It was warm and wet, either from drool or blood.

"There's buckshot in her lungs, I think," Lethe said. "The shot in the muscle tissue should come out on its own, pushed out as it heals. But the lungs..." She shook her head. "She needs surgery for that."

"I can live...with some metal clanking around in my...lungs," I managed to gasp out.

"Not this much, I don't think," Lethe said.

"Well, what the hell are we supposed to do about it?" my mother asked, sounding near-frantic in the front seat. "It's not like there's a hospital in Des Moines that's going to perform surgery on her without asking how she got shot-gunned in the back."

There was a long pause as Lethe considered her answer. "I'm not proposing we take her to a hospital. Or at least...not a-"

I lost the last word as I entered a spell of choking, the blood in my mouth, in my throat, in my lungs reaching unsustainable levels. I gagged, unable to breathe, and the world started to grow dark around me.

"Damn," Lethe said. "I need-"

I didn't hear that either, as I spasmed so hard from my coughing that I passed out, darkness enfolding me in its depths, the pain diminishing as I fell into its depths, and wondered, dimly, if I would ever wake again.

29.

Gerasimos
London

"A casino?" Gerasimos looked up from the note that Bastet had handed him.

The dark-skinned woman was wearing a smile, a glow, almost. "A Mafia casino. In an old speakeasy."

Gerasimos looked again at the faxed photograph of a scene of carnage. "What does this do for us?"

"There's blood everywhere," Bastet said. "Surveillance footage suggests Lethe and the other girl – not Sierra – did the robbery. The unidentified woman was hit in the back with a shotgun round. Badly injured, from what we can see."

"Hmm," Gerasimos said. The black and white photo suggested little to him besides carnage, but Bastet had people on the ground working with the Iowa authorities under cover as federal officers. It was all very neat, and a benefit of having fingers in every major government worldwide. "Not as tough as we thought? Perhaps her handling of Wolfe was a fluke."

"Perhaps," Bastet said, "though it's entirely possible that this shotgun attack was a lucky hit. Either way, she's injured. Badly."

"Survivable?" Gerasimos said, looking out over London. Dawn was already on the eastern horizon, and his tea was cool. He'd been awake for hours, working for most of that time. So much to do, so many projects to oversee. Omega never stopped.

"Perhaps, with medical treatment."

Gerasimos let out a bark of a laugh. "They'd be fools to go to a local hospital. Neither Lethe nor Sierra will make that mistake."

"For someone who is possibly part of their family?" Bastet's eyes gleamed. "I think they'll seek a way to treat her, even absent conventional avenues."

"This gives you an idea?" Gerasimos asked.

"It does," Bastet said, and she explained.

Gerasimos smiled when she was done. "It certainly wouldn't hurt to check." Another of the faxed photographs lay on his desk and he picked it up. It was that same dark-haired girl, the troublesome one. "This one...I like her brand of trouble." He looked up. "Get her if you can. Alive if possible. Dead if you have to."

"Will do," Bastet said, taking her cue and heading for the door.

"Oh, Bast?" Gerasimos looked up. "One other thing..."

She cocked her head at him. So very catlike.

"The blood," Gerasimos said. "Have our people collect as much of it as possible."

She nodded. "It will be done." And she was gone.

Gerasimos nodded, looking at the photograph again. Would the blood help with the Andromeda project? Perhaps, perhaps not. But there were other uses, of course. Gerasimos turned in his chair and looked out at the London skyline and pondered the future.

30.

Sienna

I awoke to pain, sharp, but not as bad as it had been when I'd passed out in the back seat of the car. My breathing was steady, not gasping, and all the muscles in my back had settled from a loud, screaming sort of agony into quiet, mewling desperation.

"Ohhhh," I muttered into a metal table, my mouth and cheek mashed against chilly steel. I looked sideways. There was no one in my field of vision. "...Hello?"

"Hey," my mother said, appearing beside me. She put a hand on my shoulder, but only for a second. "Lie still. You lost a lot of blood, and we only just finished getting the lead out of you."

"Lethe...opened me up?" I asked, trying to look over my shoulder. My back was covered in several layers of bloody gauze.

"And stitched you closed again," she said, "to speed up the healing."

"Good idea," I said. "I don't want to think about how long it'd have taken to heal if she'd just left me open to the lungs."

My mother pursed her lips. "You might not have. Your body does have limits, after all."

"Yeah, well...I keep trying to find them by hard experimentation," I said, trying to decide whether rolling over was an option. I decided after another minute of pondering the bloody swaths of my back...nope. No, it was not.

My mother's face fell. "I went through a phase like that. When I was probably your age."

I chortled, then stopped because boy, did it hurt. "You don't know how old I am."

She nodded slowly. "That's true. And you won't tell me."

"It's for your own good," I said, taking another breath, slowly, feeling the seeping pain. I hadn't realized how much of my agony had stemmed from the buckshot that had been rattling around in my lungs. Or maybe my grandmother had dosed me with painkillers. My back certainly wasn't in great condition, possibly even worse than it had been last time I'd gone out. She had been forced to crack me open to the lungs to extract the buckshot, after all, and while I healed quickly, I didn't heal *that* quickly. "No one should know too much about their future. You might end up changing it."

"Like you're doing?" she asked, and boy did it carry the pointed weight of accusation. It was pure mom, like the perfect summation of every conversation she and I ever had, all passive-aggressive Minnesotan turned into a weapon she could club me with.

"Pretty sure this is fated in some way," I said. "I don't think I'm doing anything now that I haven't...already done." I lost the plot at the end, finishing lamely. "You know what I mean. This is a predestination paradox. Lethe, in my time, had already lived these events, I'm pretty sure."

"So many qualifiers in there," she said. "You're not sure of anything. You don't even remember living this."

"No, and – hey, where am I?" I looked around. "Other me, I mean."

"Lethe is with her in the back office," my mother said. "She's still sleeping." She nodded her head behind me. "We're in an animal hospital."

I looked down at the steel table. "Oh. Well. That beats a mob hospital, though that would have been more in keeping with the theme of this evening."

"I don't know where any of those are in the area," my mother said, "and I only knew about the casino because...apparently everyone knew about the casino."

"That is some seriously rotten corruption in the upper Midwest," I said, "an underground casino everyone knows about and the cops never shut down."

She shrugged. "Sometimes that happens. We got the money, anyway. And as soon as you're a little better, we can hit the road. We have to be out of here before day breaks."

"Right," I said. "Employees will probably start showing up, and it'd be better if we weren't here for that."

"It'd be nice to get a head start out of town, too," she said. "Any idea where we need to go?"

I smacked my lips together. They were utterly dry, but I didn't want to ask for water. "Minneapolis."

She cocked her head at me. "Why?"

"It's where I grew up," I said, fighting the urge to shrug, mostly because it would cause me unspeakable pain to do so.

"Minneapolis it is, then," she said. She was looking a little grey in the face. "You know...when I saw you limping out of the casino, blood all over the place, your grandmother carrying you..." She looked down at her feet. "Well, I thought the worst might have happened."

"Seems it got a little touch and go there for a while," I said. "But hey, I pulled through."

"Yes, you did," she said, looking away. "Is this a regular thing for you?"

"I don't really get injured like this very often anymore," I said, trying to figure out how I could tell the truth without alarming her by speaking the entirety of it. I doubted it would sound like, *Back when I had Wolfe in my head, I'd almost die on a consistent basis, but now that I don't have instant-healing powers at my disposal, I have to be a little more cautious before leaping into fatal danger.*

No, that would not do at all.

"'Anymore'?" my mother asked, picking out the one word I wished I could vacuum back into my stupid mouth.

"I went through a learning curve when I first took up the trade, you know," I said, trying to be breezy and blow through it like it was no big deal. "Took some hits, some injuries I shouldn't have. I was reckless. I'm older and wiser now."

"But you won't tell me how old."

"A lady never discusses her age," I said, forcing a smile.

"This is maddening," my mother said, breaking off. "You could be twenty or a thousand for all I can tell."

"That's the succubus genetics at work," I agreed. "Though I imagine I'd be a little more aged if I was a thousand, since you were showing it a little bit by the time I was grown up."

She shot me a dark look that ended in a malicious smile. "That's probably your fault, if I had to guess."

I pondered how to answer that, settling on, "Well...you're not wrong."

"I should have known," my mother said, turning her back on me. "They say daughters are punishment for how you treated your mother. Well, Lethe's going to have a hell of a lot of laughs at my expense, I'm guessing, because I was hell on wheels for her from start to finish."

"But hey, at least you weren't crazy Charlie," I said. "Small favors."

"Charlie behaved fine as a kid," she said. "It was only after she manifested that she started to go off the rails into being psychotic and murderous. Something about getting a taste of power, especially the succubus power..."

"It does have a certain draw," I said, shifting very slightly on the steel table and being rewarded with a bout of extreme pain for my trouble. "One of the reasons I try not to use them, personally."

"Yes," she said. "Better to not have to deal with-" She froze, and I heard something clatter behind her. "Did you hear that?"

"I did," I said, using one hand to push myself up to an elbow. Stars flashed in front of my vision, and I almost blacked out. "Was that Lethe?"

"Came from the wrong direction," my mother said, turning to face the doorway behind her. "It's not her." She hunched over into a ready stance, and fumbled at the nearby table, coming up with my MP5. I could tell by the blood dripping off the strap.

"You know how to use that thing?" I asked.

"I used to use them in the Agency all the time," she said, "I'm a surgeon with an MP5."

"Yeah, well, don't use it to operate on me. I'm good already."

She pulled the sight picture up, bracing the stock against her shoulder. There was another noise, clanging, and I heard swearing under someone's breath, very quietly, in the next room.

My mother had her finger on the trigger, and we waited. I tried to sit all the way up but failed, miserably, thumping back down on my elbow. "Whatever comes through that door...probably best to open up first and ask questions later," I said, meta-low.

She nodded.

I waited for the door to open. There was definitely someone in there, moving around. They'd made loud noises twice, which suggested clumsiness. A worker, come in early? A cop investigating a reported break-in?

Or some idiot lackey of Omega's?

I held my breath as I waited to find out.

It didn't take long.

The door in front of us burst off its hinges, slamming to the ground as someone – something – burst through it.

Something big.

Something black. And metal, covering every square inch of his human figure.

Full Metal Jackass.

"So loud, Henderschott," came the hissing voice that followed the man in black armor. A large silhouette followed in Henderschott's wake, massive frame slightly hunched over like the animal he was.

Wolfe.

They'd found us.

31.

My mother opened up, pointlessly, ripping off a long series of earsplitting shots that pinged off Henderschott's armor and hurt Wolfe not at all. She readjusted her aim after the first burst, focusing in on Henderschott, aiming for the holes in his armor-

The black-armored bastard reached out and held a hand over the barrel of her gun as she squeezed off a shot. It made a noise that I didn't care for, something like steel against steel, and then he yanked it out of her hand, throwing it across the room behind Wolfe.

I was watching the whole thing unfold, paralytic screaming running down every nerve ending in my back as I tried to stand and failed, the muscle tissue still utterly shredded. I collapsed onto my side, making a noise that I wouldn't have been proud of under any circumstances.

It sounded like failure.

My mother took a swing at Henderschott, ringing his bell as she cracked her knuckles across his metal helmet to little effect. His head moved slightly under the impact, eyes anchored on her. She swung again, and he clamped a hand on her wrist.

The crack was audible, and so was my mother's gasp as he crushed her wrist.

"Henderschott, your mother screwed a pack of wild dogs about nine months before you were born," I said, affixing a long string of epithets to the end of my insult. Some of it was motivated by pain, some of it by a desire to hurt his feelings as much as I could. "That's why Wolfe tore your face off. He smelled competition, and there's only room for one alpha dog in Omega."

Henderschott cocked his head at me, then glanced back at Wolfe. "What's she talking about?"

"Just running her mouth," Wolfe said, baring his teeth. "Trying to distract you."

"Yeah," my mother said, "for this."

Leaning against Henderschott's death grip against her hand, my mother pulled down, hard, committing all her weight against his ironclad clamp. She bucked and threw her legs up as Henderschott's eyes widened in surprise. She mule-kicked him in the metal helm, and it would have registered on the Richter scale if there'd been a sensor nearby.

Henderschott staggered from the hit, letting my mother's wrist go as he stumbled back into a rolling tray with bloody surgical equipment on it. Over the crash I could hear dogs barking somewhere else in the hospital, clearly not thrilled with our little war.

"Hey, Henderschott," I said, listening, "I think I hear your father calling you."

Wolfe chuckled, hanging back out of the fight. "Such a clever girl. What should we call you, little doll?" He looked at me, cocking his head a little. "Wolfe thinks he knows. How about...Juliet?"

I stuck out my tongue and feigned a gagging noise. The best I could do right now was to lie here and try to give my mom cover to work while I distracted them. "Ugh. Don't expect me to call you Romeo, you big, hairy crapbag."

My mother, flat on her back, kicked Wolfe in the shin as he took a step toward me. It was another epically rattling blow, and it had all the effect of...nothing. Wolfe glanced down at her, then swept a quick kick at her, sending her spiraling sideways into a shelving unit, where she crashed hard enough that the top shelves bent under the force of the impact and all manner of medical supply boxes came dumping down onto her. My mother disappeared under the avalanche of stuff.

"Now...where were we, before we were so...rudely

interrupted?" Wolfe asked, creeping in on me.

"I was trying to get up to leave," I said, holding very still, not because I wanted to, necessarily, but because squirming now would only hurt like hell while doing nothing to aid my cause, "but unfortunately, I can't, which is, I'm sure, a huge bonus for you, Wolfe, a man for whom an ambulatory woman is a big, big negative." I kept my gaze steady on him as he closed, trying to instill fear in me just by his slow pace. "I know you love the hunt, but it must be frustrating for your ego that every woman takes a look at you and says, 'Oh, hell no, I want the hell away from that thing'."

Wolfe licked his lips, but I saw a twitch at the corner of his eye that suggested his defiance was taking place in the face of my insults to his pride. "You think you know the Wolfe? Just by reputation?"

"No, I've smelled your milk-bone breath before," I said, keeping very, very still and trying not to let the thought of what he'd do to me override my sense of reason. If he got his hands on me, these were very likely to be my last moments not in agonizing pain, and I wanted to use them to do as much damage as I could. "And can I just say – in the days since you were part of the three-headed dog trio, they've done wonders in advancing the cause of mouth bacteria extermination. Have you considered mouthwash? Dental strips? Maybe Beggin' Strips in your case-"

Wolfe had reached the side of my surgical table, and leered down at me, not even touching me yet. "The Wolfe can smell your fear."

"Oh, that's not fear, that's urine," I said. "I didn't get a catheter before surgery; can you believe it? Definitely not leaving this place a five-star review on Yelp."

Wolfe frowned at me just slightly. "Yelp?"

"I guess you probably don't have that yet," I said. "My bad."

"It's what you'll be doing soon," Wolfe said, getting back on his intimidation mission. He was a master at it, too. He brought his hands up now, but still didn't touch me, just hovered them over me, a single finger dancing over my body as though deciding, with such difficulty, where he wanted to touch first. "Oh, little doll. Do you like the anticipation? Wolfe loves anticipation-"

"Really?" I asked. "You strike me as a guy who'd get kind of premature with the action. Now Frederick or Grihm, they seem like men who actually know what a woman wants-"

Wolfe's eyes flared with anger, and he moved to grab me by the throat.

What could I do, lying flat on the table, my back shredded like hamburger, or, as I like to think of, pre-prepared for Wolfe?

Well...there were a few things. I was still faster than him.

I caught his hand as he surged at me. Wrestling and trying to overpower him was a futile idea, but even Wolfe had bones and joints, and while he had tremendous healing powers and an immunity to being damaged in certain ways thanks to long-ranging adaptation to injury, I had a suspicion that he'd probably never really sat down and practiced various joint locks on himself in an effort to really build up the resistance of his connective tissue to injury. Because only a lunatic would do that.

So I caught his hand, the motion sending a scream of pain down my back. It almost made me drop his hand-

But I didn't. And the force of my slap caused his fist to thump against the table about an inch from my neck, his hand clutched in mine.

I rolled my other hand over to his, bracing it against his wrist. I had his whole hand captured on both sides. His face flashed irritation, and I sensed he was about to strike back.

With all my strength, I pressed against his knuckles with one hand and under his palm with the other, bowing his wrist forcefully, pushing his palm toward the inside of his forearm at about a hundred miles an hour.

If I'd done this to a normal human, the next sound you'd hear would be shrieking as every tendon and bone in the wrist ruptured, and the tips of their fingers touched the inside of their elbow.

I didn't quite manage to get Wolfe's fingers to bend that far, but they were pretty close. In the momentary flash in which I did it, I saw the tips of his long nails hover about a quarter inch above the hairy skin of his forearm, his mouth thrown open in a silent scream.

Needless to say, I didn't stop there, because I didn't want to die.

Trying not to put too much weight on my annihilated back, I swept my right foot up and brought my calf under Wolfe's chin while pulling myself up using his arm as a lever. It wasn't dissimilar to what my mom had done and was an exceedingly dangerous thing to do under any circumstances, because I was drawing closer to the beast.

I was fresh out of options, though, and was counting on Wolfe's failure to feel pain on a regular basis to be a stunning experience that would give me a moment or two to work my plan before he started tearing me to pieces.

Locking my legs around his neck, I gave his wrist one more crank and shoved hard, pulling myself up him a little farther, my thigh reaching the underside of his chin, the far side of his neck cradling perfectly beneath my knee. Dropping my left leg down now that I was in place and no longer needed it to stabilize me during my ascent, I muscled myself up enough to grip my right ankle, forming a perfect loop – a noose, if you will – using my leg as the choking mechanism, snaked around his throat. I clamped on to my ankle hard and squeezed my knee joint as tightly as I could.

I was hurting so much, my back screaming as I dangled from Wolfe, hanging upside down, my right thigh and calf forming the perfect squeeze play around his neck. I cranked it with all my strength, closing the loop tighter, trying to bring them together so there wasn't an inch of space between thigh and calf. His neck, naturally, was in the way, but with my meta strength I tried to crush that trifling obstacle into non-existence, cranking my muscles as taut as they could go, ignoring the screaming pain all along my back and flank.

This was my life on the line. Failure meant death, and so I ignored the pain – at first.

"Nnnnnnnngh!" Wolfe grunted, lifting me, driving me up with his jacked-up arm. I slapped it with my left hand, and he screamed as I agitated the splintered tendons and connective tissue with my blow. I hit it again, and again, hard slaps to the top of his hand, trying to keep him in pain so he wouldn't think through what I was doing.

I definitely wasn't stealing his breath. His grunts proved I hadn't cut off his airway at all. Maybe constricted it some, but I was not choking him.

I was squeezing the carotid artery and jugular again, thanks to General Krall reminding me of the efficacy of that particular weak point in the human body. It was top of mind, my most recent humiliating failure, being choked out by a pint-sized pipsqueak who – not that long ago –I would have been able to burn to ash to rid myself of the literal spider-monkey on my back.

Now I seemed to be applying this particular technique everywhere, including now to the toughest son of a bitch I'd ever met. He writhed and jerked, thrashing up and down and yanking me along with him. My shoulders and back moved two feet up, then dramatically whiplashed back down after he reached the apex of his movement.

I screamed, and I didn't mean to. It just came out.

My grip was like iron on my ankle, but only by thoughtless default, only because it was locked in. Everything else on my body cried out, hurt, like I'd taken a hundred lashes to my back.

I came through a blackout, long seconds I'd somehow lost, my body now in a different angle and orientation, two feet lower than I'd been a moment earlier. Wolfe had me hanging only a foot from the ground. My eyelids were fluttering, but when they came open I found him doing a very similar thing, a flaming hatred behind his eyes that was fading as he did.

Movement out of the corner of my eye caught me by surprise. Wolfe was moving his other hand, bringing it up above him, plunging it down, claw-like fingernails catching the overhead fluorescent light with a glimmer-

He shoved his claws into my guts without mercy and I gasped as he did it. He ripped into my belly like a chainsaw through a loaf of bread, buried up to his elbow in a half-second. It was a fury move, pure anger, him lashing out as he fought against unconsciousness and against the thing causing it – me.

I tried to hold on, but gut wounds are painful when they're

small. Having an oversized lump of fetid skin and putrid psychiatric disorders ram his clawed hand through your belly and into your intestines went well beyond the "small" category of stomach trauma and well into the "catastrophic" range. I couldn't see what he was doing because my body immediately spasmed as the shockwave of pain ran through me like someone had placed a star in my abdomen and then triggered a supernova.

Every muscle in my body contracted, and the scream I let out would have been the kind of music Wolfe would normally have danced madly to. I didn't know what happened next, only that I was in the most pain I'd ever been in in my entire life. That this was definitely what death felt like, especially if it crawled up inside you and inflicted itself on every square inch of your body and your innards all at once. It felt like my stomach had been turned into a blender, the blades turned free on my tender belly, and a mountain of broken glass turned loose within, all at once.

My scream died and I blacked out, crashing against the table I'd been lying against, something breaking as I came down, Wolfe still clutched between my thigh and calf. My grip was a death grip now, because I was sure I was dying, and we both collapsed into metal and steel and pain-

32.

The slap to my face woke me to a world of agony, a galaxy of it, an infinite universe of screaming anguish-

I cried out and didn't even have the self-control or inhibition or shame to give a good damn, I just let it out as I came screaming back to the world, my head wedged against a hard metal surface and my entire belly feeling like I had been vivisected then burned for good measure.

Blood tinged my mouth and came out with the slap, along with a couple of teeth and a fair amount of spittle. It was not a gentle hit, nor a gentle hand, but one covered in steel and painted black, jarring me out of my passed-out, glorious reverie in which the pain had been at least muted.

I writhed as it all came back to me now, and I opened my eyes to a scene of horror under my breastbone, an open hole in my stomach that looked like my body had been used as a prop in *Alien* for the stomach-exploder scene.

"...Back to us now," Henderschott's husky voice came from beneath the black mask, eyes peering at me from the thin slits he used to see. He was leaning over me, hand raised to deliver another wakening slap.

Behind him, clutching his throat and grimacing with pointed teeth sticking out from beneath curled, sneering lips, was Wolfe. He was rubbing his neck self-consciously and staring at me with hatred.

He...was...*sooooo pissed* at me.

I spared a look at where my mother had landed, and she was

already bound, tightly, in unyielding chains, her eyes closed, not too far from where Henderschott had flung her before I'd engaged with Wolfe.

I wanted to say something spiteful, something horrible, but all I could get out was a weak gurgle of pain. I tried to move and failed, my body wrecked beyond my ability to overcome the nerve and muscle and tissue damage. My brain seemed to be operating at ten percent of normal, and I suspected I was experiencing at least a little organ failure to go with my wounds, because Wolfe probably hadn't just gotten my guts with his attack. The liver was in there, some other somewhat important stuff, and I'd likely lost even more blood in addition to what I'd left in the damned mob casino.

My body was spasming, almost gently (except for the anguish it brought) every few seconds. It blended into a cacophony of such pain that I could barely concentrate on anything. My thoughts came slowly, all this occurring to me over the course of long minutes in which Henderschott leaned over me, trying to ask me things I couldn't even really hear because I was so out of it.

He slapped me, probably due to non-response. I barely felt it.

My neck went slack, and my cheek found the hospital floor. It was strangely cool to the touch, an odd counterpoint to every other sensation in my body, which was hot, steaming hot, pain everywhere.

"Transport will be here shortly," I heard Henderschott through the spreading haze that was in my head.

"I want this one first," Wolfe said, still brushing his fingers against his neck, hoarser than usual. He was still staring hatefully at me. "Alone."

"No," Henderschott said. "Gerasimos wants her alive. And...as unharmed as possible."

"I won't harm her any more than she's already been."

Henderschott's eyes flicked to Wolfe, then back to me. They were cool, Wolfe's were flaming angry. "No," Henderschott said. "Take it up with Gerasimos."

"What was it...they called him...back in old...days? When he was Zeus's bitch?" I burbled, blood running down my chin and cheek, whether springing from the bleeding in my mouth or the internal injuries, I wasn't sure. "Smite? Wrath?"

Henderschott and Wolfe traded a look, but Henderschott was the one who turned back to me first and asked, in a professional, quiet tone: "How do you know about that?"

"I know...all about you guys..." I said, dribbling, speaking into a pool of my own blood and bubbling it with each spoken word. "Gerasimos's son...is Rick. And he...is definitely a little...bitch." I chuckled and the blood bubbled. "He's going to come...to a bad end..."

My brain was fading; now I was answering questions a little more honestly than I might have otherwise, all my inhibitions fading behind the pain, behind the cold touch of death that was coming over my nerves even now.

Henderschott started to ask me something but stopped midway through. He raised an armored hand, beckoned forward. "Come."

There was movement behind me I couldn't see. Something crossed into my vision past Henderschott, black boots and black pants legs, and something moving wildly between them-

Sienna.

Little Sienna.

Two Omega operatives had her clutched between them and she was crying, squirming but utterly unable to do a damned thing against them. They were full-grown men and she was a child, and I watched them carry her like she was nothing, bring her to Henderschott like she was a sack of writhing cats.

And behind her followed two more...

Dragging Lethe by the arms between them.

She was unconscious and riddled with bullets, blood dripping down her chin. She twitched as they tossed her down next to my mother, and her eyes were blank, unfocused, though she blinked when she saw me.

"...Thought she was dead...?" Henderschott asked, only part of his question making its way through the haze filling my brain.

Wolfe looked away. "It doesn't matter. Look at her. She's nothing anymore." There was a level of contempt in his voice that hit new lows, loathing that reached even deeper than the anger he was currently harboring for me.

I lost a little time, I realized, as the players on the stage in front of me were in different positions when next I saw them, as though I'd skipped through a few minutes. Wolfe was on his feet, looking at me, but now next to the two Omega lackeys that were holding little Sienna.

He brushed a clawed finger across her cheek, smiling at me. "So delicious."

I grunted, my few surviving abdominal muscles tightening in revulsion.

If he killed her right now, would I cease to exist?

If he did his usual, horrible, Wolfe-things to her now...

What the hell would be left of me in the future?

I only had enough brain power to idly consider those possibilities before the world shifted on me again. Now there were more black-clothed figures in the room, an even half-dozen, and the new ones were carting something big and metallic on a dolly. Two of the others had my mother, and were shoving her inside, a metallic THUNK! resonating through the room as they closed her into the containment unit, then clicked a lock that shut her in. She was still bound hand and foot when she'd gone in, and I blinked, staring at the damned thing as two of the newcomers tipped it back, wheeling it out the door.

"Take the girl, go with them," Henderschott said. "Bring the next unit." He turned his head to me. "She's next. Gerasimos wants her."

I wanted to decline his invitation with a spit of blood, but I couldn't even muster it, and no one was really in range of my spit right now anyway. The pool of blood before my lips seemed to have grown in the period that I was out, and I coughed up another glob.

My muscles were all paralyzed, my usual defiance all spent. I couldn't even manage a nasty quip.

I was beaten. Broken.

Finished.

I lay there, muscles all slack, feeling like I might fall into the concrete floor were it not pushing back at me just as hard as I was against it. It resisted my efforts to meld with it, to fall into it, to just drop right to hell and cut out the middleman.

The middleman, though...he wasn't having any of that.

"Don't leave us yet, little doll," Wolfe said, turning his attention to me now that little Sienna and my mother had been pulled from the room. He cast a stray look at Lethe, revulsion curling his lips. "Wolfe wants to show you the...depths of his appreciation for you."

"Guessing you mean...shallows..." I managed to burble out, a bare shell of my former self, but defiant to the damned last.

Wolfe's expression flickered with contempt, and he took a step closer. "Wolfe is going to show you-"

And he froze, mouth open, teeth bared, mid-step.

A strong grip took hold of me by one hand, dragging me. I let out a scream, but it did no good, echoing in the room, warbling in a strange way, as though the sound were bouncing off the walls.

Lethe was there, next to me, eyes fluttering, hand raised above her head, also being dragged. I couldn't quite see the figure that had us, but I lolled my head up, up-

The strain was visible on his face, his jet-black hair slightly more mussed than usual as he pulled me and my grandmother from the room, Henderschott and Wolfe and the Omega men frozen in time.

"Akiyama," I breathed. My grandmother stirred, just for a moment, then her eyes closed as he dragged us away.

A moment later, I joined her in unconsciousness.

33.

I awoke to pain, but not as grim and agonizing as it had been when I'd passed out, Akiyama dragging me from the animal hospital. I also woke to darkness, to faint dawn on the horizon, and to a ringing headache in addition to the still-rumbling anguish in my belly.

Trees swayed softly overhead, gently moving in a light breeze, and there was a chill on my skin as I stared up into a dark blue sky, the sun yet to rise. Night sweat had given way to morning dew, and I mopped my brow, feeling the chilled water resting there, salty as I disturbed a drop on my cheek and it ran down to my lips. I licked it, mouth dry and heavy with thirst.

A ripple of movement drew my gaze. Akiyama was there, then he was not, skipping in and out of view like a bad videotape. Which they'd know all about here in 1999.

"You...got me out..." I managed to croak. My voice sounded like Wolfe had scratched up my voice box while he'd been rooting around in my guts. He'd done no such thing, as far as I knew, but it had damned sure felt like it.

"I did," Akiyama said, solidifying back into this time. I almost gasped as he did so.

He looked...drawn. Dark circles were fully emplaced under his eyes, and he walked with a hunch, like an old man. Akiyama maybe – maybe – looked middle aged the whole time I'd known him, so this dramatic transformation was...well, dramatic.

"This thing I am doing...holding us here, keeping us from moving forward," Akiyama said, shaking his head. "It is different than anything I have done before."

"Dude," I said, "you once held an island in place for seventy years, suspended and out of time. You're telling me-"

"That was different," Akiyama said. "Extremely localized." He put his hands inches apart. "A very small slice of territory. This..." he pulled his hands apart as wide as they could go. "This is the whole world, and I am keeping recent events from rewriting our future, the one we left behind to come here." He shuddered. "If I let it go..." He shook his head. "It would not be good."

I squinted at him. "Wait...you're saying that the world we left behind...it's gone? Because-" I pointed over my shoulder, as if to indicate the hell that we'd left behind in that animal hospital with Wolfe and Henderschott.

He nodded. "Worse than that, I think – if I were to let go of time and let it re-run its course, right now – you would disappear from existence."

I shifted, a stick digging into my back. I moved to avoid that and a rolling spasm of pain shook my whole body, starting at the stomach and moving out in a rollicking wave that radiated from my head to my toes. I looked down at my belly; it was caked with dried blood, and there was still a wound an inch in diameter there, though it looked like it was crusted over. "You couldn't have let me disappear before the disemboweling?"

"I have done all I can here," Akiyama said. "I have stopped time to aid you...for the last time." He drew himself up a little taller. "I cannot help any further without dropping the hold I have on time. And that...would mean catastrophe for you, at present."

"I'd cease to exist," I said, musing. "Sounds like a bad deal."

"For more than just yourself," Akiyama said. "Think of all you have done in your time on this earth-"

"I think you mean 'since I got out of my house', because before that I wasn't doing much of anything."

"Sovereign," he said, solemn. "The meteor over Chicago. President Harmon. The nuclear missiles launched by Hades. To say nothing of what you did in my case, saving all of time from-"

"Yeah, I get it," I said, clutching at my stomach, trying to steady it from moving while I spoke. It didn't work, pain came with every movement of my abdomen. But less. "I've done a lot of stuff. But I've got to tell you – none of this feels right." I wished I could sit up without feeling like I was going to explode in the midsection. Having a conversation on your back with a person who's standing? It's weird. You get a straight-up-the-nostrils view, and I found it very disconcerting. I looked to my right and my grandmother lay there, unconscious, and completely still – like "out of time" still.

"What do you mean?" he asked.

"You have to keep in mind – my childhood was distinctive," I said. "I remember being locked in a house in Minnesota until seventeen. None of this – none of Des Moines, none of this childhood – and definitely not being pursued by Omega actively, at least not until I left my house." I settled my head back on the lumpy ground. "Everything I'm seeing here is in total opposition to everything I remember." I drew a taut breath. "I think we may have already changed the timeline in ways I don't know that I can change back. Because none of this fits the shape of what I remember from being a kid. And it keeps getting further and further out of whack with every encounter."

"How so?"

"Think about it. Wolfe just kidnapped me," I said. "Little me. That's a seriously traumatic event. He got mom, too. You can't tell me that has no lasting effects."

Akiyama stared straight ahead, over me. "No. I do not know Wolfe nor Omega as well as you, but it does seem it would leave certain marks on the psyche to be handled by them in such a way."

"Exactly," I said. "I don't know what to do next. And even if I did, by some miracle, track down little me and mom and rescue them..." I shook my head, and it felt heavy. "...How the hell do we restore everything to *status quo ante*?" I looked right at Akiyama. "How do we fix what is...completely screwed? Because that's what this is. Completely, irrevocably – it's just screwed, Shin'ichi."

Akiyama stood in silence for a long time, staring straight ahead over me, deep in contemplation. "I do not know," he said, finally. "But I do know this...I have watched your adventures from outside of time-"

"You reviewed the tape? Nice to be watched. Between this and the Revelen livestream, I'm really building my own little fandom."

"-and this much I know to be true." He bent, squatting next to me, his suit flexing and a faint aroma of some lightly flowery yet masculine scent coming with him. "You solve the problems that no one else seems able to. This problem certainly seems insurmountable now. And perhaps it is. But..." He smiled, just a little. "...If there is one person on this earth who can solve the insurmountable problem...I think it is you."

I sighed, letting myself go slack. A sharp, short, wave of pain followed. "Thanks for the vote of confidence. But I'd really rather you just alter the timestream so that the last day doesn't happen the way it just did. How about that instead?"

"I cannot turn back the clock any further," he said. "What has happened...seems fated to have happened. It always went this way." He rose to his feet. "From here...the future is in your hands. Act wisely."

With that, he was gone, as though he'd never been there at all.

"'Act wisely'? Really?" I called to the swaying trees above, assuming he'd hear me wherever he was, holding back the crushing tide of time trying to rewrite itself. "That's what you've got for me? Thanks a buttload." I tried to move and failed, the pain once more surging through me.

I sagged back against the earth, let it pull me back to it, and closed my eyes. Only one thought came to me, and it was one of pure desperation and uncertainty. "What the hell am I supposed to do now?"

There was no answer, so I settled back to wait, hoping I'd be able move again soon, because otherwise...

Otherwise, that future that Akiyama had mentioned, the one where no one was in place to fight Sovereign, or Harmon, or to stop the meteor over Chicago or keep Hades from going nuclear...

That future was going to arrive.

And my world – and my life – were going to be over.

34.

A long groan stirred me out of a strange torpor, a half-sleeping, half-waking state wherein my body had gone into a restful phase to try and heal me. My mind had churned for a while after I'd come to the conclusion that I was properly boned, and I'd had a nice think on possible solutions and come up with absolutely bupkis. Unconsciousness had followed, thankfully, sparing me from stewing in my physical and mental misery all night long.

My grandmother was moving now, shifting to her hands and knees, dry leaves sticking to her where the bloody gunshot wounds had scabbed over. She plucked at one now, pulling it from her chest and discarding it after looking at it blankly for a moment. "Where are we?" she asked, sounding more than a little sleepy.

"I don't know," I said. "I suspect we're in the woods a safe distance from the animal hospital. Probably about as far as Akiyama could drag us without losing his grip on time."

"Akiyama did this?" she asked, pulling another bloody leaf off herself. This one she stared at like she'd drawn an ace. Still discarded it, though.

"Got us out of the shit soup we were in, yeah."

She looked around. "What about-"

"Omega has them," I said.

Lethe's face tightened. "How does that affect things?"

"Poorly," I said, trying my hand at sitting upright. It hurt, but the wound on my belly was down to centimeters of

183

scabbing now, and most of the internal damage was, presumably, healed. "Akiyama's keeping back the tide of rippling change through the timestream, so he's a bit...overworked at the moment, I guess."

"Is there a dark future waiting if he lets it go?" Lethe asked, dropping onto her haunches. She wasn't trying to stand yet, which, from my own experience, suggested to me she'd probably lost a crap ton of blood and needed a little more time to replenish it. I was guessing she was feeling the telltale lightheadedness that accompanied that condition. I knew it well.

"Yeah, I think the darkest timeline is waiting," I said. She furrowed her brow questioningly. "No one understands me here."

"You really aren't that far from being a teenager, are you?"

"As he was kind enough to remind me, I have saved the world a time or two in my life," I said, trying to deflect her accusation by not sounding so self-involved. I got a rueful smile. "I guess I really did have a wonderful life after all. Or at least I tried to make it possible for other people to live their own wonderful lives."

"Mmm, I love that movie," Lethe said. "Kinda want to sing 'Buffalo Gals' now."

I raised an eyebrow at that. "That's not a side of you I've seen yet."

"Movies were amazing when the medium first came along," she said, stretching. "Can you imagine? You live thousands of years and the most interesting thing you see is a play or a concert, and suddenly they can project a movie on a screen a hundred feet high, with edited scenes, telling a cohesive narrative – well, most of the time it was cohesive. I still get blown away by them sometimes. By lots of little things in the modern world." She touched her chest. "Modern medicine would be a great example of that. Surgery is a wonderful thing."

"I could have used some of that to speed my recovery from Wolfe gutting me," I said, touching my stomach. "How the hell did you stand traveling all of Europe and Asia with that guy for years?"

It was her turn to raise an eyebrow at that. "How did you know I traveled with him?"

I shook my head. I shouldn't have known that, but I did. I blinked a few times, took a long breath, concentrating. "I don't know. Errr, I don't know how I know. But I do...uh, know, I mean." I blinked a few more times. "How did I come to know this?" I asked, actually sincere. Wolfe had never told me about traveling with my grandmother, at least not that I could recall.

Which meant nothing; I'd lost memories due to Rose, memories I couldn't account for and couldn't get back. It was well within the realm of possibility – and probable – that she'd stripped the underlying memory of him telling me at some point, but left the knowledge of their travels intact, just to mess with me.

Lethe gave me a suspicious look but didn't push it. "Uh huh. Sounds like you've had dealings with him before."

"Yeah," I said. "Which is why I'm suggesting that when we deal with him – and Henderschott for that matter – we can't kill them. They have to live...so I can, uh...kill them later."

Her eyebrows went way up. "You killed Wolfe?"

"And his damned brothers, too," I said under my breath, knowing she'd catch it.

Lethe let out a low whistle. "You really did grow up to be a badass, didn't you?"

"I come from good stock," I said, clutching my stomach and pulling myself up to one knee. "Man. We've got a major problem here."

"Yup," she said, similarly moving to kneeling. She cringed as she did so, leading me to believe those bullet wounds hadn't fully healed yet. Her hair curled around her head. "Got a plan for dealing with it?"

"If we weren't locked into conducting a rescue mission, I'd suggest we just bomb the shit out of whatever Omega black site they're using as a staging area here in town," I said. "Since we're a bit more constrained...hell if I know." I brushed a hand through my own hair, dislodging a few leaves and finding lots of dirt and grit. "Neither of us is in peak form, and we're facing off against Wolfe, Henderschott, and whatever else Omega has in town." I sagged, feeling a little tremble of pain roll through my guts. "We're unarmed, without a car-"

"If we're not far from the hospital, we may still have a car." There was a gleam of triumph in my grandmother's eye. "I had your mom park a good distance away after she dropped us off. And I had her hide the money in the trunk."

"Oh, good, so my shotgun to the back may not go to waste," I said, feeling around my shoulder blades. That wound had seemingly healed. "I do so hate to be gravely wounded for no reason."

Lethe smirked, but it vanished almost as quickly as it appeared. "So... we need to find Wolfe and company...and then deal with them."

"Yep," I said. "And without so much in the way of resources to our names. No one to help, no one to-"

She took a deep breath, then sighed. "That's not...entirely true."

I frowned. "Beg pardon?"

She took a long, deep breath. "I need to make a call." She seemed to take a long moment to ponder this, like it was something she didn't want to do. Decided, she pushed herself to her feet, but held herself angled, as though the pain were pulling her body in a few different directions, and she wasn't fully answering the call of any. Unsteadily, she wobbled, but caught her balance and raised herself upright, offering me a hand. She looked down at me, bright of eye and serious, so serious. "We need to find a pay phone. Now. Before it's too late."

35.

I didn't bother waiting at a respectful distance as my grandmother made her call, collect, to a Texas area code as near as I could tell, instead, leaning against the divider that wrapped around the phone. We'd retrieved the car from where it had been hidden, a short distance from the animal hospital, which was swarming with cops. Akiyama had dropped us in the woods about a thousand yards away, and we'd stumble-walked, using each other for support, until we'd made it back to the car. Driving had been an interesting, slightly wobbly experience for Lethe, but she'd gotten us to a nearby Kum and Go convenience store and gas station, where we now stood, at the pay phone out front, her on the phone and me listening to the ringing with my head against the rough brick facade for support.

"Hello?" came a muted voice on the other end of the line, a Texas twang in the female voice. Felt like I'd nailed the area code.

"Hey, it's me," Lethe said. "I ran into a problem."

"What kind of problem?" the voice asked, a little rough.

"Omega and Wolfe," Lethe said.

There was a long pause on the other end. "That's quite a problem."

"Tell me about it," Lethe said. "We lost Sienna and Sierra. Wolfe has them."

Another pause. "Shit." Sounded like *sheee-ut!*

"Yeah," Lethe said.

"Gimme a sec." A rustle.

I peered at Lethe over the divider that ringed its way around the phone in a U, a tiny privacy wall that didn't really do much for privacy. "Who is this?" I asked, not for the first time.

She shook her head at me, pointing to the phone, as though clearly, she could not answer me because she was on it.

"I'm hearing the entire conversation," I said, annoyed. "I know they're not talking right now."

She just shook her head and turned away from me. What the hell?

"I knew I shoulda come with you," the voice came back on the line. "I'm lining up a ride, but it'll be a couple hours if I'm being optimistic. Can you wait?"

"Maybe," Lethe said. "We don't even know where Omega's taken them."

"Okay, hold on." That Texas drawl was a hell of a thing. I'd spent quite a bit of time in the Lone Star state and whoever was on the other end of the line, they sounded native.

"You could at least acknowledge that you're ignoring me and keeping me in the dark on this for some reason," I said, prompting Lethe to half turn to glance at me over her shoulder. "They're not even talking to you right now. This is just you, being rude."

"Wouldn't want to spoil the future," Lethe said, then turned her back on me again.

"That doesn't make any sense," I said. "I'm the one from the future, not you."

"But you don't know who I'm on the phone with, so clearly you haven't met them yet," Lethe said, "ergo, I'm preserving the-"

The voice came back on the line. "There's a warehouse Omega uses as a staging area in Des Moines. Or did, about ten years ago. No idea if this info is up to date. It comes third-hand from an old Alpha report we managed to catch hold of." She rattled off an address.

"Thanks," Lethe said, taking it in. She turned to me. "You get that?"

"Yeah," I said, hackles rising. "Thanks for including me, finally."

"We're going to head over there now," Lethe said, turning away again. "If you don't hear from us, probably assume it's the place."

"Not sure how fast I can be there," the voice on the other end of the line said. "Definitely hours, though, even if I manage to get the...fastest route available."

"Understood," Lethe said. "We won't wait up. Time..." She looked back at me, "...is of the essence."

"Y'all get to it, then," the voice said. "I'll be there quick as I can." There was a click denoting the call ending.

Lethe hung up. "We have any guns left in the car?"

"Not that I saw," I said, still leaning. "And I have to warn you – if we get into a fight with Wolfe right now, it's going to be ugly."

She looked me over once. "How much longer do you need to heal?"

I probed my midsection gently. It was still tender, but not agonizing any longer. "Give me an hour, I'll be ready to go, probably at least 90%."

She leaned back against the divider around the pay phone. "We're going in against some deep odds, and we don't have a lot to work with. My help," she inclined her head toward the phone, "may show up in time, may not, but we can't count on it either way. You got any ideas how to level the playing field, Wolfe-killer?"

I tried to think back to all the ways I'd gotten torn up over the years. Wolfe had turned his skin into a kind of de facto Achilles's flesh, invulnerable to all sorts of assaults that would tear up a normal meta of his type.

But I'd killed at least a few Achilles types in my time, and I had more experience getting heartily shredded than most average people.

"I could maybe come up with a couple methods for effing him up on short notice," I said, looking at the convenience store behind us. "Or at least putting a hurting on the bastard."

She nodded. "What about Henderschott?"

I grunted. "He's annoying, but either one of us can put him out of the battle. He's a wrecking ball – you either have to dodge him or ping pong him out. I'm more worried about the

189

nameless Omega guards. They're armed, and as evidence by the pockmarks peeking out from the holes in your clothes, they have willing trigger fingers and bullets to spare."

She nodded. "That's going to be a problem. We go in quiet?"

I nodded. "Yeah, quiet. In the middle of the day, without night to fall back on." I looked at the gleaming blue sky overhead. "Man, talk about bad timing. How long do you think we have before they move out the captives?"

Lethe's eyes darted back and forth. "Put it this way – I wouldn't want to wait very long. This is the last transit point we know of in the Omega chain, and it's iffy. After this...who knows where they go?" She paused. "Assuming that warehouse is still an address in use by them."

"Well," I said, shoving off the divider, "I guess there's only one way to find out."

36.

The Omega warehouse was everything you'd want in an illicit safe house – isolated, nondescript, tucked into an industrial district that had seen better days. An old processing plant was next door and had clearly been closed for a while. What had they processed? Hell if I knew, but there was a smell of old animal parts that lingered in the air.

"It seems we've found the right place," Lethe murmured. We were watching from behind the processing facility, and the smell was tickling my nose.

Omega guards were circling the perimeter of the warehouse, dressed in black, the conspicuous bulge of guns in their jacket pockets. The poor guys had to be sweating, wearing jackets in the Iowa summer heat, but here they were. I couldn't see them dripping from here, but they were stopping to mop their brow every dozen or so steps in their patrol route.

"I count two on this facing," I said, looking around to see if any were going to come wandering out from behind the building. The warehouse was a corrugated metal design, two stories high, no other building close by, so we weren't going to be able to leap over to it. The guards stood at the front entrance, on the short side of the warehouse. No entry doors and no guards were along the long side visible to us from where we were hiding.

"Likely there's a loading dock on the back of the building," Lethe said, ducking back behind the building with me. "We should probably scout the whole place before we move on them."

"You see any security cameras?" I asked. She shook her head. "It's going to be tough to move past those guards without them noticing us. Too much space between buildings here."

"You want to take them out first?" she asked. "That's dangerous. What if someone comes to check on them while we're scouting the rest of the building and finds them gone?"

"The Omega crew inside snaps to alert and makes our job that much harder," I said, shrugging. "I don't see how we cross to check the rest of the building without them seeing, though."

"I don't know how we approach them without them seeing," Lethe said. "This is a wonderful defensive position. There must be a hundred feet of open ground between us and them, it's broad daylight, and we have to cover all that territory to hit them because we don't even have a gun."

"And if we did, it'd make a hell of a noise," I said, "once more giving away the game." I sighed. "Yeah. This is not great." I looked back around the side of the building. "Maybe we can go around them? Enter the building elsewhere? Try and stealth this mission?"

"We're rescuing a five-year-old," Lethe said. "They're not quiet, especially when scared. If little you wakes up, she's going to cry, and it will blow our so-called stealth mission."

"Right," I said, coming back behind the building. "Okay, well," I said, "come on." I hustled back down the long wall of this warehouse, away from the Omega facility.

"Where are we going?" Lethe asked, following me.

"Taking the long way around," I said, running the entire length of the building, then crossing the street and going two more warehouses away. I hooked long around, detouring past about five warehouses, weaving in and out of the buildings block by block at a light jog (for me) that looked like a sprint to anyone watching. I was relying on the vacant nature of this warehouse district, hoping that any Omega watchers were sticking close to their warehouse.

"You weren't kidding about this being the long way around," Lethe said as we circled back to the rear of the Omega warehouse. We'd probably run over a mile to cover a hundred yards, as the crow flies, from where we'd been at the front of the building. Here, on the short, rear facing of the building, there was a loading dock with eight big garage style doors for semi-trailers to pull up to, complete with the sunken ramps that allowed them to put the trailer loading door at ground level to the warehouse.

Two tractor-trailers were parked at the loading docks, the warehouse doors wide open, but the trucks parked close enough that there was only a few feet of space between the back of the trailer and the warehouse. I couldn't see into either trailer, and visibility into the warehouse was similarly poor from our vantage point. Because of the narrow gap, any vantage point, short of sticking our head inside, was going to be of limited utility.

"This is the blindest blind mission I've ever been on," I muttered, cowering behind a stack of rotting pallets about a hundred feet away. No guards patrolled outside the dock, probably because hanging out inside was a way smarter play. They could bushwhack anyone coming in pretty easily.

"I think we can both agree this entry point sucks," Lethe said next to me, her hands squeezing the edge of the pallets, white-knuckling them.

"Yep," I said. "It's a two-story warehouse, and there are high windows on the long sides. Maybe enter there? Break the glass, quietly, hope for a catwalk? Or a steel support beam? I mean, we could just drop to the ground, if there's cover down there..."

"It really is a black box," Lethe said, chewing her lip. "I think we need to take out the guards out front." She raised a hand. "Grab some memories, get an idea of what's waiting inside."

"Yep," I said. "If we run along the side of the building, we'll be thirty-forty feet from where they were hanging out when we last saw them. Better than covering the distance between the next building and them, right?"

"Yes," Lethe said, and grabbed a chipped piece of concrete from the ground, tossing it to me. I caught it, looking at it blankly for a second before I got it. "Easier if we have a distraction, though – something else they can focus on."

I nodded, and she broke out of cover first, running to the

side of the warehouse and sprinting along it at blazing speed. I had a hell of a time keeping up with my grandmother because – damn, she could move for an old lady.

We made it to the corner and stopped, and she let me take the lead. I clutched the chip of concrete in my hand. It was rough, about an inch long, and I gave it a quick squeeze, trying to feel my way around weight, angle, doing the geometry and physics problem instinctively in my head. "Ready?" I asked, and she nodded.

I stepped out first and heaved my rock. It made the flight between the corner and one of the guards, the one farthest away in about a second, cracking him in the back of the head like a gunshot. He took the hit and it ripped him off his feet. He came crashing down on his face, legs whipsawing up behind him as he landed.

"What the hell?" Lethe ripped at my arm, and when I turned to look at her, her eyes were wide and her face was flushed. "You were supposed to throw it past him!" She was speaking meta-low, but the urgency in her voice was apparent to me.

"Oh," I said, looking at my handiwork. The remaining guard was stooped over the fallen one; he must have thought he tripped. "I thought we were throwing rocks to knock them out."

"No, it was supposed to distract them while we crept up and knocked them out!"

"Well, they look pretty distracted to me," I said, and burst into a run. She followed behind, leaping past me at the last in time to crash into the back of the standing guard's head. He slumped, probably on his way to dead from blunt force trauma to the skull. Lethe caught him as he sagged, forcing her bare palm against his slack face.

I stooped to retrieve the guard I'd pelted with the rock. He was breathing steadily, and I mimicked Lethe's motion, pressing a hand to the side of his neck.

She stared at me in pure annoyance. "Next time, distraction. Don't go charging in like a young bull."

"Hey, I'm not a bull," I said.

"So you're a cow?" Lethe asked, lips pursed.

"In this analogy, yes," I said. "I like how you maneuvered

me into accepting that as the lesser of the two evils offered, though."

"Rhetorical trickery is one of my lesser-known skills," she muttered, eyes flitting from side to side, then rolling straight up. I recognized the look on her face as similar to the look Rose got when she absorbed memories from me – part ecstasy, part blood rush.

I hit the same feeling a moment later and my eyes rolled up in my head as I slid right into the guard's brain. I had to be a little selective, jacking the info about the warehouse and leaving aside other, less-useful stuff, like his childhood memories of being bullied into having tea parties with his older sisters. The guy was awash in resentment for that one, and I tiptoed around them, figuring it'd probably go easier on him if I removed them, and why the hell would I want to make anything easier for an Omega dipshit?

"Okay," Lethe said, letting her guard slip to the ground as I started to come out of my own memory-stealing trance. I dropped my guy with slightly less grace, but he was already out from the rock so he didn't even grunt as he hit the concrete.

"Yeah," I said. "That was..."

She closed her eyes. "Yes."

She didn't even need to say it. I knew. We both did.

There were guards scattered all throughout the warehouse. About thirty of them, all armed.

Wolfe and Henderschott were inside as well. Wandering as they pleased, though Wolfe was more the one to wander. My guard didn't even know where he was, exactly, because when last the guy had been inside, Wolfe had been mobile, pacing around. Henderschott was mostly hanging out in the warehouse office, upstairs.

"We have less than an hour," Lethe said. "And they're moving them."

"Yes," I said.

"My guard didn't know where they're going next. Did yours?"

"No," I said.

"We're completely outnumbered," she said.

"Yes."

"This warehouse is a hardened target," Lethe said, breathing deeply. "We attack, they dig in, and send the trucks out sooner. Once they're mobile...if we lose them, they're gone."

I nodded. "Yes."

Lethe looked up at me with watery eyes. "So... are you feeling as desperately hopeless about this whole situation as I am?"

I just stared at her. "No."

She looked back, blinked twice. "...What?"

"No, I'm not feeling desperate or hopeless at all," I said. "On the contrary. We just got handed the keys to the kingdom."

"What the hell are you talking about?" She stared at me as though I were about to sprout a demon out of my nose. "I just laid out what we're up against – thirty armed guards, Henderschott in armor, Wolfe. A solid defensive position. An available and mobile escape means, with an easy route to leave, less than an hour before they're gone." She looked right in my eyes. "How is any of that 'the keys to the kingdom'?"

I smiled. "Because now...I know exactly what to do." And I started to explain.

37.

When you're up against impossible odds, it helps to boil the problem down to its simplest essential elements. That had been a formula for success – or at least not dying – in my life. Facing off against Century, the most powerful metahuman army in the world, led by the most impossibly difficult and powerful meta? Divide them into their component parts and they're – if not *easy*, easier to destroy than trying to take them all on at once.

I'd killed tons of Century operatives piecemeal before I'd invaded their final meeting and blown them all up. After that, I'd taken on their boss, Sovereign, all by his lonesome. Divide, conquer. And furthermore, hit them when they're at their weakest, when they least expected it. I'd wiped out a bunch of Century people at one of their safe houses by kicking down their door and going to town with an automatic shotgun. They hadn't even seen it coming.

When you've done stuff like killing Wolfe or his brothers, mopping the floor with an Achilles, breaking a pack of mercenaries guarding a quarry or even busted up the nation of Revelen, the challenge of plowing your way through thirty guards and two strong metas to get to your objective starts to sound a little like child's play.

Which it is not. But still. One could get overconfident, especially since I'd killed the two most dangerous guys in the building before.

"You are a little cocky about this for my taste," Lethe said, clearly latching onto my attitude.

I didn't give voice to the reasons behind my well-founded confidence. "We'll get this done. No sweat."

She rolled her eyes. "You're out of your damned mind."

"Probably," I said. "But I live by that old St. Francis of Assisi quote: 'Start by doing what is necessary; then do what is possible and suddenly you are doing the impossible'."

Lethe just stared at me. "Well...you certainly got the last part right."

"No," I said, "breaking into the building and beating all the guards is impossible. This thing we're about to do? It's going to be easy, comparatively."

My grandmother shifted in the driver's seat of our purloined car, taking hold of the steering wheel and adjusting her grip so that she was holding on a little tighter. "Seems you've had an interesting life."

"I have indeed," I said, taking hold of the, "Oh, shit," bar just above the passenger door. I think it was actually called a stabilizer bar, but the only time most people grabbed it was either to hang their arm there or when they were in a situation that demanded the use of the phrase, "Oh shit!" "Let's make it a little more interesting, shall we?"

"More interesting than being transported back in time to fight an evil, superhuman criminal empire with your mother and grandmother in order to save your childhood self?" The trace of a smile lit her lips, and we peered out from behind the building to where the two semis sat, parked, several blocks away.

"Admittedly, that one's hard to top," I said. "But I've got a story or two that might come close."

"And someday I'm going to get to hear them?" There was a flicker of emotion in the way she looked at me.

"Someday," I agreed.

A slight nod. "Okay, then."

"Movement." I turned my attention fully to the scene a couple blocks ahead. We were parked in the shadow of a nearby warehouse, and someone had just come out of the loading dock and started to hop up in the cab of the second truck. They didn't quite make it before realizing that the cab was sitting a little low.

It was tough to judge faces or hear much at this distance, but there was a sound of distress, and something called out to people in the warehouse, something on the order of, "Hey, you guys!" Then the guy disappeared behind the truck and, presumably, back into the warehouse to tell his Omega squad boys he'd picked up a nail in his tire.

Which he had. I'd driven the damned thing in with my own bare fingers, and boy was that a chore. I'd had to rip the nail out of the wall of a nearby, disused warehouse, and my fingernails were still caked in blood from that particular labor, which was nowhere near as glorious as any Hercules had ever performed. Except the whole "cleaning out the Augean stables," thing. Bloody fingernails probably beat that.

"All right, let's see if they decide to change the tire," Lethe said, peering ahead.

"Driver moving to the main semi," I said, catching a flash of motion as someone hopped up on the running board of the undamaged semi, mostly hidden from our view. He seemed to be looking down at his front tire. He shouted something back toward the warehouse, then circled around his vehicle, performing an inspection. Once he'd finished, he shouted back something akin to, "Good to go!" because I'd spared his tires. And my fingernails.

"He's getting in the cab," Lethe said. And he was. A slight rumble clued us in that he was starting it up, and suddenly we had our target.

"I'll watch for movement on the second semi," I said, "but for now, it doesn't look like they're in a hurry to change the tire."

"They're lulled," Lethe said, starting up our own car as the semi started to pull out of the loading dock, ever so slowly in order to keep him from ripping up the sides of the trailer coming up out of the dock's ramp. "They think they beat us back in the animal hospital."

"Well, in fairness to them, they did," I said. "Beat the damned hell out of us."

"Beating us is not ending us," she said.

I nodded along solemnly. "Damned right. Ain't no stopping

the Nealon girls. And the people who try seem to end up real dead."

With a nod, Lethe waited until the semi had finished pulling out before shifting our car into gear, then she took us slowly around into a turn, matching the truck's trajectory, but two warehouse blocks over. I kept an eye on the Omega safe house but saw no other sign of activity. We disappeared behind a building, and I said, "We're clear."

"Good," Lethe said, taking the next turn and pushing the pedal down. She blazed us down the next block at about 50 miles per hour, then took a sliding left turn that had me both holding onto the bar *and* saying, "Oh, shit!"

My grandmother smiled as she slewed the car back into a straight line, once more parallel to the semi, but now with only a block between us. I could see the top of his trailer, about a hundred feet ahead of us, across the wide, flat-open parking lot to my right. "I have eyes on target."

"Bully for you that you're not blind," Lethe said, keeping us on course, but keeping that block between us. This was going to be the dicey part. There weren't a lot of ways that we could keep the driver from spotting us if he decided to look in this direction. Hopefully he'd keep his eyes on the road.

We passed behind another warehouse, and when we came out from behind it, we were almost to an intersection when Lethe damned near stood on the brakes, the car coming to an abrupt halt. I let out a small cry, feeling like I was about to go through the windshield.

The semi was making a right turn, and Lethe slammed the gearshift knob into reverse, squealing tires as she took us back ten feet and then threw the car into drive again. She put the pedal down, and we sped up, the tractor-trailer in front of us still making its lazy turn at about ten miles an hour, no part of the cab visible because of the twisting, snake-like turn of the trailer behind.

"Hurry up and get in behind him tight," I said. "If you can't see his mirrors, he can't see you." I was repeating something I'd seen on the back of countless semis, but it seemed likely true.

Lethe didn't waste time acknowledging what I'd said; she

sped up to what felt like Ludicrous Speed, and then tapped the brakes a few times to keep from squealing the tires coming to a stop almost at the trailer's back bumper as it completed the turn and started to slowly chug forward again.

I waited no more than a second before it dawned on me that this was the time. I clicked the button to undo my seatbelt, and Lethe shot me a sidelong look.

"He's never going to go any slower than he's going right now," I said, and caught her nod as I slid out of my rolled-down window head-first. I was up on the hood in seconds, my grandmother keeping the speed matched to the trailer's.

Wind was rushing through my hair, not too much at first, but increasing as we sped up, the driver taking advantage of a long, straight road ahead. He needed to get out of this industrial park and onto a main road, but based on the long stretch of road ahead it looked like I had some leeway, and so did he, and we'd both take advantage of it. Him by nosing the speed up, me to do...

Well, something stupid.

I braced myself against the front windshield of our stolen car, using a windshield wiper to keep me from tumbling off. Flimsy, but it'd do about as well as an, "Oh, shit!" bar to keep me stable for the moment I needed.

The semi was up to thirty already.

I needed to go now.

I took a long, slow breath, bracing my feet against the hood, then closed my eyes for just a second. When I opened them, I looked up at the back of the semi. Up at the top of the back doors, that was my target.

"Three, two, one," I said, quick-counting.

And I sprang off the hood of the car at thirty miles an hour toward the back of the semi-truck.

38.

About a second after I leapt, my fingers made contact with the back of the tractor-trailer, and then my ribs did the same a second later, driving the air out of me as I hit. As far as leaps went, it was not among my most graceful, and probably was reflective of the grievous wounding I'd taken just last night.

A sting of raging pain rang through the nerves along my rib cage as the breath was driven from my lungs by the impact. It made a loud, metallic *Thump!* and I almost released my grip.

I didn't, though. I kept hold, tight, hanging there over the doors, trying to land a foot on them. For grip. The treads of my shoes would hopefully help me hold on.

Lethe kept right on the guy's bumper, inches away, providing me a "safe" landing zone if I fell. If you could call landing on the hood of a speeding car "safe."

I hung there for a second, then pulled myself up, the semi hitting a pothole and rattling. I didn't let it dissuade me; riding atop the vehicle had to be better than hanging off the back.

Once I'd executed my perfect pull-up, aided just slightly by doing a vertical mountain climber, I landed on top of the trailer, rolling to my knees and plopping to all fours as the wind streamed into my face. My eyes watered a little; the driver was really picking up speed now.

Now was the fun part. I had to crawl the length of the trailer without falling off, then seize control of the vehicle. No big deal, no pressure.

Until the driver started decelerating, and I almost went

202

tumbling. I looked up. There was a turn approaching. Looked like a main road, not one of these side alleys that wove their way between warehouse properties.

"Shit, shit, shit," I said, hurrying my ass up. All I needed right now was for him to make a turn and see me up here on top of his trailer. Could I cover the fifty-foot length of the trailer and catch him by surprise in the seconds I had before he made the turn? Because all it'd take would be one look at his side mirror – or, hell, a glance out the window when he was right-angled to his trailer – and he'd see me up here.

I'd only made it halfway up the trailer when he started into his turn, and that made the decision for me. I waved Lethe back, caught her nod through the reflection on the windshield, and hit my knees, rolling to my right.

I dove over the left side of the trailer, catching myself by one hand, stretching sideways there as the driver went into his turn.

It was a tense moment, hanging there like Spider-Man as he pushed the trailer into a slow turn. Looking back, I couldn't see Lethe or the car. Which was good.

Until the trailer shuddered in the turn, the truck's downshifting running through the whole vehicle, and I almost let go out of surprise at its vehemence.

I held on, though, hanging there off the side, muttering, "Tread, please don't fail me now," like it was some kind of prayer. My breaths were coming a little strained from, well, the strain of holding myself sideways in place along a flat surface. I looked like I was in push-up position on the side panel of the trailer. If anyone had been watching, it probably looked ridiculous.

The trailer eased onto the main road, straightening out, and once again I was left with a timing issue. I needed to be back up on top before the cab and trailer came back into alignment or I'd be visible in the side mirror.

Who knew hijacking a trailer would be so much damned work? If I'd known it was going to be this much trouble, I'd have opted to storm the warehouse unarmed and let the chips fall where they may.

I kid, I kid. Also, doing that with my kid-self around? Not

smart. Even if she made it out alive somehow, who wants to know you're going to meet your bloody fate defending your own past? That's pretty grim.

Rolling my body back atop the trailer, the metal dinged and crackled as I made my landing. I only took a second to catch my breath before rolling to my feet again, ready to besiege the cab, but-

The revving of the semi's engine was matched, overlaid by the sound of a car engine behind me. I looked back to see a van almost sideswipe Lethe as she swerved to avoid the oversized vehicle bearing down on her from behind.

Damn.

There was movement at the back of the van as it took up position behind the trailer. Its rear doors were open, swinging in the wind, and someone was suddenly atop it, taking two solid bounds before leaping through the air toward me-

And landing behind me on the trailer, sending a mighty shudder through the whole vehicle.

He stood taller than me, his matted, tangled hair blowing in the wind as the semi got back up to speed, the driver flooring it in a mad effort to – get away? Shake off Lethe? Make my life a living hell?

Who knew? Either way, he was speeding up.

And there I was, staring down my oldest foe, fifteen feet off the ground, the world speeding by around me.

"There you are, little doll," he said, his sharp teeth in a wide, delighted grin. "The Wolfe has been looking all over for you."

39.

"Found me, you ha-"

I started to smart off, Yoda-style, but Wolfe, apparently having learned his lesson about wasting time listening to me be a dickweed to him, attacked.

He came at me with a swipe of his long arm, claws glinting in the sun. I had to retreat, stumbling over my feet. I was faster than him, but only by a hair. He caught nothing but empty air, and I shuffled, readjusting my position, clomping on the trailer's thin metal roof.

"You're going to have to be quicker than that," I said, not coming up with a better quip before he reset. His feet set, he swiped for me again.

I was limited in my ability to retreat. Anything fancy like a flip, or getting too aggressive with my jump back, and I'd likely end up splattering onto the pavement below.

Well, maybe not splattering, but definitely ending up in a heap of broken bones. That probably wouldn't be the high point of my trip. Probably. Which I say since it's Des Moines, and really, what else is there to do that's exciting besides getting blasted in the back with a shotgun, gutted by a homicidal psycho, or getting into a rumble in the local Walmart's dairy aisle?

Come to think of it, I'd pretty much hit peak Des Moines. It had to be time to leave after this death match atop a semi-trailer...which was now turning onto the freeway, rattling me and Wolfe as we tried to catch our footing.

The driver wasn't slowing down much on the turn, and he hopped the curb with the rear tires. It sent a jarring thump through the whole vehicle. I let out a gasp as I nearly lost my balance.

Wolfe, also off balance, used the opportunity to slice at me with his fingers again. He nearly overdid it, falling to one knee just before he spilled over the trailer's edge. He landed with an open hand, fingernails catching the metal.

I stared at where he'd landed his fist. As he withdrew it, I saw five perfect holes in the metal where he'd torn through.

With his freaking *fingernails.*

It shouldn't have surprised me, since he'd recently done something similar to my belly and intestines, but seeing it done to metal caused me to hesitate. What the hell had he been strengthening his fingernails against? Adamantium?

Wolfe came at me again, a sneering smile plastered on his lips, and I dodged back again.

With Wolfe, it wasn't safe to make even one mistake. One missed dodge, and he was so powerful and vicious he'd eat my lunch.

Also: my face. Because, duh, cannibal.

The trailer bumped again as though it had been hit by a car, and I looked past Wolfe. I half expected to see Lethe's car bouncing away, but no.

A black-gauntleted hand emerged at the back edge of the trailer, heralding the imminent arrival of Full Metal Jackass.

"There really are no easy days for me," I said, getting a really bad feeling as Wolfe launched at me again. He was being aggressive, but also tentative given his size. He could have made much larger leaps. Much longer swipes.

He was being cautious. He knew the game was his to lose and losing meant falling off. Because that would be the end of his game, at least for now.

"Easy days are for retirees," Wolfe said. "Are you retired, little doll? How old are you?"

"What are you, an idiot? You never ask a lady her age," I said. "Everyone's so rude here. This explains why you've yet to find a nice girl you can settle down with and bring home to mama. Also, you keep eating all of them, so there's that..." I snuck a look behind me using only my peripheral vision.

Gulp.

Wolfe was no idiot. He was maneuvering me perfectly, predator chasing down prey.

I was about ten feet from running out of room to run.

Full Metal Jackass launched himself onto the rear of the trailer, rocking the whole thing. Wolfe shot him an angry look, turning his head to throw it-

I took advantage of the distraction, going to the legs-

It was a hard sweep, the kick that I laid across the back of his ankles. I went down to pull it off, not one of my most optimal moves. Getting on the ground when Wolfe was at hand? Easy formula for suicide.

But in the second it took him to cast his furious, boiling glare at Henderschott, I threw myself at his ankles like I was kicking through concrete.

The blow landed across the bottom of my shins and just above my kneecaps. I felt it, like dual sledgehammers at the points I intersected his legs.

I didn't care. I'd punched through metal, through concrete, through all manner of impossible barriers in my life.

I wasn't letting some faux-invulnerable jackass slow me down now.

Wolfe took the hit, head snapping around in surprise. I doubted it did a whit of damage to him.

But it didn't have to.

All I needed was momentum.

I cut his legs out from beneath him like a combine running through a corn stalk, and that sonofabitch went down like a middle school boxer in the first round of a fight with Floyd Mayweather.

He landed on his back, slamming into the trailer top, feet above his head where I'd kicked them from beneath him. Before he had a chance to recover, I landed on my elbow and bounced, flipping back over and bringing my knee to my chin.

I was chambering a kick, and just like any exercise involving application of force, it helped to get a little running start at it. Throwing everything I had into the kick, I planted it right in Wolfe's crotch at highest speed.

He grinned when he saw it coming. I knew in that moment that this sick, sick bastard had – big surprise – applied all manner of cruelty to his own genitals in a bid to make himself invulnerable down there.

I didn't care if it hurt him or not, though I was hardly agnostic about it. If I could have caused him agonizing pain, I would have done it without a single regret.

But for now I settled for kicking him off the side of the trailer. Which I did as I planted my foot in his groin, landing it like I was battering down a metal door.

He took it like a champ for the first second, grinning at me as I hit. "Can't stop the Wolfe with that, little doll. Can't stop him from wanting to use it to-"

His eyes widened as he started to move, my kick's momentum transferring to him. He reached out frantically, trying to stop himself moving, but I'd punted him right in the balls, and while it might not have hurt him, it still hit with as much force as this damned semi-trailer could have brought to bear right now if it had struck him.

Wolfe tumbled over the side, leaving claw marks in the trailer where he frantically grabbed at the metal as he fell. Judging by his shouts, I hadn't completely dislodged him, but for the moment he was a man overboard.

I could work with a moment.

Vaulting back to my feet, I staggered as the numbness radiated out from the spots on my legs where I'd hit Wolfe with everything I had. My right foot was numb like I'd been sitting on it for a week, and the two places on my left leg where I'd struck his immovable, concrete limb felt...dead, honestly. Like the nerves had just died in those places.

I almost overbalanced, but I corrected a second before I would have face-planted into the trailer roof. I caught myself on one knee, bringing up my hands.

Full Metal Jackass was making his way toward me, eyeing the rips in the metal trailer where Wolfe had gone over. He'd left several good gashes, strips of metal just hanging there like little pillars where his individual nails had shredded between them.

"You know what I like about you, Henderschott?" I asked, regaining my balance. He was about ten feet away now and cocked his head at me. "Nothing, really. There's not a damned thing I like about you, you soft-skinned little pus-and-turd bag."

He straightened, and I saw his eyes narrow in the slits of his mask. "You think you're so funny."

"Compared to you, elephant man, I'm hi-frigging-larious," I said, waiting for him to make a move. I couldn't wait long, though, because I really needed him dealt with before Wolfe climbed back up behind me.

A pincer between these two? That'd be death, or as near to it as not to make a difference.

We were rattling along the freeway now, wind rushing from behind me, the semi fully up to speed. The driver was shifting lanes, sending us both slightly to the side. Nothing too crazy, fortunately; it appeared he didn't want to send his Omega teammates over the edge.

Cars were passing by on either side of the trailer, streaming past, and I caught some funny looks. One kid was right in the middle of pumping his arm to get the driver to blow his horn when he caught sight of us. His little mouth dropped open, and I imagined him swearing in exclamation in the back seat.

That was all the time I got to contemplate what he would have said, though, because Henderschott made a swipe at me.

Unlike with Wolfe, I didn't get wide away from Henderschott, trying desperately to dance out of his range. I dodged small, his blow missing me by inches.

I couldn't afford to let this dance go on. I needed Full Metal Jackass out of here, needed him to dismount immediately. If he did, I could turn and deal with Wolfe, kicking him in the face over the edge and dropping him into traffic. Then I could take control of the semi and drive off to victory, mission accomplished.

As soon as Henderschott reached full extension of his arm, I caught him by the wrist and cranked it back, planting a palm at his elbow. I dragged him around by brute strength, barring his arm as he let out a grunt.

I didn't think Henderschott was stronger than me, but metahuman relative power levels were tough to gauge. He strained, but I had the advantage of leverage.

He, though, had the advantage of weight. And that dovetailed into another advantage of his.

Henderschott dropped to a knee, pulling his arm with him. If he'd been a normal Joe on the street battling me, his elbow would have dislocated instantly. I could almost imagine his grunt turning to a scream as the pain kicked in.

Unfortunately, though, he was wearing armor plating from fingers to toes.

His upper arm plate clanked against his lower arm plate, his joint having reached maximum extension. I felt the metal strain, but not give, and he pulled his arm forward, with me still attached to it.

My feet left the trailer top and I went airborne, unable to let go in time.

I hit the trailer shoulder-first, rolling all the way to the far left edge. I hung half off, rolling back just before I lost my balance and fell off.

On my belly, I looked up to where Henderschott stood, rising back to his feet, an implacable black figure between me and the truck cab.

And there, next to him, finishing his climb back up the side...

Was Wolfe.

Damn.

Now I was outnumbered.

40.

"This really isn't going my way," I said, coming back to my feet, staring down Henderschott and Wolfe, united in their mission to smear me across the concrete seams of Interstate 35. "Any chance we could change things up, boys? Maybe resolve this in a way more favorable to me? Battle of wits? Game of Boggle?" They stared, unimpressed. "Pictionary?"

"The little doll thought she was so clever," Wolfe said, alighting his hate-filled eyes on me. And I could tell it was hate, too, the kind that bordered on hungry animal lust with him. I held in the shudder of revulsion. "Popping that tire. Probably thought we'd be too dumb to realize it was you."

"I'm guessing a lot of people have made good money betting on you to be dumb," I said. "Hell, Frederick and Grihm always counted on it-"

That did it. Wolfe always was sensitive about his bros.

Wolfe's eyes blazed and he broke for me, lunging, claws extended in a massive leap.

The trick to dealing with a bull charging you is to not be there when its horns and bulk and weight all come speeding into the planned intersection of its body and yours.

For most people, this is easier said than done.

I am not most people.

Dropping low, I went under Wolfe's feet, rolling sideways to keep out of Henderschott's reach. It was a neat move and sent the black-armored giant scrambling. Something I'd realized after all these bouts with him-

The big dumb bastard couldn't see peripherally all that well thanks to his stupid eye slits. Up, down, left, right, and anything in the diagonals between those directions?

The stupid bastard was as good as blind.

I scrambled beneath him, avoiding his leg as I went, keeping out of his sight as I rounded his right knee. His head swung around, like a robot trying to re-acquire his target.

But it was too late. I was behind him now, and he was leaning over, looking down for me.

I rose up and delivered the heartiest metahuman-powered shove I could deliver, planting both hands against his shoulder blades. He lost his balance instantly, lost his footing against the roof of the trailer, hell, he probably lost gravity for a second, I shoved his ass so damned hard.

He damned near bowled over Wolfe as he hit, the momentum of the semi moving at sixty-plus miles per hour catching him like a kite in the wind as soon as he surrendered his footing. He gasped audibly and hit the trailer with a clang, indenting the ceiling and rolling out of it through sheer momentum from my shove, not any intent of his own.

Wolfe leapt to clear him, pulling his knees up to almost his chin. The big ball of Henderschott rolled under him like an obsidian boulder, limbs tangled and flying in every direction as Full Metal Jackass tried to get a grip on something, anything to keep from flying off the trailer.

He didn't quite make it. On his second roll, face up in the air, he flew off the back edge, arms and legs windmilling in hopes of discovering his heretofore unrealized powers of flight.

Alas, he found naught but disappointment.

And the pavement, at sixty miles an hour.

It was loud, like a car accident happening behind us, followed by the squealing of tires as someone swerved to miss the sudden, black piece of human artillery I'd launched off the back of the trailer.

Someone did not succeed in dodging, and the next sound I heard was an actual car accident, and I caught a glimpse of the Omega van flipping end over, the hood smashed and the rear doors still hanging loosely. A couple of human bodies were flung, but I only caught sight of them for a second before they disappeared below the trailer's edge, presumably into a maelstrom of blood and bone and metal and – well, what I like to call a "Reed blender" these days.

"Have a nice trip," I called behind us. "See you next fall."

Wolfe's eyes flashed with malice and worry for just a second before he regained control of himself, feet planted as he stared at me. "So clever, little doll. But you've arranged for us to be alone together." He smiled, and it was as ugly as ever, filled with malice, lust, a desire to gnaw my flesh and taste my blood. "Henderschott would have stopped the Wolfe from tasting you, from...feeling you..." He brushed clawed fingers against his chest and shivered. "Now...there's nothing to stop us from the fun."

"Remember this moment when you're screaming in pain," I said, staring him down. "Remember it. And remember that unlike all the people you've preyed upon all these years, when the pain starts for you – remember you actually were begging for it, sicko."

"The Wolfe doesn't beg," he said, leaping for me, but more reserved this time. Less of a grand leap, more of a hop and swipe. He was keeping his center of gravity low, probably to keep me from shoving his ass off like a metahuman projectile.

Like Henderschott.

But that wasn't the plan I had for Wolfe.

No, I had something much, much worse in mind for this sick bastard.

Years of having him in my head had taught me to never lose respect for his utter maliciousness, not for a moment. There was no dropping your guard with this savage. He lived to eat and rape and sometimes do both at once. He was easily one of the most prolific serial killers of all time...

And I'd had his voice in my brain for the better part of a decade.

I'd been free of it for six months...

And I really didn't miss it, not even a little.

Except maybe when I was feeling wantonly cruel and wanted a co-conspirator. Those were never good times, though.

I dodged sideways, rolling past Wolfe toward where he'd

gone overboard and left his gouging claw marks down the side of the trailer. Some of them were still hanging there, like light metal banners in the dark gap between claw marks. I came up and scrambled, reaching for them, seizing hold of two of them, these flimsy peninsulas of metal several feet long and bound only to the trailer further down the side, where Wolfe had arrested his momentum and the gouges stopped.

They cut into my palms as I grabbed hold of them, two long pieces of independent metal just hanging there-

My balance tipped as Wolfe snarled, spinning around to face me where I teetered on the edge, so close to falling. He pivoted, teeth exposed as he set his feet, ready to spring at me again only a second after turning. He readied himself to spring-

And then I tipped, my weight carrying me just a little too far.

With only those flimsy pieces of metal to hold to, I fell over the side.

41.

Falling off a speeding semi was a thrilling, terrifying experience. I was hanging onto the threads of the trailer Wolfe had shredded, little pieces of metal only an inch or so wide where his claw-like nails had passed on either side. They dug into my palms, tearing skin as I held on frantically, ripping them down with every foot I fell.

About two feet down I passed the point where Wolfe had arrested his fall, and the threads I was holding ceased to be independent, rejoining the solid metal structure of the trailer. They let out a squeal I could barely hear over the thundering rush of wind and tires on road. The ground was blurring beside me, the driver having shifted back to the far right lane.

I stopped falling very suddenly, reaching the end of the metal "ropes" and jerking to a stop. I'd thrown my legs sideways, and as I felt the metal start to resist, I kicked out and caught hold.

That's when I found myself standing on the trailer's side, horizontal, and hanging from the shredded metal pieces that Wolfe had carved out.

Just where I wanted to be.

The metal threads holding me up squealed their little protest at holding my weight. But they held.

For the moment.

Keeping my grip tight, blood already slicking my palms, I clamped on, refusing to let loose in spite of the stinging pain in my hands.

Then I started to run sideways along the trailer, toward the front of the vehicle.

The metal threads resisted me right off, and I knew they would. It was a battle of my grip and weight versus the compromised structural integrity of the metal.

I won.

Using the resistance of the metal, I hauled ass diagonally back toward the roof of the trailer, and leapt back up in a flip, ripping the metal pieces free with my last great leap and about a half a second before my ass (and the rest of me) went tumbling down under the semi's wheels. Which would have been unfortunate. And also probably painful, if not fatal.

I caught a glimpse of my grandmother speeding up alongside the semi mid-flip, the two metal threads like miniature swords in my hands, blood running down the white surface of their "blades."

Catching myself in a superhero landing, I came up immediately, the metal pieces dripping red, one in each hand, like my escrima sticks of old.

Wolfe just stared at me, poised almost at the edge, about to look over. He'd seen me flip up and back to the top of the trailer but just stood there, his mouth partially open, unable to believe what he'd just watched.

He finally caught his words, nodding at the "blades" in my hands. "Those won't help you."

"On the contrary," I said, bringing them up and slapping my hands together so that they met, the flat sides pressed one against another, "they're going to do more than help me – they're going to allow me to completely whip your ass, Wolfie-boy."

Sliding a hand up the "blade," I pulled them in front of me like a staff, a hand now at each end, and gave them a hard, cranking twist that only exacerbated my bloody palms. Adjusting my grip, I did it again, and again. Wolfe watched, befuddled, as I braided the two pieces of metal together into one twisted length of aluminum about four feet long.

He just stared at me, brows furrowed in the most bizarre, curious look I'd ever seen on his face. "That won't help you either," he said, gravelly.

I gave the metal one last twist and admired my handiwork. "No?" I looked at it, then looked at him. "Why don't you come at me, dog, and we'll find out."

He didn't need my invitation, but he damned sure took it, leaping for me, teeth bared and nails exposed. He wasn't messing around anymore. He meant to get me, to do his sick business with me-

To end me.

All I had going for me was an edge in speed.

But that was all I needed.

I ducked under his attack, my braided steel coil gripped in my right hand. Once I'd made it under his arm, I thrust my braid of metal up at his throat like a dagger.

He dodged it, the steel missing his throat by about an inch-

As I slid around behind him and grabbed the other end, completing my garrote.

The braided metal bit into his throat without effect, and he raised his hands immediately to counter it, trying to dig his fingers in between the newly minted aluminum cord and his skin.

I yanked as hard as I could and planted a foot in the small of his back as I rolled onto my own, taking my own legs – and his – from beneath us.

Slamming spine-first into the trailer with Wolfe's entire weight on my right foot?

Not fun.

Fortunately, I was already numb there, and my leg held, carrying his entire bulk and balancing him atop it, several feet off the trailer top. I added my other foot to his upper back, trying to spread the weight as I started to tighten my grip on the braided metal.

Wolfe tensed as he realized he'd gotten himself into a situation that he just didn't have a clear way out of. My garrote was tight around his throat, and he couldn't get his fingernails into the wound metal enough to shred it. Blood started to drip down from above as he tried, though, tried to claw his own throat out to get rid of the steel noose I'd made for him.

"Fuck you," I said, bracing my left foot against the base of his neck, pulling even tighter. "You hear me, Wolfe? I hate

you. I never forgot what you were, you filthy piece of murdering, raping trash. You were never better than this, ever." I twisted the braided steel tighter as he gurgled. "You were always a serial killer, always scum of the lowest order, and all the help you gave me never balanced the scales, because there is no taking the weight off the scales for the cruelty you inflicted in all your years." I was almost yelling at him, and he had given up digging his own throat out and was trying to reach me but couldn't get his hands around except to scratch at my calf. I ignored it, because the pain was so pathetically minimal compared to what he'd already done to me this trip. "I know what you are. I've always known what you are. And it's what you always will be. No amount of time in my head could ever fix your broken-ass, broken-glass soul. I don't even care how you died, because this is how you lived – like scum, through and through."

His hands went limp, his body slack, and all the fight went from his body.

I didn't let up. Wolfe was powerful enough that I could choke him to death and he'd revive when his brain got oxygen again. A little more feral, maybe, but probably not enough that anyone would notice the difference, since he was already a wild dog.

We sat there, him balanced on my legs, for at least two minutes as I counted, slowly, trying to make sure his sorry, angry ass was dead, at least for the moment. Once I was sure he wasn't just faking it, I rolled him off and he landed with a heavy thump on the trailer's roof.

Twisting a heavy braid into the metal on the side I'd gripped, I tied a knot in its end. Where he'd ripped into the trailer was a heavily shredded section of metal, almost like a slot.

Taking the newly-improvised lump of a knot, I slid it down into the impromptu slot, and it clanked, the metal squealing-

But it held.

And Wolfe dangled, lifelessly, off the side of the trailer.

Coming back to my feet, I looked around. Far, far behind us, I could see red and blue lights flashing, which was a bad sign.

"Time to wrap this thing up," I said, and sprinted the length of the semi, sliding off the air dam atop the truck cab. I grabbed the smoke stack and hung on, slinging myself down and around toward the passenger window.

I hit the passenger window feet-first, shattering my way through the glass and rolling into the front seat. I hit the Omega flunky driver with both feet on my way in, and he screamed and bounced, crashing into the door as I landed on him full-force.

Throwing an extra elbow, I grabbed the driver's side door handle and tossed it open, sending the driver out without mercy, remorse, or a single damn about his humanity. "Bye," I said, taking control of the big semi-truck wheel and steering the heavy vehicle back into my lane.

I saw a green EXIT sign proclaiming that there was a way off this highway just ahead. I took it, sliding off the interstate with my wounded truck, my grandmother following behind. By the time I made it to the bottom of the off ramp, I saw the flashing lights streak by, cops still on the freeway, chasing whatever ephemeral threat they were after as I calmly drove off to the right, leaving the interstate behind me.

Made it.

42.

Finding a place to safely park turned out to be less of an ordeal than I'd thought it would be. There was a truck stop a hundred feet off the exit ramp, and I'd steered right in there, taking care to keep the "Wolfe" hanging decoration on the side of my trailer faced away from the restaurant and truck stop at all times. I'd sidled the truck up to a facing right by the woods that surrounded the place, as far from the truck stop as I could get without going off-road and leaving the parking lot.

My grandmother pulled the older car in behind me as I dismounted, looking more than a little harried. "You squeezed that a little close, didn't you?"

"You talking about the cops?" I asked, striding toward the back of the trailer. "Or me falling off the trailer trying to fight Wolfe?"

"That it could go either way seems worrisome," she said, beating me to the back of the trailer doors. She ripped them open, clearly antsy to make sure we'd gotten the right truck.

We had.

I swept a hand out, taking the legs out from the guard who'd been poised to shoot my grandmother, perching just inside the door. He fell, surrendering his grasp on his MP5 in order to try and catch himself, sparing us from an accidental discharge of rounds that might warn everyone in the truck stop that shit was going down out here. He landed face first, before he could scream, and Lethe put a foot behind his ear, crushing his skull before he could make much in the way of noise.

220

"Go team," I said, leaping up into the trailer. There were only two things inside the trailer, light leaking in from the shredded holes in the side that Wolfe had made. Lethe landed beside me a second later, dragging the body of the Omega guard up with her and loosing it with a thump.

One of the things – the biggest – was the steel containment unit that held my mother. I recognized it instantly, even in the faded, washed out light of the trailer interior.

The other item was much, much smaller.

"I'll get mom, you get – me," I said, springing for the big container. I unbolted it in an instant, hesitating only a moment as my hand brushed the cool metal lock.

Pulling the door open, I found myself staring into a dark enclosure. In the shadows I could see my mother's outline, her eyes wide as the beams of light streaming in from the hole in the trailer roof hit her. She flinched, and I grabbed at her restraints, unbinding them with a simple yank. They'd been tightened to the point where strength mattered little, her arms twisted behind her so she couldn't get a single inch of leverage to rip free. As soon as I'd undone the ones up top, I knelt and unbound her legs.

"Thanks," she said, ripping the gag out of her mouth and taking a full, deep breath. "What happened?"

"A scene out of Mad Max," I said as she ripped her legs out of the restraints. "But it's all good now."

"Where's Wolfe?" she asked as she stepped out of the metal sarcophagus they'd trapped her in. I looked away, turning my attention back to where my grandmother huddled over a smaller variant of the confinement apparatus, ripping the lid off like she was resurrecting the dead and had no time to spare. "And the man in the armor?"

"Henderschott took a dive on the freeway a few miles back," I said, then stepped over Lethe to test the knotted coil of metal hanging in the carved slot on the side of the trailer. It was still heavy; Wolfe was, presumably, still hanging there. He didn't move when I tugged on it. "And Wolfe...well, he's just hanging out." I sidled over to the other gash, a few feet further in and started ripping more metal bindings out with my bare hands, threading and twisting them together. "For now, anyway. I need to deal with him on a little more permanent basis."

"Why don't we just get in the car and go?" Lethe asked. She was leaning over the metal apparatus, taking great care with where she placed her bare skin. Gently, she lifted out little me, and I saw a shudder of motion and wide, panicked little eyes in the darkness.

I looked past her and my mother. "We can't. Not yet." I twisted another length of metal fiber together. "Wolfe can't remember this." I looked down at my younger self, shaking against my grandmother's chest, almost convulsing. "None of it."

My mother took a staggering step over to Lethe, her leg apparently numb from the tightness of the bindings. She reached down to rub it but shot me a hell of a look while she did so. "Why not?"

I shook my head. "Because the next time we meet, he can't remember this encounter. Even if he might think I'm – I don't even know who he thinks I am, honestly – he *cannot* remember me when I fight him in the future. He'll rip me into tiny pieces and use me for stew meat if he thinks I've kicked his ass in the past. I need him to assume that I'm weak and useless and act accordingly."

My mother shot a look to my grandmother, who produced a shrug. "You raised her," Lethe said.

"I guess," my mother said, sounding a little uneasy. "Not sure I quite recognize the girl standing in front of me, though. You're going to take his memories?" There was no amusement on her face. "You want to carry a little Wolfe around in your head?"

"No." I kept my expression cool, trying not to give away that I'd carried more than a little Wolfe around for years. "But it's what has to be done."

"What are you going to do with him after that?" Lethe asked, cradling little me against her shoulder. There was no sound, no movement from Sienna the child, which was scarily unsurprising. What effect did immense trauma have on memory formation, I wondered? "It's not like you can just leave him here for the cops to find. He'll go nuts and slaughter people, the moment they let him loose from whatever you do to him. And they will let him out, sooner or later."

"I need to incapacitate him for a little while." I stood there for a second, trying to concentrate over the highway noise. "There's a... river or creek in the woods a little ways off. I'll tie him up and throw him in after I rip his memories, let the water carry him away."

My mother reached out for little me, and Lethe surrendered her without any fuss. My mom took her up, and little Sienna was still shaking, still catatonic. She looked into my little face, then up at me – big me: "You sure everything's going to turn out all right?"

I pursed my lips as I finished threading the metal pieces together. I had enough to bind together Wolfe's hands and feet in addition to the noose already around his neck. It was all covered in my blood, and my palms were still dripping wildly, all over the inside of the trailer. "Yeah," I said, nodding as I stepped past them, heading toward the light at the end of the trailer. "I've got it all figured out now." I threw the binding metal threads over my shoulder like a rope. "I'll be back in a few, and then..."

I didn't say it. Didn't want to speak it aloud, necessarily.

There was just...so much to do to set things right.

"'Then' what?" my mother asked, calling after me as I hopped out of the trailer and started around to deal with Wolfe.

I didn't answer.

She didn't chase me to ask again.

They'd find out in time.

43.

Wolfe was a heavy bastard. This came as no surprise to me, given that I'd already lifted his ass once today in a leg press when I choked him out. Once I bound him, hand and foot, I dragged him by the aluminum noose down the wooded embankment away from the truck stop parking lot. It wasn't a lot of woods, or a lot of hill, for that matter, but it was a little more geographically diverse than most of Iowa, so credit to them for that. It was maybe a 10 degree slope, which in Iowa constituted a mountainous bit of topography.

And Wolfe...his dead-ass weight made not a step of it easy. He just hung there, purple, eyes bugged out and dead, tongue lolling out of his mouth. He truly was dead, at least for the moment, and it was probably a testament to how messed up I was as a person that looking him right in his ugly face bothered me not at all.

I found the river about a hundred feet down the slope, woods occluding it the whole way down. It wasn't much, just a running current about a hundred feet across, fast enough moving that it'd carry his sorry ass out of sight in a few minutes, but not strong enough to produce whitewater rapids or anything of the sort.

When I reached the shore, I paused, sick of dragging this dead weight sack of meat. Being very careful to keep the noose tight so he couldn't get a single molecule of oxygen to his brain, I turned him over and looked for something convenient to bind him to.

I found it in the form of a dead log about thirty yards up the bank. Hanging Wolfe from a nearby tree branch, I set to work dragging the log down and then unbinding and rebinding his hands and feet around it, careful not to let any tension out of the noose while I worked. It took a good twenty minutes to do all of this, and I probably slowed my progress by spending at least ten checking and rechecking his noose every thirty seconds.

Once I finally had him on the log, ready to go for his Viking funeral (minus the fire, unfortunately), I stared at his face, which had turned a shade of violet not usually found in nature. At least not since we had started sending our dead to morgues instead of burying them ourselves.

"You know what I said earlier about you being a piece of serial killing shit?" I asked his lifeless face. Naturally, he did not respond. "I meant it."

Casting a slow look up the embankment, just to make sure my mother or grandmother hadn't made their way down to see how I was doing, I turned back to him. "But..." I said, taking a breath, "...I didn't hate you at the end. I didn't love you, either, but...I didn't hate what you became. Just what you chose to be before that."

Shaking off the slightly gross feeling I got from saying that, I planted my hand on his forehead, which was already room temperature, the warmth gone from it. I took a deep breath, in and out, counting the seconds until-

Shit.

After a minute, I had to concede...

I couldn't draw out Wolfe's memories with him dead.

"Dammit," I said. This was not optimal.

I rolled the log over so that Wolfe was facedown, the weight of the tree planted firmly atop him, his face crushed into the earth. I got astride it, the whole ten foot or so plank of wood...

And started to slowly – very slowly – let the tension out of the binding around his neck.

I wanted him to get a breath, maybe two, and that was about it. Letting Wolfe fill his lungs sounded like a recipe for disaster, and I wanted to be able to choke him off in a heartbeat if he started to really stir.

With one hand firmly on the metal twist-tie, ready to make it taut again with one good turn, I took another slow breath, my fingers planted on his cheek.

Easy peasy. I'd just bring him back to life for a second, drag the memories of the last few days out of his oxygen-addled brain, and it'd be straight into the river with him. He'd get loose somewhere downstream, probably wondering how the hell he'd gotten there, and his life would go on. At least until the next time we met.

I felt the burn start a few seconds later as enough oxygen got to Wolfe's brain to restart his higher brain functions. I tried to make my own breathing go slow and steady, easy, as the feel of my brain matching up with his began to-

Uh oh.

The log wobbled, jarring my grip on Wolfe's face, and I blinked in surprise as the connection was broken. I pitched forward, catching myself with my left hand before I shattered my face on the downed tree-

But in catching myself...I let go of the noose.

There was a bellowing roar as the log flew off the ground and I was launched into the air. It rolled and flipped, smashing me beneath it as it came back down, blood filling my nose and mouth as something broke in my face and something else cracked in my back.

I lay there, drooling and bleeding, as the sound of sheering metal filtered in through my daze.

Oh, man.

The log was ripped from where it rested on my face just a moment later, and there were dark eyes inches from mine when my vision cleared, the light flooding in from above blinding me for a moment.

Wolfe.

Was.

Free.

"And now, little doll..." he said, breathing, a fleck of drool dripping onto my cheek as I lay there, unable to move, "...you're all mine."

And he licked my cheek.

44.

My face felt warm, wet, where Wolfe's slobber lay on my cheek, then suddenly cool after it had been out of his body for a moment. I lay there, staring up, past his long, matted hair that hung over me, looking into the blue sky past the treetops.

I couldn't hear anything over his breathing. No rustling in the trees to indicate my mother or Lethe was charging down the slope to come save me. No hint that they'd heard the trouble I'd started, or the thundering of the log smashing me.

They were probably consoling little Sienna, still catatonic and twitching, up in the parking lot. Maybe they'd taken her in to the truck stop bathroom, trying to clean her up. She'd looked about as messy as you'd expect a five-year-old to look after being imprisoned by shitbirds like Henderschott and Wolfe for hours without food or water or a toilet.

And here I was, flat on my back, stunned and out of it...

With the world's most dangerous man hovering over me.

He licked my cheek again and scratched it with a fang, drawing blood. I jerked in response to the stimuli, and another wave of pain rushed over me. He smelled like sweat, like filth, and I almost retched at the scent of him. It was so heavy, so musky, I could almost taste it over the peaty smell of the woods.

Water ran in the background as I tried to marshal a defense. I struck at Wolfe, blindly, with a spasming arm.

He batted it away, giggling. "Oh, little doll. No stopping the Wolfe now. This...is happening."

I couldn't see what he was doing, but it didn't take a genius to realize it wasn't good. There was a warm trickle along the back of my head, and the blurring at the edge of my vision told me I'd been concussed. Even for a meta with my healing ability, that didn't heal immediately.

It felt as though someone had come in and laid thick carpeting all along the inner surfaces of my skull, fuzzing my brain. I blinked, blinked again, it didn't help.

The log must have partially crushed my skull when it had landed. All that weight, and it'd caught me in the middle of the forehead. A twitch ran through my body. Wolfe was on me, pressure on my hips.

I balled a fist. Swung again.

He laughed. It didn't hurt him at all.

"Ooh, brains." He lifted my head, licked me somewhere on the back of my skull. "Oh, little doll. So tasty."

"Z... zombie," I managed to get out, my synapses firing very poorly indeed, but that thought somehow escaping.

Wolfe didn't even laugh. He always lacked an appreciation for humor.

"We should go somewhere more private," Wolfe said. "Where your little gal pals can't find you." He picked up my ankles and started to drag me.

Bump. Bump. Bump.

My head hit every rock and uneven place along the slope, and then, suddenly, I was in the water.

"Shhhh," Wolfe said.

I floated along for a little while, unable to see anything but sky and tree tops. He kept me above the water – mostly, except for a couple of moments of snorting and spitting and panic where water ran down into my nose and I choked.

Then, suddenly, I was on dry land again, being dragged up a slope, trees rising above me.

"We need privacy, doll," Wolfe said in a whisper. "We're far enough away now...they'll never find you in time." He was a towering shadow, dragging me by my ankle, hand gripping the pants leg. "Lethe and her little water-blooded offspring will get away, true, but...the Wolfe has you."

I wanted to heave, but I just got dragged along instead.

"All for himself, the Wolfe has you," Wolfe said, smacking his lips together. "The little doll has no more sass, with her brains leaking out. Wolfe likes that."

I wanted to say something to that but couldn't form the thought.

"They'll never find you now," Wolfe said, dragging me behind a little berm. He peeled his shirt off once he had me situated, and I found myself staring up at the hairiest chest I'd ever seen. "Never. The Wolfe will keep you alive for days. Days and days. Weeks. Years, maybe."

A stray thought drifted through my brain: *Akiyama.*

But he couldn't help me anymore. He'd said so.

Lethe?

Mom?

Both busy, and even if they weren't...

Wolfe had dragged me away, possibly far away, from where I'd taken him.

They were good – for all I knew Lethe was an expert tracker – but tracking him downriver?

In time to save me?

There was no chance.

Wolfe was an expert predator. He would have made sure to cover his tracks.

"Just you and me, little doll, together...forever," and he licked my cheek again, slurping at me. A shudder of revulsion ran through my body, causing me to spasm in pain again. "Or at least...as long as you last."

And his shadowy face came down, again, on mine. His breath stunk like rancid meat, and the trees swayed overhead, a rush of wind running through them to my left-

No.

Not wind...

Wolfe stiffened a moment before it happened. He started to turn his head-

But it was too late.

Wolfe was lifted, bodily, from me, ripped from the ground. His legs pinwheeled as he rose, shadowy, curling boughs from the trees surrounding us wrapping his arms, his torso, his upper body and yanking him from the ground and into the air.

He hung there, suspended, trapped between two of them, a few feet off the ground, in crucifixion position as three trees seemed to gang up on him. One had seized him by each wrist, wrapping him up with branches and vines, leaning in impossibly to make this miracle happen. He hung there, legs still riding an invisible bike as he tried to free himself with the only two appendages he had free.

It didn't work.

The trees overhead rippled and shifted, and a shadow came moving through like a great hawk overhead, passed between rustling boughs as easily and as quickly as if it were flying. I blinked, staring up, dimly aware that it was not a hawk, not a bird. The shadow was-

Human?

And thin, feminine, long, dark hair wrapped into a tight ponytail. She was tanned, I could see as she descended, carried like an empress on the branches of the surrounding trees. As she came closer into view, a look of cold disgust played out on her features, which showed age mingled with anger.

Even without knowing her...

I knew her. Instantly.

And as if I needed any further proof, she spoke. "I warned you a long time ago, Wolfe," she said in a Texas drawl, so coldly it felt like all the world might freeze at her anger, "if you ever touched any of my girls with those filthy stinking meat hooks of yours...well..." She balled a fist, and a tree branch slithered like a snake around his neck, and Wolfe started to make squealing, choking noises as he began to turn purple again. "...You can't say I didn't warn you, you hairy turd."

It was Persephone.

My great-grandmother.

45.

Wolfe was going to die.

Branches wrapped his neck like a thick noose of wood and green shoots, twisting and pulling, and his hairy face was turning a shade of lavender – again – that just didn't look natural at all. His tongue was hanging out, but this time it was different.

My savior, the Goddess of the Underworld, Persephone – my great-grandmother – was going to rip his damned head clean off. Her face was twisted, mottled with rage, and she clenched a fist tight in front of her. So tight I thought I saw a drip of blood running down her wrist.

"Don't..." I managed to get out. "Per...sephone...don't..."

She looked at me like the goddess she was, and drifted down, trees branches passing her to the earth. She landed next to me, and the stray weeds and shrubs that poked out of the ground around me seemed to dance closer, trying to touch her. She knelt at my side and her fingers brushed my face.

I sucked in air, gasping, as the fuzzy feeling in my head left me suddenly and I coughed, sputtered, really.

"Don't kill him," I said, once I recovered, thanks to her healing touch. "You can't kill him."

"Oh, I can," she said, "and I oughta." Her Texas drawl seemed to come out even harder with the rage that rimmed her eyes.

"No, please," I said, brushing her hand away from me before I drained her. "I have to kill him...in the future."

She chewed that over for a second, then nodded. She squeezed her hand, and Wolfe choked, but she kept from squeezing his head entirely off. Which would have been cool to watch given what he'd just tried to do to me, but also hazardous to my existential health. She shot him a long, disgusted look. "Your grandmama told me you came down to the creek to dispose of him. Reckon you ran into a little trouble on the way?"

"I was trying to absorb his memory of...all this," I said, brushing at the back of my head. It was bloody, crusted, and I felt a knot where Wolfe had fractured my skull. "Of me, of...little me. Lethe told you...?"

"She told me everything," Persephone said, looking straight into my eyes with her own. They were so bright and green. They reminded me of Kat's. How many generations from Persephone was Kat removed? It couldn't have been many, not with those eyes. "When she called, you know."

I nodded. "I kinda put it together. How'd you get here so fast? Hell, how'd you find us?"

An impish smile formed on her lips. "Well, you ain't exactly hard to track, my darlin'. But I caught a ride on a Hermes. You know what that is?"

"Speedster," I said, blinking a little grit out of my eyes. I stood, and she rose to follow me. She didn't look any paler for having touched me. She'd healed me and didn't look any the worse for the wear.

I could smell the power wafting off of her. It figured. She'd stood toe-to-toe with ol' Hades, my great-grandfather, after all. He was a hell of a pill; I doubted a lesser woman would have been able to survive his bullshit.

"You got a look on your face," Persephone said, giving me a shrewd stare. "You got questions."

"A million of them, probably," I said.

"Save 'em for later," she said, and nodded at Wolfe. "I'll keep him bound up 'til we're good and gone, but you're going to have to do your memory thing, because all I've got in that department is the ability to choke his ass until he don't recall much besides his own name. I'm guessing that ain't what you have in mind."

232

"Right," I said, and branches snaked their way to his legs, wrapping his ankles and ripping them apart. One of the boughs, a fresh, green one that looked like it had popped out this morning, lifted Wolfe's pant leg for me, and I placed my hand on his hairy leg.

I was in his thoughts in seconds, and out in a few more. I took everything from the past few days – every disgusting brain wave that had flashed through his head, every wretched impulse, every daydream, all the filthy, nasty plans he'd made for what he was going to do to me now that he'd gotten his execrable hands on me.

When I had it all, I ripped my hand from his flesh and the burning feeling in my palm tingled on. I looked up at his face, but it was blank. Persephone had squeezed the consciousness out of him, and now the sleeping Wolfe looked surprisingly relaxed. Not quite dead, but not quite living, either.

"I'll hold him 'til we're out of here," Persephone said, beckoning to me. I took a wobbly couple of steps back to her and she reached up and patted my cheek. "You goin' to be all right?"

I spared a last look at Wolfe. Nope, I didn't miss him, at least not for what he was. "I'm going to be just fine," I said, and I knew it was true. Persephone snapped her fingers and the trees came to life, lifting me up along with her, and passing us like the wind was guiding them, carrying me away from the beast that had once been my greatest nightmare.

46.

"You look like hell got his teeth into you," Lethe said as the trees set us down at the edge of the parking lot. She was standing next to the shredded trailer, giving me a once-over as I landed a little unsteadily. Persephone caught my arm, and I smiled as I got my balance. She let me go.

"He damned sure tried," I said, once I was steady.

Lethe nodded. "But it's done now?"

"It's done," I said. "Where's mom and...?"

"In the trailer," Lethe said, lowering her voice. "The little one is, uh..." She shook her head. "Well, it's not good."

I glanced around, standing in the shadow of the trees, then looked to Persephone. "Where's your ride?"

"I told him to head on home," she said with a shake of the head. "Ain't nothing here we girls couldn't handle on our own, right?" Her green eyes twinkled.

"Maybe," I said, eyeing the trailer.

"Can we get out of here now?" Lethe asked, folding her arms in front of her. "Or do we need to hang around a while longer? Because as much as I love a good truck stop greasy spoon, remaining near where we took out an Omega ambush? Is just asking for more trouble."

"Agreed," I said. "But there's a problem." They both looked at me. "Where do we go?"

Persephone cleared her throat. "Well...I've been here in this country for a mighty long while, long enough to develop a little bit of a network 'round here. And while I don't have anything available in Iowa, if we could hit the road and head up north to Minneapolis...I got an old safe house there that ain't in use. We could hunker there for a spell if need be."

"Where is it?" I asked. "In the city, I mean. What part?"

She thought about it for a second. "South of Minneapolis somewheres." She rummaged in her pocket and pulled out a piece of paper. "I wrote down the address in case I needed it."

I looked at the scrawl on the paper.

832 Hamilton Ave, Minneapolis, MN.

Cold chills ran down my arm as I took it out of her hand. "That's the house I grew up in."

Persephone just stared at the paper, then back up at me, those green eyes bright as summer fields. "Well..." She smiled, wide. "I guess we were fated to meet this way, then, huh?"

"Maybe more than you know," I said, all the pieces falling into place now. I made my way past Lethe, around the back of the trailer, which still hung open.

I could see my mom, just inside, cradling little me in her lap. Someone – presumably Lethe – had removed the guard's dead body, and my mother sat on the side of the trailer, rocking little Sienna back and forth. "Shhhhhh," she was saying, but little me wasn't making a sound. Her eyes were wide, and she was just...

Shaking.

"Do you think they did anything to her?" I asked.

"You don't remember?" Persephone asked.

"None of this, no," I said. "But apparently it happened in my past." I brandished the scrap of paper. "This proves it to me, anyway."

"She's probably just scared witless," Lethe said, looking into the back of the trailer with me and her mother. "There's not a mark on her but imagine it from her perspective. She watched her mom get imprisoned, got taken by some of the scariest people in the world – it leaves a mark."

"Yeah," I said, looking past my mother and the little girl that was me, at the piece of the puzzle I'd done my best to ignore up to now. I shook my head and turned to my grandmother and great-grandmother. "One of you needs to go buy a pickup truck. One with a big bed and a king cab. Pay cash out of our casino robbery money."

Lethe exchanged a look with Persephone. "Why a truck?" she asked. "If we're going to Minneapolis, can't we just get in the car and go?"

I shook my head. "No." I pointed into the back of the trailer, at the shadowy rectangle lingering in the darkness. "We need to bring that, too."

They both looked at it; my mom, too, looked up from her soothing of little me. "You want to bring that...thing...they imprisoned me in?" she asked in a hushed whisper.

"Yes," I said, staring at it. Its steely edges were visible from the gouges in the side of the trailer up at the front. "We need it."

"For what?" Persephone asked. "I mean...it ain't nothing but a slab of metal made to hold a person in, sweetheart. What could you possibly need that thing for?"

"I don't," I said, cool prickling running over my skin.

This really was fate.

And I was walking right into it with every choice I was making right now.

"But she does," and I pointed at my mother.

And myself. My littler self.

"What the hell for?" Lethe asked.

"Because..." I said, climbing up into the back of the trailer and slowly sauntering my way over to it. It was only a little taller than me now, and cool to the touch as I ran my hand over its metal, unyielding surface.

If my mother had been unbound, no way would it have held her. She'd have smashed her way out in no time at all.

Just the way I had...the way I *would*...when I got my powers.

"Because this is the way it was when I grew up," I said. I looked back in the darkness. My mother, grandmother and great-grandmother were all there, shadows and light, with the little me held tight against my mom's chest, barely breathing. They all listened in silence. "This...this is it." And I ran my hand over the side, like I was saying hello to an old friend I knew well...

And really, I was.

"...This is the box."

236

47.

The house looked better than I remembered it. Of course, it was over a decade newer than when last I'd seen it, and before fire had claimed it, leaving it – in the present – a scorched shell of its former self. A week ago – that felt like a month, or years - I had sat in the back yard with Angel, thinking wistfully about how far I'd come since I'd started my journey on a fateful day in January by stepping out my door for the first time in a decade.

Now here I was, standing on Hamilton Ave in Minneapolis, putting things in place to seal myself inside for over ten years.

"You sure about this?" Lethe asked as Persephone unlocked the front door for us. When she opened it, a wave of stale air came out, a smell like the place hadn't been used in a long while.

I looked at my grandmother, whose eyes were rimmed with concern. We'd argued, a lot, on the drive up from Iowa. I'll spare you and say that it boiled down to two camps – me versus everyone else. Their point: "You don't have to do this."

My point: "This is the way it was done. Mess with it, and you erase my history – and thus me, and possibly the world."

I won.

But it went on a long, long time, and I could tell I hadn't really convinced anyone on the merits of my case. Which was understandable, because essentially I was arguing for child imprisonment, and that my grandmother and great-grandmother had to get the hell out of our lives and let us –

and me – struggle and suffer for the next twenty years.

"This is not a sacrifice you should have to make," she whispered. I could feel Persephone nodding her head over my shoulder, standing. "What you're going to go through in the next however many years-"

"Is hell," I said, nodding along. "I know. I lived it."

There looked to be a big lump in her throat. "But you shouldn't have had to. The things you're talking about...the things your mom did...there was no call for all that." She shot a look over her shoulder to where my mom still held little me. Little Sienna had fallen asleep somewhere south of the Iowa state line, and except for the occasional twitch or moan, slept peacefully.

Good for her. I couldn't imagine processing that much trauma was easy. I had a feeling I'd be having Wolfe nightmares next time I slept, and I was twenty years removed from her and had been through so much shit since then it would have made that little girl die of fright.

But that was the point of my upbringing. Every step I took, every trauma my mother inflicted, every punishment, every day spent training...

All of them had combined to form me.

It was like a Jenga tower. Pull one little brick from the wrong spot...

Sienna falls down. And maybe she doesn't get up again. Which, self-servingly, would be bad for me.

But – and I say this without ego, or at least try – it'd be a hell of a lot worse for the world.

"Without me being who I am," I said, driving home the point again, "without me doing what I learned to do in these next ten plus years...the world dies at the hands of men who can't be stopped by anyone else." I looked past Persephone into the dark of the living room.

Shit. Even the furniture was the stuff I grew up with.

"I have to do this," I said, and walked past her to go inside.

It all looked so familiar. It lacked so many of the homey touches mom had probably added later, but it was...

Home.

I put my face in my hands because I didn't want my

grandmother and great grandmother to see my eyes getting wet. A rush of feelings hit me – uncertainty, fear, stark terror, mingled with the hints of nostalgia that a moment like this couldn't help but produce.

"It's...not bad," my mom said, stepping inside behind me, little Sienna huddled over her shoulder, sleeping.

"It's yours if you want it," Persephone said, a little uneasily.

"We need it," I said, and she held out the keys. I took them, let them dangle in my hand for a moment as my mother came alongside me, then pushed them into her hand.

The look in her eyes...it was like she died a little.

"I need to go put her down," my mother said, looking around. "Which room-"

"Right there," I said, pointing at my old room. I could see a bed in there. Looked like mine.

She went inside, and I saw her stoop to put down little me. She stayed down for a second, then turned her head. "Debra?"

It took me a second to remember that was me. "Yeah?"

"She's asking for you," my mother said, rising to her feet. I could see little eyes peering past her.

My grandmother caught my arm, and I looked Lethe right in the eye. "I already said my goodbye to her."

"So did I," Persephone said, and I saw in her bright green eyes the same look her daughter was giving me.

They knew.

I nodded as my grandmother let loose of my arm. Without another word, I slipped quietly into my old room, passing my mother in the door frame. She didn't say anything either, just gently closed the door to a thin slit behind her, leaving me alone with my childhood self.

48.

"How are you doing, kiddo?" I asked, sitting down on the edge of the bed. It was a little dusty in here, obvious to my meta senses but hopefully not to hers. It wasn't like she'd be able to develop asthma, given her destiny of meta powers.

"The bad men scared me," she said, looking down at the bed. "I didn't like them."

"I know, sweetheart," I said, running a hand through her hair. "I made the bad men go away, though."

She looked up at me, and I saw a reticence in her eyes. "Will they come back?"

I felt a lump in my throat and found I couldn't lie to a five-year-old, even when that five-year-old was me.

"Yes," I said, around that lump in my throat. "But it'll be when you're big enough to...to kick their butts yourself, okay?" I squeezed her hand, real quick, just a few seconds of skin-to-skin contact, then went back to safely stroking her hair. "You're going to grow up so big and so strong...those guys won't be ready for you."

Her eyes stayed on mine, so blue, but then wavered. "I don't think I can do that." She bowed her little head in shame. "I'm not big and strong like you."

"Not yet," I said, voice getting a little husky. "But someday...you will be. It's going to be...so tough...getting to that point." My voice was cracking. "But you..." And I looked her in the eyes. "You're going to be tougher."

"You think so?" So innocent. For how much longer?

"I know so," I said, brushing her hair back from her eyes again. "Now...you go to sleep, okay?"

She nodded and put her head on the pillow. "Will you stay with me? While I'm sleeping?"

"Kiddo...I'll be with you always," I said, dabbing at my eye with my shirt sleeve.

I waited there until she fell asleep, brushing her hair every now and again.

And as soon as she was out, that little face relaxed...

I moved my hand to her cheek. In a few seconds, I felt my powers start to work.

And as quickly as I could, I took all the memories of my childhood that I could part with and leave her a whole person.

Everything about Wolfe and Henderschott.

Everything about Des Moines, about Lethe and Persephone, about Debra.

I took the memories of the sky, and outdoors, and playgrounds and sunny days.

And I left her sleeping, peacefully, in the dark.

49.

"I don't want to do this," my mother said as I shut the door to my room. Her eyes were already red, and she shook her head at me. "The things you described on the way here..." She just kept shaking her head. "I don't want to do this. I don't want to be this kind of parent." She sniffed. "It's not worth it."

"Sierra," Lethe said quietly, drawing an ireful look from her daughter. "If you don't do this...imagine having Wolfe after you all the time."

"There's other ways," Persephone said, looking at each of us in turn. "I got a nice setup in West Texas. A whole town of metas. Push comes to shove – we can hide y'all real well down there."

"Hell, dad would happily take us over in Revelen," Lethe said, "if you're really just looking to dodge Omega. But that's not what this is about." She looked at me. "Is it?"

I shook my head. "No. Omega's bush league compared to the shit that follows. They're petty criminals. Hell, Gerasimos bit the big one before I even had a chance to kick his door down. The people I have dealt with – they're of the world-ending variety." I looked straight at my mom. "And I can't deal with them unless I'm trained. Unless I'm ready." I shifted uncomfortably as I walked over to join them in the living room. "Unless I go down the path I know, the world ends."

My mother's shoulders shook violently as she put her head down. "Sienna...what you are asking me to do is..." Her shoulders shook repeatedly, like she was spasming. "It's inhuman."

"Well, I'm beyond human," I said coolly, because the last thing we needed was me falling to pieces with her. "So I can take inhuman. Think of it this way – what you'll be doing to me is a pittance compared to the hell I go through later. It's all preparation, done for love and not out of malice."

My mother went quiet, but she didn't stop shaking her head.

"I don't like that you're going through hell," Persephone said, looking me right in the eye. "I don't like that you're telling me to stay out of it, either. I've got half a mind to-"

"Come on," I said. "You know nature, right?"

My great-grandmother was apparently taken aback by this change in conversational topic. "I reckon I know a thing or two about the workings of nature, yes. Why?"

"A butterfly in a chrysalis," I said. "You ever hear what happens if you try and 'help' it out before it can get out on its own?"

She relaxed everything but her frown. "It dies, because it never builds the muscle to-"

"Solve its own problems," I said, staring her down. "Same thing with a baby bird that gets taken out of its nest. Oh, you can fly it around with your bare hands, but sooner or later it has to learn on its own."

"This is your life we're talking about, girl," Persephone said, taking a step closer to me, absolutely serious. "Your grandma and I are here, now, and you're telling us to butt out until – when, exactly?"

"You'll know when," I said to her.

She didn't look convinced. "I don't like one bit of this. And a whole lot of baby birds end up smeared on the ground, you know, trying to learn to fly."

"Well...I'm still alive," I said. "So you don't need to fear that. At least in this case."

"I-" my mother started to say something but stopped because something dramatic changed in the room.

Someone...dramatic...appeared in the room.

"Apologies," Shin'ichi Akiyama said, looking even more worn than when last I'd seen him. "Our time here is growing very short." He looked right at me. "We need to...wrap this up. Swiftly, if possible."

"My ride's here," I said, looking at the three women now arranged in a rough circle with me. "And as much as I'd like to argue this – or drink a toast of...well, water is about all I can manage these days, honestly – I can't stay."

"You can't just leave me like this and expect me to do...any of it," my mother said.

"I don't," I said, looking her right in the eye. "I don't. If you want me to...I'll take the memories you need gone in order to make you a harder person." I pursed my lips. "If I can."

My mother blinked at me. "You mean...I won't remember any of this? At all?" She swallowed, and then turned redder. "You can't do that to me. Sienna, you can't. I want to remember this." She looked me up and down. "I want to remember you. If I have to do terrible things to that little girl to keep her alive..." She balled her fists and bowed her head. "How am I supposed to do that if I can't at least remember that it all turned out okay for you?"

"I am afraid your choice is even more stark than that," Akiyama said, surprisingly straitlaced given that he'd been holding back time for days. "The only reason I knew about...all this, this incident," he waved a hand at us, "is because on the night of your death, you told me a message I give you now: 'the next time we meet will be on the day of your death. But your death will save your daughter's life'."

My stomach dropped like I'd been flying along and Gavrikov had been sucked out of my head midair. "Wait, what?" I looked from him to her, then back, in disbelief. "She knew?"

He nodded.

I looked to my mother. "I - I had no idea that you-"

"I... die?" she asked, looking the calmest she'd been since we'd left Des Moines. "Between now and..." She looked at me. "And when you get back?"

I almost couldn't look her in the eye. "Yes," I said, finally. "You die in... well, it's a hell of a fight. And yeah...you do save my life."

She took a long, hard breath, then covered her mouth with her hand. "I die."

"We all die sometime," Lethe said quietly.

"Oh fuck off, mom, you're still alive," my mother said. "And your mom is still alive."

"I'd die in a heartbeat to save any one of you," Persephone said.

"Same," Lethe said.

My mom thought, then blinked, then looked right at Akiyama. "How much time do I have?"

Akiyama just shook his head. "No one should know when their hour is at hand until it is arrived. But...you have some time." He looked at me. "Enough to see your daughter grow up."

"You help me save the world, mom," I said, and I realized in that moment that my mother had known... that she'd been cruel to save me...she'd known that she was going to die saving me, and...

She'd done it all anyway.

"I've got some time, then," my mother said, straightening up. "I do want you to take some memories from me, yes." She nodded. "But...not this." She looked at Persephone, then Lethe. "You can take the surrounding events, take Wolfe – hell, gladly take Wolfe – but don't take this." She looked at each of us in turn. "I want to remember *this*. This moment, with the four of us."

"The day four generations of our women stood together and kicked Omega in the balls," Lethe said with a smile.

"I can do one better than that, I bet," Persephone said, and disappeared behind the kitchen counter for a minute. She rummaged in a drawer and came back around with a silvery camera the size of a land mine. She looked at Akiyama. "Any chance you'd be kind enough to oblige us on this?"

Akiyama gave a nod, and we all shuffled over to the couch as he stood before it, camera in hand. I didn't plan it, no one did, but we ended up with Persephone on one end, then Lethe, then mom...and finally me. Chronological order. We barely fit, but we did make it, just.

"It really does help me to know you're going to be okay," my mother said as she settled in next to me. She wouldn't look at me, though, at first. "I can endure almost anything if I know you're going to be okay."

"I'll be okay," I said, thinking of the world ahead, and how surely...surely it must be worth the sacrifice. Seven billion people were still alive because of her death, after all.

"I'm not sure I quite believe you, with all that enthusiasm," she said, looking at me sidelong as Akiyama fiddled with the camera. It was an old model. Maybe new to him, though, since he'd given up on modern life around the fifties. "You know there's more to life than just saving the world."

I thought back to how my life had been going before Akiyama had pulled me out of time. That room in DC, with the blank, bare walls, and no one talking to me. Just when I thought I'd finally gotten clear of that stupid fugitive business...

"I know. And it will be all right," I said, mustering confidence I didn't entirely feel. "I've been through a lot, but things are coming together. And there's...someone...now."

A little hint of sadness settled in around her eyes. "Good for you." She looked around. The picture still wasn't happening. "You're the stronger succubus? Of the two of us?"

"Yes," I said.

"I guess that tells me a little something about our future relationship," she said.

"It turns out just fine," I said. "I love you, mom."

"I love you, Sienna," she said, putting her arms around me and giving me a squeeze, her cheek directly to mine. As she pulled back, before my powers started working, she looked me in the eyes. "Your father would be proud of you, too." She sniffled. "When he's done..." she brushed her back and gestured to her neck. "Take what you need to, okay? Before you go."

Lump in the throat like a stone the size of a coffee cup. Gulp. "Okay."

"I think I have figured this out...maybe," Akiyama said, lifting the camera.

"It's an old model," Persephone said. "I ain't been here for a while."

"Whenever you're ready, ladies," Akiyama said, pulling up the camera. "It would appear we have twelve exposures remaining."

"Have at it," I said, settling back into position next to my mother. Out of the corner of my eye, I could see my grandmother and great-grandmother.

Four generations, right there. Not a wimp among us.

"You know, if you ladies don't have any plans later, we could probably take over the world together," I said, and that prompted a round of giggles as Akiyama snapped away.

50.

"How did it go?" Lethe asked as I walked out into the waning summer sun. She was waiting with Persephone and Akiyama, both of whom were blinking at a brightness that would not have been a problem if this had been January. Ah, Minnesota.

"I took what she asked me to," I said, not looking back. "Any memory of you two being alive." I nodded at her and great-grandma. "Part of me wanted to leave her with it, but she didn't recall you being alive when we talked about it, so I sort of sculpted the memories as best I could. Not sure what she's going to actually remember, but I think I left her the impression you're both dead. Which is going to be an interesting issue for you to deal with, since now she doesn't know where this house came from, or how she got here, or where all that casino robbery money came from. I tried to suggest a few logical items, plant some ideas, but I'm not sure I'm capable of inception."

"I don't know what that is, but you're very capable," Lethe said. "I'm sure it'll all come out fine."

My gaze fell on the small roll of film clutched in Persephone's hand. "What are you going to do with that?"

"Develop it," Persephone said, eyes glittering. "Hope it turns out all right given that it's such old film. Hang onto it for a bit...til you're ready to come get it. Which will be when, exactly...?" She was wearing a teasing smile.

"I don't know how to say this to you," I looked at Akiyama for guidance, but he was Sphinx-like. "Use your best judgment

248

for trying to contact me. You've saved me multiple times in the last year," I pointed at Lethe, "though I didn't know your actual name and relation until very recently."

"Hmph," Persephone said, looking at her a little judgy. "You're back working for your daddy, then."

Lethe scrunched up her face and turned to her mother. "How could you possibly know that?"

"Because I wouldn't have you lying like a dog if you were doing whatever it was on behalf of me," Persephone said, pure southern grandma pronouncing judgment. She looked over to me. "How do things end out between you and your great-grandaddy?"

"We got to an understanding," I said, trying to be careful of how much I divulged here. Especially since the last time I'd seen him, his face had been mush and he'd been forced to belly-crawl away from me while bleeding from the beating I'd given him.

"I just bet you did," Persephone said, drawing another one of those looks from Lethe. Two parts suspicious, one part, "What the hell, mom?" I recognized that myself from when my mother would say something questionable or overly blunt around other people.

"So... we'll see you again," Lethe said.

"You will," I said. "For sure."

"Soon, right?" Persephone asked, sidling closer to me and putting an arm around my waist. "Because I know I don't look it, but I'm an old lady now, and I could go any time, so you really need to come see me, y'hear?" She was smiling as she said it, that perfect combo of guilting and love that I'd never known growing up.

"Just...keep your distance until it's time," I said. "Yes, I will come to you. But I need time to grow up. Time to become...well, me."

"I don't like this," Lethe said, folding her arms in front of her, "and if it was coming from my five year-old granddaughter...there's not a chance in hell I'd let you go through what you've proposed."

Persephone nodded along. "It's a little different, though, coming out of the mouth of a grown-ass woman who knows she's about to be put through hell and is willing to walk right on into it for the sake of the world."

"Every day of hell I went through made me a stronger person," I said, looking down at my hand, then over at the box, which rested on the back of the trailer on the back of the truck we'd driven here. Mom could move it in later; she knew what to do with it now. "Every adversity I went up against...I kicked the ass of. I lost a lot along the way, but life has a tendency to do that to you, y'know? Even when you're not trying to save the world."

"It can be a little tough sometimes," Persephone said. "Like beef spareribs if you don't cook 'em long enough."

Akiyama cleared his throat. "My strength is waning."

"I've gotta go," I said, and Persephone stepped forward to give me a hug. It was strong and snug and perfect.

"You come see me, girl," she said right into my ear, sounding a little choked. "I'll keep my distance from you as long as I can, but I swear to you, if you don't come see me as soon as you get back – I'm going to jerk a knot in you, I don't care how old or strong you are. You saw what I did to Wolfe – you know I'll do it." She put her hands on my biceps and pushed back, looking me in the eyes. "I'm in New Asgard, Texas, all right? You're welcome there anytime, you just show right up and I'll roll out the red carpet, y'hear?"

"Loud and clear," I said, and she let me go with more than a little regret.

Lethe came at me next, wrapping me up just as tight, maybe a little less warmly than Persephone, though we both took care not to touch skin to skin. "You can still call me anytime."

"I might need some alternate numbers for you in the future," I said, trying to hedge on giving too much away about what happened in Revelen.

She pulled back, studying my eyes with some intensity. "You don't need a phone."

I blinked. "I don't?"

She peered at me, and there was a little knowing to her look. "You're a succubus, aren't you...?"

"Oh, dreamwalk, right," I said, nodding. "Duh. Of course. Yes. I will dreamwalk to you when I get back." I looked at

Persephone. "Both of you."

"You better," Persephone said, a twinkle in her eye. "I don't have that many great-grandbabies that have kept in touch. I ain't letting go of you, girl, so you best get used to that. If I don't hear from you, I'm going to find this fella," she seized Akiyama's arm, hauling him off balance and making his eyes go ridiculously wide cuz she was stronggggg, "and I'm going to come back in time and kick that door right down and give that little girl in there some serious hugging, consequences be damned." She let go of Akiyama and wagged a finger at me. "You take that to the bank."

"Consider it banked," I said, trying to hide a smile.

She waved her hand at me, the little film canister clutched in her fingers. "You can consider this banked, too. 'Til then."

"If you are ready?" Akiyama asked, having regained his balance. He brushed some of the lines out of his suit where Persephone had messed it up when she grabbed him. He made a couple attempts, then finally seemed to write it off as hopeless, because he looked at me. "If we could, please."

"We can," I said, and moved to stand by him.

"Don't you go forgetting us," Persephone said. "Because I promise you, however long ahead it is for us to get to your time...we ain't going to forget you, Sienna."

"We'll be waiting," Lethe said as her mother put an arm around her shoulders.

"You ain't alone in this world, ever," Persephone said, her face starting to get hazy. "If you don't remember anything else, you remember *that*." Lethe nodded, silent, emphatic agreement.

"I will," I said, as they started to fade, their faces taking on a hazy quality, like mist rolling in.

Because this time...I would remember.

51.

Gerasimos

"We retrieved Wolfe from a nearby truck stop," Bast said, her head nearly hung. A proud woman, she was not the sort prone to humility. "He had been hung from a tree, he said. Our resulting investigation yielded the trailer that was used to transport the girls as well as the vehicle used by Lethe and the unknown assailant to stage their attack." She pursed her dark lips. "They struck while the vehicles were in transit. The unknown subject-"

"We still have no name for her?" Gerasimos asked, his fingers templed in front of his lips. "Even after all this?"

"No," Bast said. "She appears to have taken Wolfe's memories of her. He has no knowledge of the last few days. He does not appear to even recall that Lethe is still alive."

"She's another succubus, then?" Gerasimos asked.

Bast half-shrugged. "Lethe could have done it. Succubi are rare. Lethe, Charlie and Sierra are the only three we have on record outside of...Andromeda. Though this new girl could be another of Lethe's offspring."

Gerasimos nodded, contemplating. "I dislike that there are four possible succubi not in our control."

Bast raised an eyebrow. "Incubi are the same, and I don't see you scrambling to gather them up. You let Fries parade around doing whatever the hell he wants, leaving me to clean up more bodies than Wolfe." She paused, thinking. "Of course, that's because Wolfe eats his leavings, but still...Fries makes a mess. This is known."

"There is always a cost associated with doing business," Gerasimos said, "especially with the powerful people with whom we deal, and whose appetites require more...latitude. We will pay this cost gladly, for the alternative is to deal only with the powerless, whose appetites are never satisfied for they have no strength with which to make their will manifest."

Bast surveyed him with a wary eye. "You finished?"

Gerasimos smiled. Few would talk to him as she did. "For now. What of Henderschott?"

"Thrown from a truck, but retains his memories," Bast said. "However..."

"Yes?"

"There was...an incident," Bast said. "When they retrieved Wolfe. He remembered nothing, of course."

"So you have said."

"Henderschott pressed him," Bast said, with distaste. "Regarding his lack of memory. Wolfe...did not appreciate it."

"And what happened?"

"Wolfe tore his face off," Bast said, hands clapped behind her. "Or tore his mask off and brought his face along."

Gerasimos did not raise so much as an eyebrow at that. Wolfe had long been in his service, and he had done considerably worse than this to considerably more powerful people. "Make some accommodations to Henderschott to satisfy him. He is a valuable member of the team and I would hate to see his loyalties waver over this."

Bast nodded. "It will be done, but...this project of yours?"

Gerasimos eyed her. He knew what was coming. "Yes?"

"It exacts a heavy toll."

"All worthwhile ends require a certain amount of sacrifice," Gerasimos said after a short pause for thought. "Surely you agree, having been one who once received great sacrifices in your very name?"

"I agree to a point," Bast said, "for I was never making sacrifices in anyone's name. This project...it drinks our monies like a beggar through the choicest wine."

"We have plenty of money," Gerasimos said. "And if the

worst comes, you will be glad I have stewarded our monies in this way. It is the future, the Andromeda project, you see. A bulwark against coming troubles." He touched his face. "Against the worst troubles, in fact."

"We have many troubles that are unrelated to your fears about the offspring of Hades," Bast said, "and your belief that at some point they will seize their true legacy."

Gerasimos just smiled. "You say that because you have perhaps never dealt with an unleashed incubus or succubus, or a Hades that has drunk a hundred metahumans." He wagged his finger at her. "If you had, you would know...there is nothing more fearsome, more dangerous to our species. Even a Gavrikov is limited in the scope of their destruction. An unleashed child of Hades, willing to feast upon the souls of our kind?" He shook his head. "There is no limit to the carnage they can achieve." He stared at the outline of London on the horizon. "It would be the end of everything we have built. The whole world, even, maybe."

"As you will it," Bast said, and he heard her surrender. "I will leave you now, if there is nothing else."

"One final thing," Gerasimos said. "This...other woman. The other daughter of Lethe, the one foiling our efforts these last few days?"

"Yes?"

"You said we had collected her blood?"

"A great deal of it, yes," Bast said. "I had some of it transferred from our agents on site to-"

"Get all of it," Gerasimos said.

That raised Bast's eyebrow. "All of it?"

"All of it you can lay your hands on," Gerasimos said. "Send it to Eagle River. To the Andromeda project. It will give them more, perhaps, to work with in their studies."

Bast considered this for a moment, then nodded, almost a bow of her head in pure deference. "As you wish."

Then she left him be, and Gerasimos settled into an easy silence. He often found himself in silent contemplation, considering the future. It was always a dark contemplation, for darkness was all he saw. Myriad threats, lingering beyond the horizon, always seeking to destroy his empire, one that had its roots in the olden days of gods and men, when men knew their place.

Now...men did not know their place, and that was fine, for their place was to be guided from the shadows. Gerasimos had long made his peace with the reality that the world had changed, that they could no longer sit atop a pyramid or temple and rule as in days past. It mattered little, even as it irked him slightly, for he would still gather all the power he could lay his hands upon. He had, in fact, taken control of this empire after Poseidon's death...

But for now, he sat, and he thought again of the future. It must surely be dark, for things always grew darker before the dawn.

And in his imagination, Gerasimos had a very bright dawn in mind. All his planning, so much of his resources had gone toward it. It sat across the globe, in a place called Eagle River, Wisconsin. How amusing that his bright dawn would begin in the west, how counterintuitive. It should have begun in the east if it followed the laws of nature, but...

Metahumans did not follow the laws of nature. They were exceptional, and they were the exception to all those laws.

Gerasimos smiled at that thought and contemplated this girl...this troubling girl. He looked at the black and white photo on his desk. She had never been seen before this, but surely...surely she would be seen again...? One as powerful as this could not hide her face forever.

Nodding once more, he knew it had to be true. Yes, she would be back. No one with such power as hers could remain hidden for long. She would return, someday, yes...

And Gerasimos would be ready for her.

52.

Sienna
Washington DC
Now

I jerked as my ass hit the hard chair, the world resolving into four smooth walls and a mirror. I blinked, the scent of stale air conditioning hitting my nostrils, replacing the summer warmth of Minneapolis with the chill of an office building where someone had turned the thermostat down a little too far.

Looking into the mirror opposite me, I seemed a little worse for the wear. With a glance, I realized my clothes had somehow changed back to the shredded mess I'd been wearing before I'd "left."

How the hell did that work?

It threw me for a loop for a moment, looking at my filthy, damaged clothing. This was not what I'd been wearing when I'd left 1999.

Had my adventure in the past even happened?

Had I just had a massive hallucination of an excursion through time?

Or had Akiyama somehow returned me to my present clothing when he snapped me back into this room?

Sleep tugged at my eyelids, and I realized, not for the first time, that it had been quite a while since I'd slept, truly slept rather than falling unconscious due to injury. Probably since

256

that first night in Des Moines. I blinked a couple more times, eyeing the table, then the mirror. These people hadn't killed me yet...

I settled my head on the table, felt the hard pressure of it against the side of my skull. It should have been uncomfortable, but somehow it wasn't.

One of the things Lethe said to me before we'd parted ways came back to me now: *You're a succubus, aren't you?*

And I thought of her as I drifted off into sleep.

"You picked a grim setting," Lethe said as she appeared in my black and quiet dreamwalk. Her hair was back to its familiar curl the way it had been in Revelen, and she'd picked up just a couple wrinkles in the intervening decades. "How are you?"

"I'm okay," I said, looking around. I was still wearing my shredded clothes. "Just got back from a little sojourn to Des Moines...with Akiyama."

Her right eyebrow inclined slightly upward, and she nodded, slowly, once. "Oh?"

"Yeah," I said. "How's Persephone?"

She smiled. "She's just fine. I'm on a plane, heading to her now. When are you coming to...?"

"I don't know," I said. "I'm in a room in Washington DC. They brought me here after I surrendered."

She bristled. "Do you need us to come get you? Because we'll be there in hours. As soon as I land, I can-"

"No," I said, shaking my head. "Gondry promised me clemency, and I don't think..." I shrugged. "I don't know what's going on, but...don't come get me yet."

Her eyes blazed. "I'm going to get things into position. If I don't hear from you, or hear that you're all right soon..."

"Sensible." I nodded. "Hopefully it'll all turn out all right." I smacked my lips together, wishing I'd gotten a drink of water before I'd left 1999, because suddenly I was thirsty. "Thank you. For being there when I needed you. For giving me the space to grow up...well, like I asked."

She took my hand in the dream, and I fought the urge to recoil away. She smiled. "No time limits on touch in a dreamwalk, remember? And I'll always be there for you. Like

I said."

"Now I know why you stayed out of everything," I said.

"It was very difficult," she said, looking me right in the eye. "For me and Persephone both. We talked about ignoring your wishes quite a few times. Even tried to make contact with you a few years ago, though it didn't go very well."

"That's when I fought you," I said, getting it. "That's a memory Rose must have stolen."

She nodded. "We wanted to help you...so many times. I really was on my way to Minneapolis when you fought Sovereign. I couldn't stand it anymore."

"I'm glad you held off," I said. "And I'm glad you're both still here."

"Apropos of that," she said, and her eyes glistened, "I've got something for you. For next time we see each other."

"Oh?" I asked.

She fussed about with her hands for a second, and suddenly she was holding a wooden frame in them. She handed it to me, and I took it. "This is just an approximation, you understand. But I have the real thing, waiting for you in Texas when you get down here."

I looked at the thing she'd handed me.

It was the picture of the four of us – Persephone, Lethe, mom and me – sitting on the couch in my house back in 1999. It had the slightly dyed look of an old photo, but still...

There it was. Four generations. One picture.

"I miss her," I said, looking at my mom. She was smiling, so different from how I remembered her in my upbringing. Of course, she'd been that way in my upbringing because I'd made her. "Maybe now more than ever."

"I know," she said quietly. "But like she said...and I know she'd feel the same if she knew all you'd done since..." She smiled encouragingly, "*We*...are all so proud of you."

I didn't know what to say to that, so I just looked down at the photo, trying to burn it into my mind even though it was blurring from tears. "Thank you, grandmother," I said, looking up. "I can't wait to-"

A door slammed and I jerked off the table, back to the four walls and the long mirror. Someone was standing in front of the door, had come in while I'd been sleeping, not making a sound until they'd slammed the door behind them.

It was a woman, painfully thin, in a dark suit, a slightly impish look on her face like she was here doing God's own work. "Oh, sorry," she said, not remotely sincere, "did I wake you?"

"Yes," I said, figuring I'd have to be the one to carry the honesty bucket between the two of us. "But I wouldn't worry yourself about it." Because plainly she wasn't, so why expect it?

"Do you know who I am?" she asked.

I did, but based on her attitude, hell if I was going to give her the satisfaction. "Uhm...lemme guess, you're the Special Assistant to the Undersecretary of Masturbation, here to talk to me about all the very dangerous criminal behavior I've done in that department over the years."

Her mouth dropped slightly, then tensed as she forced a smile. "I'm the Director of the FBI. Heather Chalke."

"Oh." I pretended to be disappointed. "That's way less exciting."

"Do you know why I'm here?" she asked, settling her arms in front of her. She hadn't moved from in front of the door yet.

"Because all is totally calm and peaceful on the federal law enforcement front at the moment?"

Her mouth tightened into a thin line. "You're as feisty as everyone has said. Do you know how much trouble you could still be in?"

I yawned. "Oh, sorry, were you saying something? Because someone woke me up in the middle of a nap."

Her eyes flashed. I was guessing FBI Director Chalke was the sort of mini-fascist who wasn't used to having her authority shat on right before her eyes. "So you've decided to be uncooperative."

"Maybe if you told me why I was here, I'd have some notion of what I'm supposed to cooperate with," I said, leaning back in my chair, folding my arms in front of me. "As it is, I'm still not convinced you aren't the Special Assistant to the Undersecretary of Wanking, because from where I'm sitting, with a presidential pardon on offer...all you've got is dick."

That wiped the smirk off her face. "You got a pardon once before. How long did that last?"

"Until some asshole in the Oval decided to frame me for a bunch of things I didn't do," I said, not backing off an inch. I cocked my head and rested a finger on my chin, pretending contemplation. "Say...I wonder what ever happened to that guy?"

"Is that a threat?" Her eyes lit up.

"No, it was a genuine question," I said, letting my own smugness melt off. "Because I'm guessing you were in the FBI at the time, so...what happened to the president? On your watch, no less."

"The president is the responsibility of the US Secret Service," she said. "That's Department of Treasury."

"Not the Department of Wanking? You sure? Because Harmon, he was a hell of a wanker if ever I met one-"

Whatever residual patience she had left evaporated before my eyes. "I told President Gondry this was how it was going to be with you, but he didn't believe me. He thought you could be reasoned with-"

"I can be reasoned with just fine, if you send me a reasonable person and not some Obergruppenführer who's spent so long in the bureaucracy that she's never even tasted the possibility of getting fired for her smug stupidity." I stared her down, she stared back. "But he sent you, Cocky McCockerson."

Her eyes narrowed. "My name is-"

"You said it once already, but I still don't care," I said. "If you just came to threaten me with prison...skip it." I laid my head back down on the table. "I surrendered because I intended to face justice. If that means a pardon, fine. If it means jail, that's fine, too." I turned my head on the table so I could look at her. "But if you think it means I'm just going to lay down and let you – or someone like you – pull the crap you tried last time you sent me up the river without putting up a hell of a fuss...you have sadly underestimated me. Again. Because I will make a mess of you and your Department that will be so epic in the annals of Washington that it'll make Second Manassas look like the White House Easter Egg Hunt.

And then you really will wish you were the Assistant to the Undersecretary for Wanking." I turned my head away from her.

"So that's how you want to play it?" she asked.

"You threaten me, I threaten right back. What's the matter?" I asked, not dignifying her by looking at her. "You got too used to your unlawful detainees just folding when you get all bossypants on them? Because I've been nearly killed by the best, so it's really hard for me to sweat over some pantsuit-wearing, over-promoted lawyer with badly failing antiperspirant vaguely promising me more of the same crap I've already beaten. Say something new and exciting...or just go screw your mediocre self."

She didn't say anything for a while after that. "You're awfully jaded for twenty-six."

"I've lived a full life," I said, still not bothering to raise my head to look at her.

"And now you're ready to die?" she asked.

"Always have been," I said coldly. "If that's what it takes." Like my mother before me, I didn't say, choking down the emotions that came with that thought, so freshly in mind.

"You don't have a job."

"Oh, but I do," I said. "And I always have." Now I raised my head up to look at her. "That's something that maybe you've never quite gotten through your collective heads in this town. I'm going to save the world whether you like me or not, I'm going to stop the bad guys whether you want me to or not, and I'm going to be there when people need me..." And here I stared her down. "...No matter what. So... threaten me. Sideline me. Cage me, if you think you can. Try and bury me, if you think you've got the brass to pull it off. I'll be back when I'm needed. And I don't care whether you're the Assistant Undersecretary for Wanking, the Director of the FBI, the President of the United States, or the Goddess of Justice. If you push me...you can count on me to knock your ass the hell off."

"So... that's how it's going to be?" she asked.

I put my head right back down. "That's how it's always going to be. So put that in your pipe and smoke the hell out of it."

"Okay, then," she said.

But she didn't leave.

I just sat there, head on the desk, wondering if she'd say something first or I'd fall asleep. Either way, I was well past caring. We could wait all night, all year, for the rest of our lives if need be. Mine would be a lot longer than hers, probably.

Fortunately...I didn't have to wait that long.

Epilogue

Reed
Eden Prairie, Minnesota

"Where the hell is she?" I asked, for the thousandth time, pacing the bullpen like I was a bull, and someone had penned me in. No one had, of course, I could leave any time I liked, but staring at the four walls around me, I felt like I was in non-solitary confinement, heat crawling up the back of my neck and the agitation filling me like excess blood. I was flushed, warm, bordering on angry.

"Still nothing on her whereabouts," Jamal said, shaking his head, his phone delicately clutched in his hand, finger on the charging port so he could interface directly with the internet. "Last known position was Joint Base Andrews in DC. After that..." He shook his head again. "It's like she disappeared off the face of the earth."

I thrust out a hand and blew a chair across the room, leaving an impression in the drywall and scattering a half dozen papers.

"Oh, hey, thanks for messing up my desk," Olivia Brackett said, stooping to retrieve some of them. "Like I don't have to clean up after my own powers enough of the time," she mumbled, though everyone could hear her.

"How does someone as high profile as Sienna Nealon just disappear?" Augustus Coleman asked, hand over his face. I couldn't see his eyes, but he looked tired. Which made sense,

ROBERT J. CRANE

given that most of us had been running on very little sleep for the last week or so.

"Federal Court has no record of her in the system," Miranda Estevez said, appearing from the entry. She, too, looked tired, tossing her briefcase onto the nearest desk. "Wherever she is, she's not in holding, or in jail, as near as I can tell."

"I could have told you that from here," Jamal said.

"J.J.," I said, "Abby. Anybody?" I looked around the faces crowded in the bullpen. "She went to Revelen, she survived, she was on a military plane – HOW DOES SHE DISAPPEAR HERE IN THE US?" My voice hit the highest registers. "How does nobody – not the government, not the press, nobody – know where she is?"

"I know where she is," Guy Friday said, arms folded in front of him as he sat, surprisingly calmly, in a chair.

I sagged. "Don't mess with me right now, Friday."

"There." He didn't show any sign of hesitation, just raised his finger to point at the TV. "She's there."

I looked to the TV out of pure habit of looking where someone pointed, not because I thought there was a chance in hell that Friday knew a damned thing. "What are you-"

I froze.

Because there she was.

"Turn it up! Turn it up!" Augustus lunged out of his seat and swiped the remote like he'd been launched out of a catapult. He speared the volume button and sent the little bar at the edge of the screen shooting into the stratosphere, from 0 to 50 in a half second.

It took me a second to realize what the hell I was looking at, because it was such a surreal scene. The president was there, on a stage, with a half dozen other people, including...

My sister, right behind him, framed by the gold curtains in the background, dressed neatly in a suit with jacket and everything. It was surreal seeing her like that after two years of her disguises, of casual dress Sienna, of fugitive Sienna. She was all cleaned up, her hair nicely done and pulled back in a ponytail, and she stood on the stage behind Gondry without expression, listening to him speak, arms folded in front of her.

That posture, at least, looked authentically Sienna.

264

"...I'm pleased to share the stage with Ms. Nealon after all this time," President Gondry said from the presidential podium. He turned to indicate her with a hand. "I know we've had our misunderstandings, but given her recent actions, I have nothing but praise for Ms. Nealon. In speaking with her, I've found her to be a dedicated servant of the people, someone who has the best intentions at heart."

He paused for a round of applause from the crowd, and I felt sour. "What the hell is this?" I asked.

"Gondry kissing your sister's ass," Augustus said. "Probably hoping if he stands next to her, it'll make people forget that we almost got nuked to hell yesterday."

"But why is she even there-" I started to ask.

But my question got answered first.

"I am pleased to announce," Gondry went on, "vis a vis this lovely ceremony, the creation today of a new unit of the FBI to replace the old Metahuman Policing and, uh..." He froze in the middle of it, seemingly trying to conjure the name of the old agency we'd worked for. "The...uh..." Finally he gave up. "In any case, effective immediately, we begin creation of a new legacy, one to wash away past failures and half measures, one focused on upholding the newly-passed laws surrounding metahuman conduct with their powers. It will, of course, carry forward the highest tradition of ethics, coupling that with an emphasis on proven leadership and keeping the public safe. To that end, I'm pleased to announce the new head..." He looked back behind him, right at Sienna. "...This very minute, in fact. Please give a hand to Ms. Nealon."

There was a round of applause, long and stunning. At least, to me. My ears rung with the clapping, filtered through the television.

"Are you freaking kidding me?" Kat asked, eyes narrowed to thin slits, staring up at the TV.

"What...the...hell...?" Jamal asked. Maybe it wasn't just me.

Sienna unfolded her arms like she'd just come back to life and stepped up to the podium. There seemed to be almost nothing in my sister's expression – no joy, no anger, just...

Nothing.

"Thank you, Mr. President," she said, and finally a small,

familiar smile appeared on her face as she clutched the edges of the podium and looked right into the camera. It gave me a little chill, like she was talking to me...even though I almost didn't recognize her at this point. "It's good to be back."

Sienna Nealon will return in

COLD

OUT OF THE BOX
Book 24

Coming February 8, 2019!

Author's Note

Thanks for reading! If you want to know immediately when future books become available, take sixty seconds and sign up for my NEW RELEASE EMAIL ALERTS by visiting my website. I don't sell your information and I only send out emails when I have a new book out. The reason you should sign up for this is because I don't always set release dates, and even if you're following me on Facebook (robertJcrane (Author)) or Twitter (@robertJcrane), it's easy to miss my book announcements because...well, because social media is an imprecise thing.

Come join the discussion on my website:
http://www.robertjcrane.com!

Cheers,
Robert J. Crane

ACKNOWLEDGMENTS

Editing was handled by Lewis Moore, with Jeff Bryan and Jo Evans batting cleanup. Many thanks to all of them.

Once again, the illustrious illustrator Karri Klawiter produced the cover. artbykarri.com is where you can find her amazing works.

Nick Bowman of nickbowman-editing.com provided the formatting that turned this into an actual book and ebook.

And thanks as always to my family – wife, parents, in-laws and occasionally my kids, for keeping a lid on the craziness so I can do this job.

Other Works by Robert J. Crane

The Girl in the Box *and* Out of the Box
Contemporary Urban Fantasy

Alone: The Girl in the Box, Book 1
Untouched: The Girl in the Box, Book 2
Soulless: The Girl in the Box, Book 3
Family: The Girl in the Box, Book 4
Omega: The Girl in the Box, Book 5
Broken: The Girl in the Box, Book 6
Enemies: The Girl in the Box, Book 7
Legacy: The Girl in the Box, Book 8
Destiny: The Girl in the Box, Book 9
Power: The Girl in the Box, Book 10

Limitless: Out of the Box, Book 1
In the Wind: Out of the Box, Book 2
Ruthless: Out of the Box, Book 3
Grounded: Out of the Box, Book 4
Tormented: Out of the Box, Book 5
Vengeful: Out of the Box, Book 6
Sea Change: Out of the Box, Book 7
Painkiller: Out of the Box, Book 8
Masks: Out of the Box, Book 9
Prisoners: Out of the Box, Book 10
Unyielding: Out of the Box, Book 11
Hollow: Out of the Box, Book 12
Toxicity: Out of the Box, Book 13
Small Things: Out of the Box, Book 14
Hunters: Out of the Box, Book 15
Badder: Out of the Box, Book 16
Apex: Out of the Box, Book 18
Time: Out of the Box, Book 19
Driven: Out of the Box, Book 20
Remember: Out of the Box, Book 21
Hero: Out of the Box, Book 22
Flashback: Out of the Box, Book 23
Cold: Out of the Box, Book 24* *(Coming February 8, 2019!)*

World of Sanctuary
Epic Fantasy

Defender: The Sanctuary Series, Volume One
Avenger: The Sanctuary Series, Volume Two
Champion: The Sanctuary Series, Volume Three
Crusader: The Sanctuary Series, Volume Four
Sanctuary Tales, Volume One - A Short Story Collection
Thy Father's Shadow: The Sanctuary Series, Volume 4.5
Master: The Sanctuary Series, Volume Five
Fated in Darkness: The Sanctuary Series, Volume 5.5
Warlord: The Sanctuary Series, Volume Six
Heretic: The Sanctuary Series, Volume Seven
Legend: The Sanctuary Series, Volume Eight
Ghosts of Sanctuary: The Sanctuary Series, Volume Nine
Call of the Hero: The Sanctuary Series, Volume Ten* *(Coming Late 2018!)*

A Haven in Ash: Ashes of Luukessia, Volume One *(with Michael Winstone)*
A Respite From Storms: Ashes of Luukessia, Volume Two *(with Michael Winstone)*
A Home in the Hills: Ashes of Luukessia, Volume Three *(with Michael Winstone)*

Southern Watch
Contemporary Urban Fantasy

Called: Southern Watch, Book 1
Depths: Southern Watch, Book 2
Corrupted: Southern Watch, Book 3
Unearthed: Southern Watch, Book 4
Legion: Southern Watch, Book 5
Starling: Southern Watch, Book 6
Forsaken: Southern Watch, Book 7
Hallowed: Southern Watch, Book 8* *(Coming in 2019!)*

The Shattered Dome
(with Nicholas J. Ambrose)
Sci-Fi

Voiceless: The Shattered Dome

The Mira Brand Adventures
Contemporary Urban Fantasy

The World Beneath: The Mira Brand Adventures, Book 1
The Tide of Ages: The Mira Brand Adventures, Book 2
The City of Lies: The Mira Brand Adventures, Book 3
The King of the Skies: The Mira Brand Adventures, Book 4
The Best of Us: The Mira Brand Adventures, Book 5
We Aimless Few: The Mira Brand Adventures, Book 6
The Gang of Legend: The Mira Brand Adventures, Book 7*
(Coming Late 2018/Early 2019!)

Liars and Vampires
(with Lauren Harper)
Contemporary Urban Fantasy

No One Will Believe You: Liars and Vampires, Book 1
Someone Should Save Her: Liars and Vampires, Book 2
You Can't Go Home Again: Liars and Vampires, Book 3
In The Dark: Liars and Vampires, Book 4
Her Lying Days Are Done: Liars and Vampires, Book 5
Heir of the Dog: Liars and Vampires, Book 6* *(Coming November 2018!)*
Hit You Where You Live: Liars and Vampires, Book 7* *(Coming December 2018!)*

* Forthcoming, Subject to Change

Made in the USA
Middletown, DE
24 August 2020

15995074R00156